El Macho

Jessica Watts Southwest Suspense Series

Kathryn Dodson

Renegade Reads

Contents

Chapter 1

Tela, Jessica's Catahoula Leopard Dog, growled low in her throat as Jessica pulled into the parking lot. Two men Jessica didn't trust stood near the building entrance. Dick Saunders, the ex-mayor of El Paso, clasped the shoulder of a tall blond-going-gray man in a sheriff's deputy uniform. Dick's eyes moved to Jessica as she turned into a parking space. He frowned and quickly stepped back from the other man.

The man with his back to Jessica could only be Deputy Mayfield, whom she hadn't seen since he interrogated her several months earlier. Half-crazed with hunger and fear after she'd crossed the Rio Grande and trekked through the desert to escape her kidnappers, she'd landed in the sheriff's department. It should have meant safety. Instead, Mayfield had treated her like a criminal.

Jessica already suspected corruption among some of the deputies. Seeing these two together set her instincts on fire.

With that fire came a new confidence. She'd trained for this, honing her body and learning new skills that would allow her to defend and attack. No one would take her hostage again.

Dick said something to Mayfield, and he turned toward her as well. Then, Mayfield trotted down the stairs to the parking lot. For a moment, Jessica feared he'd approach, but he climbed into a black-and-white SUV with the sheriff's logo. Dick spun toward the door of the building that housed not only his wife's gallery but the insurance company he'd run since marrying into the family. Jessica waited until Mayfield drove away to leave her truck.

Tela bounced and pulled at her leash when Jessica opened the gallery door and the dog spotted Clarice, Jessica's mom. With her stood Robin, the gallery owner and wife of Dick Saunders.

"It's great to see you," Jessica said, stretching her hand to Robin, a woman with a sharp blond bob, perfectly tailored suits, and a passion for art, family, and friendship that Jessica had come to admire. Robin had discovered her mother, sold Clarice's paintings, and leased her a studio/cottage.

"Jessica." A young woman with long dark hair hustled in from the office hallway. "I'm so glad you're here. Robin just gave me a promotion. I'm going to manage the gallery!"

"That's fantastic," Jessica said as Araceli approached. Jessica marveled at how much Araceli had changed since she'd met her on a hidden ranch in Mexico while trying to uncover the cold-case disappearance of Robin's father.

Since then, Araceli had enrolled at the University of Texas at El Paso, moved into a small house near the university with several friends, and begun working in the gallery. She'd even told Jessica about a boyfriend the last time they'd had lunch together.

"Yes, about that," Clarice said, "Robin just told us she's moving to La Jolla."

"California?" Jessica asked. "You're leaving El Paso?"

If El Paso had a power couple, Robin and Dick Saunders held the title. They ran in the upper echelons of El Paso society: country club members, symphony and orchestra patrons. Together, they'd held every top political and social position.

"Our son has already moved out there with his girlfriend." Robin's cheeks reddened as she spoke. "He's hinted that he's going to ask her to marry him—and you know how important family is to me."

"What about your mom?" Jessica had met the cranky old lady on several occasions. Robin seemed devoted to her.

A wave of sadness crossed Robin's features. For a moment, Jessica thought she might break down. But then she straightened and set her lips in a firm line.

"I'm trying to convince her to come with us. Until then, I'll visit as often as I can." Robin glanced at her watch. "Speaking of moving, I've got to finalize some details with Dick upstairs. It's been nice seeing you ladies."

She disappeared before Jessica could ask another question. Jessica glanced at her mom, who shrugged.

"I just heard about the move myself," Clarice said.

"Me too. I can't believe it." Araceli practically vibrated with excitement. "I will work very hard to make sure the gallery does well."

Suddenly, Jessica found herself enmeshed in her mother's hug. Tela wrapped her leash around them both, pulling her into her mom and furthering her discomfort. She'd never been much of a hugger.

"Enough about us," Clarice said. "How are you doing? Are you surviving all right without Angus?"

Everything in Jessica's world stopped as her mom hit her with the one terrible thing she couldn't overcome. She steeled herself against the loss. Told herself it had only been a few months and she'd find a way to get him back. In fact, she'd put a plan in place soon after he left.

"So far, so good." Jessica managed to push out the lie. "I've been training with Sal every weekend. Hopefully, my new skills will convince Angus I'm serious about protecting myself."

"Oh, Honey," Clarice pulled back from Jessica and stared into her face. "Angus isn't interested in your skills. He just wants you to care about yourself as much as the rest of us do."

Jessica stared back at her mom, utterly confused. She'd busted her butt every weekend learning self-defense maneuvers. Soon she'd move on to tactical weapons. A whole new world had opened to her. Angus worried about her safety, and this had to be the key to getting him back. "I don't even understand what you're saying."

"I'm sure you and Angus will get back together," Araceli said. "You should meet my new boyfriend. He's as nice as Angus, and so handsome."

Her mom disentangled the dog from them while Jessica tried to figure out how to respond to Araceli. It thrilled her how easily the young woman had adjusted to the changes in her life, but comparing some college kid to the man Jessica had spent her life in love with didn't compute.

"I'll take Tela and give you girls a few minutes to talk." Clarice tugged Tela's leash and headed toward one of her paintings. Jessica hadn't seen the work before, which depicted El Paso's desert mountains in bold strokes of plum and mauve as a storm cloud threatened and the last rays of the setting sun sent golden shards across the canvas.

Araceli took Jessica's arm and led her to a magenta faux leather bench. "Jessica, I have to thank you. I didn't know my whole world would change when we met. I thought I would stay on the ranch forever like my grandmother and aunts. Maybe I'd teach English in the local school. But my dreams were always so much bigger than that."

Passion shone from Araceli's eyes. Here was one good thing Jessica had done.

"I've made so many friends and love the girls I live with," Araceli said. "And you just have to meet Travis. He might be the one."

"Haven't you only dated him a few weeks? You don't want a relationship to tie you down when you're just getting started." Jessica suddenly wanted to meet this guy. Araceli's excitement about her new life might leave her vulnerable. She had so little experience, and guys could be dicks.

"It's new, although we've been together over a month now. I have a good feeling about him. I'd love to tell you more, but I need to get back to campus for my last final. After that, he's taking me for ice cream to celebrate."

Well, that was kind of sweet. Jessica and her friends had usually gone out and gotten wasted after finals. Still, she wanted to know more about this guy—not to mention learn about why Robin decided to leave town. Jessica glanced at her mom, who leaned over to pet Tela's head.

"Hey, I have an idea," Jessica said. "Mom's taking Tela home to play with her dogs. After work, I'm picking up tamales and heading there for dinner and to bring Tela home. Why don't you join us? That is, if you can tear yourself away from this new guy."

"I'd love to. Travis has plans with his friends later tonight."

A red flag popped up in the back of Jessica's mind. Why wouldn't this guy include Araceli in plans with his friends? She should definitely learn more about him.

"Great. Come by my house at six thirty."

"Perfect. I'll see you then." Araceli wrapped Jessica in a firm hug before popping up from the bench and striding out the door. She really had come a long way.

Jessica crossed the room to her mother. "I hope you don't mind that I invited Araceli for dinner."

"Of course not. That will be wonderful. That young lady really has it all going on. The promotion, and have you met her boyfriend, Travis? He's a real cutie."

"Not yet, but I'd like to."

"Speaking of meeting people, sometime, I'd like you to meet my new friend Eduardo." Clarice could barely contain her smile.

Uh-oh. Her mom had dated a few men since moving back to El Paso, but none of the relationships lasted more than a date a two. Now Clarice's eyes sparkled in a way Jessica hadn't seen in decades.

"He's a well-known artist from El Paso. You've probably seen some of his paintings. He's—well, I haven't felt this way about anyone in a long time." Clarice's smile lifted her whole face upward, sculpting away years better than the best plastic surgeon. Uh-oh.

"How long have you been seeing him?" Jessica asked, surprised she hadn't heard of him until now. She'd spent more time with her mom in the last two months than in the last fifteen years.

"I didn't want to tell you about it because you've been so sad about Angus. But honey, Ed's really great." Clarice's gaze flickered between worry about Jessica and the gooey look of a sixteen-year-old with her first crush.

Emotions swirled around the hollow pit in Jessica. Her mom pitied her so much she'd held back information. But damn, she hadn't seen her this happy since long before her parents decamped to the remote town of Fort Davis, Texas. The sadness present in her mom's eyes since her dad's death a couple of years ago had disappeared, or at least been glossed over with joy.

Funny how everyone around her grew happier while Jessica stewed in her foolish decision to go to a dangerous part of Juarez, Mexico, to retrieve her truck. Angus had asked her not to go. She'd gone anyway, and it had almost gotten her killed. When she returned, he walked out the door.

She couldn't take another minute of love songs breaking out around her. "I've got to get back to work. Thanks for taking Tela, and I'll see you tonight." Jessica looked straight into the hurt she'd caused in her mom's eyes. She could tell Clarice saw Jessica's pain and wanted to apologize, but Jessica pulled on her big-girl pants. "I'm happy to meet him whenever you want."

Her mom stepped in for another hug, but Jessica raised her hand in a wave and backed away. "See you tonight, Mom." Then she turned and took her tattered heart away.

Chapter 2

Alone and bored, Jessica ordered the tamales at six thirty, even though Araceli hadn't arrived yet. The empty house made her antsy. She loved the small adobe cottage with its long lot, giving Tela a huge backyard where she raced the fence with the neighbor's dog and occasionally dug holes.

She'd wanted this house so badly a few years ago. She'd needed to finally set down roots, to have something of her own to come home to, something to love and take care of. That had been the house. And it had been Angus. Once full, her life now seemed as empty as the walls that enclosed her.

As the minutes passed, the loneliness pressed in, making her wish she could go for a run. But she'd already done that. Normally, she'd crack open a textbook to keep her mind off the loneliness, but summer session had ended and her law school classes wouldn't start again for a couple of weeks.

After fifteen minutes, she texted Araceli, Then, she called her mom. "I'm running late, still waiting for Araceli."

"I'm surprised," Clarice said. "She's usually so responsible. Maybe she's in love. That can make you forget time."

After the call and the love comment, Jessica returned to finding ways to bide the time. She moved a coffee table out of the way and practiced her martial arts footwork. For months now, she'd been taking self-defense classes with Sal Guerra, an ex-sheriff's deputy she'd met shortly after she'd survived being kidnapped. He'd promised to help her gain the skills she'd need if she ever encountered something like that again. She probably would. Danger had a way of tracking her down.

Hopefully, she could avoid any more perilous cases while she finished her law degree and focused on mending her marriage. She'd graduate in less than a year and move from receptionist/paralegal to full-blown attorney as soon as she passed the bar exam. Maybe then she could trade her boss-approved side hustle of finding lost things—usually people—for the more mundane saving clients through legal means. Either way, the self-defense classes wouldn't hurt.

She imagined different scenarios: someone attacking her from behind, running at her, surprising her with a knife. Her body followed her imagination, dancing away, throwing a block, spinning out of danger while using an elbow for the first strike, a fist for the second.

She would turn herself into a weapon. She'd gain the skills to protect herself and then show Angus. When he left, he'd said he didn't want to see her die. By showing how she'd learned to protect herself, she'd steal that argument away. Plus, Sal would teach her to use a gun. She'd hated guns after running into the wrong end of them one too many times. But if it showed Angus how seriously she took his concerns, she'd become an expert shot.

The phone rang, pulling her out of her plans. Her mom's face lit up the screen. Jessica glanced at the time before answering. Araceli was now forty-five minutes late.

"Hey, Mom," Jessica said. "She's still not here."

"She must have forgotten. Have you tried calling her?"

"I've texted her twice, but I'll give her a call."

"I'm sure she's with that young man. Why don't you leave a message that you'll catch up with her later?"

"Sure. I'll be there soon."

Worry replaced the relief that should have come with finally getting to leave the empty home. Araceli might only be twenty and in love, but not showing up wasn't like her.

Her belly full of masa, pork, and red chile, Jessica settled back to quiz her mom. She spared a quick glance at the three dogs. They'd stretched out together in order of size on a giant dog bed. Her mom's wiry-haired Chihuahua mutt leaned against Tela, who lay next to Sheba, her mother's gentle giant that Jessica had found at the animal shelter. They all chewed on hard, bone-shaped dog treats. A pang of gratitude hit Jessica that her mom would be safe in her isolated home as long as she had her canine protectors at her side.

"You seem to be doing great out here. I'm glad." A mix of feelings washed through Jessica, happiness at her mom's fresh start and concern about why Araceli hadn't answered her texts or calls. Surely, her mom was right—she was out celebrating her promotion and the end of classes with Travis and had forgotten about Jessica's invitation. And hadn't looked at her phone.

Jessica flipped her phone over on the table so the screen pointed down. "So, tell me about Robin leaving. That really surprised me."

"Me too. She hadn't even hinted at it before today, although I hadn't been in the gallery for a few days. She says she'll keep an eye on things from afar while Araceli manages the day-to-day. She told me not to worry about sales, that she knows lots of gallery owners in southern California and might even open a satellite gallery there."

"Why would she move at all? She and Dick are practically El Paso royalty. And why La Jolla?" There had to be more to the story.

"They've had a home in La Jolla for years—you know, it's one of those wealthy, artsy, southern California enclaves. I've met several of their friends in El Paso who also have second homes there. Besides, like she said, their son moved there."

"That confused me. I thought he was going to run the family insurance company." Jessica had met the young man once. He seemed to have more of his mother's friendliness and less of his dad's ego. Unlike his dad, Justin had welcomed Araceli into the family after he learned they were cousins. Dick had treated Araceli's family like second-class citizens and accused them of going after the family money—even though they never asked for anything. Plus, Jessica had tracked them down—they hadn't come knocking.

"Oh, I thought you knew," Clarice said. "They're selling the company to one of the national insurance firms. I think they're making a fortune off it. When Justin's college girlfriend moved, he followed her to La Jolla. I believe he has a job with an investment firm there."

"Huh." That put a different spin on things. Robin would do anything for that kid. Although why you'd want to follow your twentysomething to another state, she had no idea. "I guess maybe I can see it, but it does seem kind of sudden." Perhaps Dick talking to that sheriff's deputy had meant nothing. Still, her gut squeezed, hinting at something more nefarious.

A groove between Clarice's brows deepened. "I am so thankful for all the opportunities Robin has given me. She sells my work and lets me lease this wonderful home studio, but Ed wants to introduce me to other gallery owners in Texas and the Southwest. Now, with Robin making this announcement, I think that may be a good idea. I just don't know."

Jessica couldn't tell if the concern on her mom's face related to Robin's leaving or Ed's advice. "Can you trust this guy?"

A smile turned Clarice's lips, but sadness lit her eyes. "I really like him, and yes, I think he's trustworthy. He's a well-known and respected artist."

"Then why the almost sad face?"

"I miss your dad."

Jessica's heart plummeted. Her parents had married young and seemingly had the perfect marriage, at least to Jessica's young eyes. Then her father broke the law by destroying evidence while serving as El Paso's district attorney. That, in turn, broke their family. After his conviction and house arrest, her parents moved to a small town in the middle of nowhere, Texas. At sixteen, Jessica refused to go with them.

For years, she'd considered herself abandoned and dealt with the pain in unhealthy ways—drinking too much, picking up guys in bars. She refused contact with her parents until years later, when an extremely wealthy business mogul asked her to find his missing daughter.

That case was like looking in a funhouse mirror, the woman's life opposite hers yet somehow far too similar. Jessica reexamined her life, got back in touch with her parents, and asked Angus to marry her. Since then, her father had died, and Angus had left. That left Jessica and her mom.

"I miss Dad too. I do know he'd want you to be happy."

"He would. It's just so much. There's so much change." Clarice sighed heavily, and all three dogs looked her way.

"It is a lot. Your world in Fort Davis was really small. You had to take care of Dad after his stroke, and you told me you didn't leave the house much. Now, you're back in the city, and you have this whole new career. I'm so proud of you."

"I'm happy. I really am." Clarice wiped a tear from her cheek. "I just always had your dad to share things with before."

"Thanks for sharing them with me. I know I haven't always been the easiest person to deal with." Far from it. It had taken Jessica long months to stop blaming her mom for all that had gone wrong in her life. Months more to forgive herself for her role in their rift.

"Jessica, you have a good heart. I see the way you are with Araceli. She's also going through a lot of new—I'm sure that's why she forgot about tonight. But you've really helped her this summer. She told me about how you've introduced her to people and had her over. She really appreciates that."

Jessica flipped her phone back over. No messages. "She's a smart young woman. I just hope she's okay. Do you know anything about this guy she's seeing?"

"Not really. I met him at the gallery once. He's super cute, enrolled at UTEP, grew up in El Paso. He seemed to really like her. I'm sure everything is fine."

Jessica hoped her mom was right. Still, her gut rumbled. Danger lurked, as always. Hopefully it was coming for her and not someone she couldn't protect.

Chapter 3

B ack home, Jessica pulled into the driveway and stared at the dark house. Tela whined beside her. It seemed like neither of them wanted to go inside to another lonely night. Not yet.

She checked her phone one more time. Nothing. Then she put the truck in gear and backed out of the driveway. She'd met Araceli's roommates when Jessica had helped her move into the small house near UTEP, but she didn't have their contact info. So she drove there instead.

Fifteen minutes later, she parked in front of a cute brick house with an inviting front porch. Lights glowed warmly from the windows. Tela looked confused, but excited.

"Come on, girl. Let's go see who's home."

As Jessica stepped out of her truck, she noticed a twenty-year-old maroon Toyota Corolla parked across the street. She recognized Araceli's car. Maybe some easy explanation existed. Araceli had lost her phone and forgotten about dinner. Jessica attempted to fan the flame of that small hope, but it smoldered for a second, then disappeared.

The laughter of young women reached her as she stepped onto the porch. Again, she hoped to find Araceli inside, all of this a big mistake. She knocked.

A short woman with a mane of wavy brown hair opened the door. Jessica recognized one of the roommates.

"Hi. I'm Jessica. Araceli's friend."

"Of course, come in. Cute dog." The woman stepped back from the door, opening it wide. "I thought she said she was going to dinner with you tonight. Is everything okay?"

A fresh stab of fear sent adrenaline sliding through Jessica's veins. Araceli hadn't forgotten. And she wasn't here. "She never showed up. I've been texting and calling. I hoped she'd just forgotten and was here."

The background noise of a TV switched off. As Jessica stepped into the house, she saw the other roommate on the couch, remote in hand, a worried look on her face.

"That doesn't sound like Araceli. She's the most responsible of the three of us," said the woman on the couch.

"Oooh. I'm worried about her," the first roommate said. "She's way too trusting."

"She was going to meet her boyfriend earlier. Do you know if she did?" Jessica asked. "Also, do you have his number?"

"I knew that güero was bad news." The wavy-haired roommate shook her head. "He came through here all blond and shiny, and Araceli, she's not used to that. Thought she was a princess and he was the prince."

"Yeah," the second woman said. "Hang around El Chuco long enough and you'll get burned by those white guys."

Jessica would have laughed at the slang term for white men and for El Paso if worry hadn't grabbed hold of her. Araceli definitely had a lot to learn from these ladies.

"Do either of you know how to get a hold of him?" Jessica asked. "I'd love to find out if she's with him."

"I've got a friend who knows him. Give me a sec." The woman on the couch bent to her phone and texted. Less than a minute later she recited Travis's number to Jessica.

Jessica immediately punched the number into her phone, already preparing to chew out Araceli for worrying her so much. Surely, she was with this guy, and hopefully she hadn't done anything she'd regret.

"Hello?" A male voice crackled in Jessica's ear.

"Hi. This is Jessica Watts. I'm looking for Araceli Gamboa. Is she with you?"

Silence. Jessica looked at her phone. The asshole had hung up on her.

She pressed the button to phone him again. It rang and rang but no one picked up.

"Fucking asshole."

She tried calling again, then texted him.

I need to speak to Araceli. Now.

Jessica wanted to reach through the airwaves and strangle this guy. She called again. This time, the phone went straight to voicemail. She wondered if he'd turned it off, and if so, what that meant.

She texted him one more time. *If something is wrong with Araceli, you're looking pretty guilty. I think it's time to call the police.*

"This asshole's gone AWOL," she said to the women watching her. "Let's exchange numbers. The first person who hears from Araceli lets everyone else know."

Back in her truck, Jessica had no idea what to do next. She drove home, figuring at least Tela could get some sleep.

But once there, her anxiety heightened. She moved from the sofa to the kitchen and back, constantly checking her phone. Tela lay on the dog bed, but her mismatched eyes watched Jessica pace the room.

Jessica thought she'd grown used to dangerous situations. In the past, just when she should be most scared, a calm overtook her, an icy feeling that slowed down time. But this time, each passing moment brought fear closer, the fear that someone who didn't deserve to might get hurt. She started to unpack that thought, wondering about the different standards she held for herself and everyone else. But this wasn't a time for selfishness. She turned her thoughts back to Araceli.

Finally, she called Angus. He couldn't solve Araceli's predicament any more than Jessica could, but she needed someone to talk to before she crawled out of her skin with worry. A mix of hope and guilt pierced her as she pressed his number on her phone. Hope that he'd understand her need to talk, that they'd have a good conversation, that it might lead somewhere positive. Guilt because she should leave him alone. He'd made it clear when he left that he'd tired of her dances with danger. And Araceli's disappearance had brought the scent of trouble to the night.

Angus knew her too well. So many times, she'd taken on cases that had almost gotten her killed. The last time, Sal had risked death as well, or imprisonment in a room that still haunted Jessica's nightmares. But Jessica had relied on luck one last time, and it had held. That well of fortune had to be bone dry by now. She knew it, as did Angus.

She'd promised herself not to bug him until she'd learned how to fully protect herself. Then he wouldn't have to worry. She'd spent months training with Sal, becoming her own weapon. The journey would take many more months. Sometimes it seemed the more she learned, the farther she had to go. But she'd get there, and then she'd get Angus back.

Tonight, she needed to stray from her plan. Surely, he'd understand once he knew she worried about Araceli, not herself.

"Jessica." He sounded happy to hear from her. Well, if not happy, then at least not angry. His voice sped years of memories past her: falling in love in high school, doing something about it in college, the dark years of hurting him and loving him at the same time, the glorious years of marriage.

"Hey. It's really good to hear your voice." It was a wonder she could talk at all.

"Is everything all right?"

His question slammed her back to the reason she'd called. "It's Araceli. She was supposed to meet me for dinner tonight, but she never showed up and hasn't returned messages. She's got some new boyfriend. Her roommates gave me his number. When I called him, he answered and then hung up. Now his phone is off."

Empty air followed her words. Had calling him been a mistake? Maybe she was overreacting. But she wasn't. Even if she hoped she was.

"If anyone else were worried about a college kid being out too late with their boyfriend, I'd tell them not to stress about it until morning. But it's you, and you have a nose for this stuff. How can I help?"

Relief sank through her bones. She wasn't alone.

"I don't know. It's too early to call the cops, but I'm going crazy just sitting around waiting for news."

He chuckled, low and raspy. "I bet. Patience has never been your strong suit."

She'd heard that before. From him. From others. For Jessica, waiting physically ached.

"How about I come over and sit with you until you hear something?"

"I'd love that, and Tela would love to see you too. Thanks." Part of her glowed with the thought of seeing him again, especially here. She glanced toward the kitchen, saw the spot by the table where he'd told her he was leaving cast in a permanent shadow.

"Be right over." The line went dead but her body came alive as his words scraped through her hurt places and wrapped her in silk all at once.

Not ten minutes passed before headlights swung into the driveway. Jessica popped up from the couch and Tela, who'd been snoring on her bed, joined her at the door.

When Angus hopped out of his truck, the dog shot across the yard and leapt into his arms, almost tackling him into the grass. Jessica wanted to do the same.

Instead, she stood on the stoop, awkward, like a teenager inviting a boy over for the first time. Should she hug him? Shake his hand? Strip his clothes from him and mount him in the front yard the way she wanted to?

"Hi. Thanks for coming over." Fully inadequate, the words were the best she could do. She envied Tela wiggling in circles around his feet so clearly joyous at his return. It would break that dog's heart when he left again.

He gave her a smile that cracked her heart open. "It's good to see you. I'm glad you called."

"How did you get here so quick?"

"I moved into Robbie's back cottage a couple of weeks ago."

"You live half a mile from here and didn't even tell me?" She did her best to sound annoyed, but her heart did a little flip. She led him into the house. Offered him a drink—beer, water, tequila—the things she always had on hand.

"Just water. Thanks. Why don't you catch me up on the story?"

She recounted the day: Araceli's promotion, not showing up for dinner, the speculation about what might have happened. Angus tried Travis from his phone but failed to get a response.

They sat on the couch together, turning the problem over. Tela splayed across Angus's lap, but reached a paw to touch Jessica as well, as if she could put them back together with her love.

Jessica tried calling Araceli again. Futile, but something to do. She made up her mind to call Jaime Castro in the morning. A lieutenant with the El Paso Police Department, he'd been a force for good in Jessica's life since her parents left. Maybe he'd have some new ideas.

Chapter 4

Jessica's phone rang, startling her awake. Her head rested on Angus's strong shoulder, just the way it used to, and relief flooded her senses. She relaxed into his chest, her dark hair spilling down his white T-shirt, her pale arm against his cinnamon-colored skin. Then the phone rang again, snapping her into reality.

She and Angus both sat up, still on the couch where they must have drifted off. Jessica pulled her phone from the coffee table.

She didn't recognize the number that flashed on her phone. "Hello?"

"Jessica, it's me." The voice sounded vaguely like Araceli's, but a new sorrow smothered the once bubbly tone.

"Oh my god! Araceli. Where are you?"

Only the muffled sound of crying came through the airwaves. Asking if she was okay seemed cruel—clearly not. A raft of tragedies ran through Jessica's mind, but in the back of them all loomed the shadow of a man. Travis must have hurt her.

The sobs lessened. "¿Dónde estamos?" Araceli asked, although not directly into the phone. She must be with someone else. And didn't know where she was.

Jessica heard a garbled answer. Then Araceli returned to the line. "I'm at Hacienda Nopal. It's a salon de eventos, I'm not sure exactly where. Just a minute."

Araceli might be across the border in Juarez. Event centers littered the outskirts of the city. They usually had a room you could rent for parties, and often featured large outdoor barbeque areas, swimming pools, even water slides. The spaces held everything from corporate parties to weddings. If Araceli had made it across the border, she was a long way from home.

Jessica's phone buzzed. The screen showed a text with location co-ordinates. Jessica pressed on it and a map appeared. Not Juarez. The pin lay far east of El Paso, miles outside of the city limits.

Jessica held the phone to her ear again. "Is that where you are?"

"Yes. I need help." The sobs started again.

Jessica looked at Angus, her chest aching with the anguish in Araceli's voice. "I'm right here. Angus is here with me. We can come get you. Are you safe?"

"No! I'm safe, but you please come alone." Louder sobs, ones that must be wrenching the poor woman's body apart, tore through the phone.

The worst of what could happen to women went through Jessica's mind. Araceli needed a friend.

"It's okay. I'll come alone. I'm leaving right now, and I'll stay on the line with you." Jessica jumped from the couch, desperation pushing her into action.

"No," Araceli said. "I have to give this woman her phone back. I'll be in the parking lot. And please bring me some clothes."

The line went dead but Araceli's pain still echoed through Jessica. She slid the phone into her pocket.

"I've got to go get her, and she wants me to come alone." She wanted to bring Angus into this, to keep him involved and close. But she respected Araceli's wishes far more than her own whims.

"I know. I heard her. She sounds traumatized. You should go. I'll head home, but if you need anything at all, just call."

"I will." She wanted to throw her arms around him. He'd come when she'd called, when she really needed him. "Thanks for being here tonight."

"You bet." He paused before leaving. The moment when he normally would have told her he loved her stretched between them. He didn't say the words, but they flooded into her heart anyway. She couldn't say them back but hoped he saw them in her eyes. The bond between them still held, as strong as the sun and as solid as the mountains. She'd find a way back to him.

He turned to leave and she darted for her bedroom, not wanting to see him walk out the door. She grabbed sweatpants and a soft T-shirt and made it to her truck in less than a minute.

On the road, her anger blossomed into a black rose whose thorns pricked her veins, flooding them with poison. Araceli needed new clothes. What had that asshole done to her? Probably only one thing would necessitate new clothes. One of the oldest crimes in the books.

Her rage grew with each mile. But her sorrow grew alongside it. Jessica had a hand in the tragedy. One of her cases had led her to Araceli, but Jessica hadn't had to stay friends with her. She didn't need to propose that Araceli move to El Paso and enter the university. Sure, Araceli had wanted these things, but if Jessica had never shown up on her doorstep, she wouldn't have begun the journey that led to this night.

Jessica forced her mind from that path. The blame for this lay squarely at the feet of Travis. Even though Jessica didn't know the details, she could imagine them. A young, naïve woman from Mexico, an entitled white kid from El Paso. A shudder went through her. She'd make sure Travis paid for whatever he'd done to Araceli.

Even speeding, it took her an hour to get to the event center. By this time, it was after two in the morning, and only a few cars remained in the parking lot. People stood in groups talking to each other, and Jessica scanned the lot for Araceli. Finally, she saw her leaning against the trunk of a sedan, an old woman by her side.

Jessica almost didn't recognize Araceli. Red eyes stared from a face surrounded by ratted dark brown hair. A shawl over her shoulders partially hid a ripped blouse, and her blue jeans had turned the color of sand and were filthy with streaks of gunk. Shame burned through Araceli's eyes.

Jessica grabbed the clothes and rushed to her side, but Araceli just held her hand out for the clothes. Then, she disappeared into the courtyard of the building.

"What happened?" Jessica asked the old woman.

"She came in from the desert." The woman's frail voice sounded as dry as the sand surrounding them and matched her wrinkled skin and the halo of gray hair. Her somber black dress matched the shawl she'd taken from Araceli's shoulders and which she now wrapped around her own.

"When? Did she tell you what happened?" The need for answers drove Jessica's words, the desire for retribution following quickly behind.

"No sé. She wouldn't tell me anything. Just asked if she could borrow my phone."

How could the woman have stayed with Araceli through Jessica's long drive across El Paso without knowing more?

"Was there a party here? Was she a part of that?"

The woman stared at Jessica with eyes that had seen too much trauma over the years. "No. My great-grandson turned one year old today. The celebration was for him. I tired of the drunkenness and arguing of my family and came to the parking lot for quiet."

Jessica became aware of the conversations around her for the first time. Loud voices spoke in English, Spanish, and the pocho middle ground. She'd seen this movie before. Children's birthday celebrations in El Paso came with kegs of beer, food for days, and kids eventually falling asleep under tables, in corners, and occasionally on the dance floor as the party continued around them. This one had probably ended at two a.m. when the salon closed. She'd attended ones that didn't end until guests stumbled home in the morning light.

Araceli returned to the parking lot wearing Jessica's sweats. She walked straight to the dumpster, threw her clothes in, then got in the passenger side of Jessica's truck.

Jessica wanted to dive after the clothes and the evidence they might contain. But Araceli looked broken, and going against her might result in one more injury.

"Thank you for helping my friend." Jessica said.

"Take care with her," the old woman replied. "Someone has trampled her spirit."

Jessica nodded, afraid of that very thing.

She steered the truck away from the party and back onto the road that would eventually take them home. "Do you want to talk about it?'

Araceli had curled against the far door, making herself as small as possible. She shook her head.

"I can tell you've been hurt. Can I take you to the hospital or to the police station?"

Araceli shook her head harder this time while tears leaked from her eyes. A guttural sound ripped itself from her throat, but no words came out.

"Do you want to go to your house? You're welcome to stay with me." Jessica hoped the trauma hadn't made her friend mute.

Araceli remained silent for at least a mile. Finally, Jessica heard a sigh.

"Is Angus at your house?" Araceli asked in a small voice.

"No. He went home."

"I want to stay with you."

Jessica glanced at the woman beside her. Her eyes had closed, and she hugged her torso as if she was cold or needed protection.

"Of course," Jessica said. "You can stay as long as you'd like."

Chapter 5

Araceli barely spoke when they got home. She wanted to shower. With her clothes in the dumpster, the only remaining evidence of the crime could be on her body. Jessica asked again if they could go to the police. Araceli just shook her head, her eyes shining pits of despair.

She needed gentle treatment and the space and time to deal with whatever she'd suffered. But Jessica bent toward justice and action, and postponing a rape kit until after a shower might destroy evidence. How did one balance care and responsibility when the offense occurred to someone else?

Jessica removed a fluffy towel from the linen closet and a pair of flannel pajamas from a drawer and offered them to Araceli. The young woman set her lips in what looked like a failed attempt at a smile.

"Your fingers . . ." Jessica stared in horror at the swollen, red fingertips and scraped knuckles.

"Do you have tweezers and aloe? I used sap from a prickly pear on my wounds, but my hands shook. Some of the spines got me."

"Please, let me help." Jessica led her to the bathroom, the brightest room in the house. She had to bite her lip to keep from asking what happened. Araceli would talk when ready.

Araceli sat on the toilet lid and Jessica on the edge of the tub. As tenderly as possible, Jessica examined each hand, pulling the tiny barbs from Araceli's fingers. They didn't speak, and somehow the moment seemed ancient, both traumatic and healing. Jessica hated that since the beginning of time, women helped each other through the worst of what men dealt them.

Jessica had lived a fortunate life, often the pursuer instead of the pursued. She took what she wanted, in a bar, in the desert night. She'd always considered herself a different kind of woman, one who preferred the adrenaline of a fight to running, who would destroy others rather than become a victim. Despite her bravado, it had happened—she'd become a victim—even if she hated admitting it. Bad guys had drugged her more than once, had punched her, confined her. But she'd survived. And she'd help others do the same.

Jessica tried again. "I really think you should consider going to the police. I'll be there with you."

Araceli's eyes fell to the floor. "They didn't rape me. I appreciate your help, but I really don't want to talk about it right now."

Relief, and even more worry, flooded through Jessica. She'd wait Araceli out for now because trauma sometimes required holding yourself together before sharing. But each minute that went by, accountability for those who had done this slipped further away.

When Jessica's alarm went off at eight thirty, her body ached as if she hadn't slept at all. She hauled herself out of bed, surprised that Tela wasn't huffing her impatience from the bedside. Regardless of when Jessica got out of bed, that dog acted as if she'd been forced to wait eons before getting breakfast and a trip outside.

Jessica peeked into the guest bedroom through the slightly ajar door. Tela looked up, then rose, glancing at the bed where Araceli slept before joining Jessica. The dog deserved a hug and a few extra treats this morning. Somehow, she knew Araceli needed her.

Jessica opened the door to the backyard, poured dog food, and brewed coffee. So much had happened last night that needed sorting. But Saturday mornings meant self-defense training. In under an hour. All the way across town.

She considered cancelling. After all, she could use a few more hours of sleep. But she'd made a commitment to Sal, to herself, to see the classes through. While the training might save her life someday, she mostly hoped it would save her marriage. For that reason alone, she wouldn't skip a single class. It was like when she stopped sleeping around and committed to Angus—even one slip-up could cost her everything. She'd adopted a no-tolerance policy for herself back then, and she'd do it again now.

Of course, that thought led back to Angus and the previous night. He'd arrived so quickly after she called and now lived practically around the corner. Was it a sign? Did he want to get back together? A part of her despised pining over a man, but unlike girls who grew up dreaming about their perfect man, she had evidence of how the right one could turn a broken life into something whole.

She'd wasted so many years living in a glorified shack, drinking too much, fucking around, her life not going anywhere. Then came Angus. She tried to shake free from the memories of what she'd lost. Whether the lack of sleep or the yearning caused the ache, it pounded as if her brain wanted out of her skull. She took two aspirins.

What had he said? That he didn't want to worry about whether she'd come home hurt or not come home at all? She'd remedy that. She would become a machine too hard to kill—like that woman in *Terminator*.

She downed the rest of her coffee and headed for the shower, determined to become a better, more badass version of herself. She noticed Tela slipping back into Araceli's room. Jessica vowed to find out what had happened and help Araceli move past it.

Once she'd showered and dressed, she stopped by Araceli's door one more time. The woman needed to sleep, but Jessica also didn't want her waking up with no one home and feeling abandoned.

Jessica knocked on the door frame. "Hey, Araceli. We need to talk."

Araceli opened her eyes and looked at Jessica. She seemed alert, like she'd faked sleeping. After whatever happened last night, sleep probably didn't come easily. Tela rose from the floor and rested her muzzle on the bed.

"I've got an appointment for self-defense training across town. You're welcome to come with me," Jessica said.

"Do you mind if I stay here?"

"Of course not. I brewed a pot of coffee, and there's cereal and a few other things if you get hungry."

"Thanks." Araceli's hand reached for Tela's head. "Do you mind leaving the dog?"

"Of course not. She can be really good company. Believe me." Tela had helped Jessica through many ugly, lonely nights.

"Thanks," Araceli said then rolled over to face the wall.

Jessica stared at her a minute longer. The monsters in Araceli's head might shrink to a manageable size if she shared them. Stuck in one's head, they stoked fear and grew. Jessica had plenty of experience with similar demons from her recent cases: an overbearing father, an evil priest, a house that kept her trapped for days.

But she wouldn't have recovered if she'd left the demons in her psyche. When she got back, she'd speak with Araceli and find a way to get her on the path to healing.

"Good girl," she whispered to the dog. "Take care of her, and I'll be back in a few hours."

Jessica left the house, wishing she had a sentry to stand guard and protect Araceli. Fortunately, only Angus knew the woman was here. Jessica had told Araceli's roommates she'd found her, but kept her whereabouts vague.

She texted Angus on the way to the truck. *Thanks for being here last night.* She'd already let him know Araceli was safe and staying with her.

Sure. I'll always be there when you need me, even if we're not together.

Well that was a razor blade to the heart. At least he hadn't asked for a divorce. Tears threatened Jessica's eyes, but she brushed them away and bucked up. She had a plan to win him back, and she'd stick to it.

Plus, she needed to get enough information from Araceli to go after the boyfriend who'd hurt her. She hadn't missed that Araceli had said "them" more than once, not "him." That deserved retribution.

Jessica rounded the corner of Sal's house, heading to the back where they usually practiced. Laughter drew her eyes to one of the lounge chairs surrounding the pool. In it lay her boss, crack attorney Linda Reed. And Sal. Spooning her boss. At least they both had clothes on.

Jessica almost turned around and fled the scene. They'd started dating a few months ago, and Linda's demeanor had changed from fierce to unreasonably happy. She also looked years younger. Great for her. Jessica sure missed that glow from getting laid on the regular. She'd probably turn into a shriveled old woman by thirty-five if she didn't get her man back. That was a great reason to stay, even given the embarrassing situation.

"Uh, hey," Jessica said, announcing her presence.

"Ah, Jessica." Sal jumped up. "Would you like some coffee?"

She swore he turned red. "Sure."

Sal disappeared into the house and Jessica sat on the chaise next to Linda. "Didn't expect to see you here this morning. I take it things are going well with Sal?"

"I can't believe I've lived in this godforsaken city for almost my entire life and dated every loser in town, only to learn he'd been here all along." Linda swung her legs around and sat up. "So, you're here for your training? You know, Sal showed me a few moves last night."

"Gross. I do not want to hear about that."

"Martial arts moves! Get your mind out of the gutter. Although, some of those holds are pretty hot. In fact . . ." A wicked grin spread across Linda's face. "Well, you don't want to hear about that."

"I really don't. Not when the whole world is getting laid except for me." As soon as she said it, she thought of Araceli and wished she could take the words back. Yes, there were a few good guys out there, but women played a risky game in trying to find them when the number of jerks and dangerous men seemed to have exploded in recent years.

Something about the ease of trolling on social media had made them more vocal if not more active.

Sal returned with a steaming mug of black coffee. Jessica brought it to her nose and inhaled, the New Mexico piñon giving it a rich aroma she loved.

"Keith should be here in a few minutes. You're going to practice with him today," Sal said.

"Why?" Jessica had warmed to Sal's nephew, a sheriff's deputy who'd arrested her for trespassing the first time they'd met. She had trespassed, although for a good reason. She'd been searching for a missing girl. As they'd run into each other over the following year, she learned he was one of the good guys. In fact, he seemed almost as eager as she to get to the bottom of that case.

As if he'd been summoned, Keith rounded the corner of the house. "Good morning."

Jessica startled. She'd only ever seen him in his uniform. Now he wore a pair of navy basketball shorts and a white tee. She'd known he was built like a linebacker, but the clearly defined muscles in his calves and arms surprised her. He looked like he'd arrived straight from an early morning workout.

Jessica scanned her own bare legs and tank top. August in El Paso brought afternoon monsoon rains and more humidity than any other month. For natives used to the dry desert heat, the sheer sweatiness of this time of year made it uncomfortable.

But that didn't compare to the discomfort of sparring with this guy. Especially since he seemed to have a bit of a crush on her. She glanced at Sal, waiting for an explanation for this unwanted addition to her lesson, but no emotion crossed his face.

"You can't just practice with me," Sal finally said. "Your opponent could be any size or shape. Let's go."

"Can I watch?" Linda asked.

Great, a peanut gallery. This day couldn't get any better.

"Really?" Jessica asked as she stared down her boss.

"That's a great idea." Sal turned to Jessica. "Learning to fight when you're uncomfortable will be good for you."

"No problem there." Jessica took a long sip of her coffee and looked around at the ridiculous situation. If this was what it took to become a fighting machine, then she was in.

They tramped into a large studio at one end of the house. Jessica removed her shoes and bowed at the wooden tiger guarding the carpeted dojo. Large windows high on the sides of the room flooded it with light, while the mirrored walls below them reflected one's stance, posture, footwork, and every block and hit.

Jessica moved to the center of the floor and faced Keith. She positioned her feet shoulder-width apart, with one slightly behind the other. Power surged through her body. At the same time, calm seeped through her like mist. Something about this room, light reflecting off mirrors, the floor a light blue-gray carpet, transported her to a different space in her mind. Everything dissipated except the strength of her body and the desire to learn this new dance.

She'd thought she'd hate learning to fight. Instead, it became an outlet for negative emotions, and she threw them into each block and hit. In the dojo, the empty spaces Angus had left filled with watchfulness and quick thinking. Yes, she learned rote moves, but as soon as she knew the basics, Sal encouraged her to prepare for his next move, anticipate it, and plan her response. She could often stay a step ahead now, although he always seemed three or four steps down the line. She yearned for that ability, and striving for it kept her deeply engaged in the moment.

When Keith stepped onto the mat in front of her, he tore through the room's special aura. She squared up against him. He had at least five inches on her five-ten frame, and easily outweighed her by fifty pounds. Probably more, given the muscles she'd seen earlier.

Sal matched her height and had a wiry frame, which differed from the mass facing her. She reset her feet, sticking them to the carpet and the earth beneath it. She relaxed into a slight crouch, ready to dance away. He appeared even larger as she looked up at him. Sparring with him would require speed instead of strength.

He matched her position, his black eyes glittering. He probably found it fun to spar with someone smaller. As Sal's nephew, he'd likely been taught all her moves long ago. But he might not expect her aggression. She would not let him best her.

He moved first, quick as a snake. One step, then a long arm aimed for her chest. She blocked it and spun away. Somehow, he was right there, spinning the same direction, then catching her from behind. As his arm closed around one shoulder, she lifted her foot and smashed it onto his with all her strength. Had she worn boots, it would have kept him from walking. Barefoot in the dojo, he barely stiffened against her. But she continued into her next move without a break and brought her free elbow sharply into his hip, right at the tender spot. He jerked at the hit, and she used his surprise to slip her wrist under the arm holding her and spin away.

This time, she danced far out of his reach. She couldn't outcompete him on speed or strength, so she'd have to come up with another plan. She glanced toward the room's perimeter where Sal and Linda watched. Linda offered her a quick wink. Sal's lined face betrayed nothing.

Jessica returned her gaze to the tower of muscle before her. He moved in quickly and threw the same hit again. This time, she leaned out of reach while sending her heel into his shin. The kick rebounded a pulse of joy up her leg as she quickly backed away.

She'd never expected to like hitting things. But the explosion of power always left a heady rush in its wake. If she'd learned to attack and defend as a child, she might have turned into a different person.

She suppressed the thought as Keith advanced again. This time, she surged forward, hoping to surprise him with the attack. A blow to his thickly muscled chest wouldn't hurt him, so she tried an uppercut to the chin instead.

Her mistake became immediately apparent. In her long reach toward his jaw, she'd left her right side wide open. He jabbed her ribs while simultaneously blocking her hit. She tried to back out of reach, but he followed, grabbing her upper arm with the hand he'd used to block her punch while wrapping a foot behind one of hers as she stepped back.

Rather than slamming her to the ground, he used his grip to slow her fall, sinking to one knee as she gently hit the floor. Two things pissed her off. First, his gentleness when she needed to learn to fight. The second was how he practically straddled her, smelling like freshly mown grass and boy sweat. It reminded her of the schoolyard playground, and Angus, her constant playmate. She pulled her knee up hard.

"Geez, Jessica," he said, grasping his crotch and rolling off her.

"Way to go!" Linda yelled from the sideline, clapping.

Jessica stood and would have offered him a hand, but he still lay curled in the fetal position, hands cupping his battered balls. Instead, she walked over to Sal, worried about how he'd react to her low blow.

When she stopped in front of him, Sal looked her up and down, shaking his head. "That was painful to watch, but smart."

She continued her workout with Sal. He took her through each of the moves Keith had made and gave her an arsenal of ways to deal with them. Finally, the lesson ended. A sheen of sweat covered her body, and she luxuriated in the heaviness of her tired muscles.

As they walked into the backyard, Linda waived them over to a table under the deep veranda. A large bowl of fruit and a full pitcher sat in the middle of the table. Keith stared at her from one of the seats.

"Sorry about that," she said.

"I'll live. I'll never trust you again, but I'll live."

"Why would you trust her? Why would you trust any opponent?" Linda asked.

Keith shrugged. "She's new to martial arts. I didn't want to hurt her."

Jessica poured iced tea from the pitcher as Linda passed her a bowl of fruit. "Yeah. If I don't get to trust men, men shouldn't trust me." She hadn't thought of Araceli's trauma when she made the comment, but it immediately came to mind.

"Fair," Keith said.

"Never trust anyone, not even your best friend." Sal almost whispered the comment, but everyone heard. All faces turned toward him. "I mean it."

Or your boyfriend. The words almost slipped out of Jessica's lips. She couldn't talk about Araceli, although everyone at this table could probably help the woman: Linda, a sharp attorney focused on women's rights; Keith, a sheriff's deputy; and Sal, a retired sheriff's deputy, all-around badass, and great self-defense teacher. Perhaps Araceli would feel better if she also learned to protect herself.

Jessica would mention it. All of it, as soon as she could get her to talk.

Chapter 6

Jessica returned to her house with a bottle of aloe vera gel and an actual aloe plant, at least according to the store clerk. The plant had the spiky leaves of an agave native to the surrounding desert, but without the deadly barbs. Instead of scratching or puncturing, the aloe healed.

Araceli took the gel and the plant with a grateful thanks, then disappeared into the bathroom. Jessica put several tea bags in a clear glass pitcher and set it on the back deck to catch the midday sun. Tela followed her out, did her business, then returned to the house. Normally she would have played for hours before coming inside to pass out from exhaustion.

Jessica followed the dog back inside. The dog's behavior pointed to her worry about their guest, and Jessica felt the same. Bringing Araceli medicine wouldn't address the internal hurt. Plus, someone needed to pay for what they'd done to her, and the more time that passed, the harder it would become.

Jessica found Araceli on the sofa in the front room. A shaft of light from the window lit her brown hair and formed a halo around her.

Tela leapt onto the couch and curled up next to Araceli, her head resting on the woman's thigh. Although she gently stroked the dog's head, the tension in Araceli's shoulders and her tight posture revealed the turmoil inside.

Jessica sat on the couch next to them. "We need to talk about last night."

Araceli nodded, but a tear rolled down her cheek. "I don't want to. I'm still processing what happened."

"Believe me, I understand the difficulty of getting past a frightening situation." Jessica might not ever completely overcome the nightmare of being locked in a room she couldn't escape. But she had survived and so had Araceli. They both needed to keep moving forward. "Sometimes it helps to talk."

Araceli said nothing. Her hand kept returning to the dog's head like a metronome, stroking from forehead to neck over and over. Tela's wary eyes watched Araceli as the pets continued.

Jessica had to get her past the silence. "Did Travis hurt you?"

Araceli's hand hovered an extra beat above Tela's head before dropping to fur. "No. I was kidnapped by a group of men. I tried to fight them off, but they put a pillowcase over my head and tied my arms behind me. I screamed, but no one heard me."

Jessica's stomach turned. This was so much worse than she'd thought. "Where did this happen?" The sun hadn't set when Araceli first went missing. It was pretty brazen to kidnap someone in broad daylight.

"I was an at old warehouse off of Paisano, near the racetrack."

"What were you doing down there?" Jessica knew the area well. Only a few miles away, Paisano ran along the Texas/New Mexico border and then the Texas/Mexico border past UTEP and into downtown. The only place with warehouses sat halfway between her house and the university. And miles and miles from where she'd picked up Araceli.

"I had to go there for something. It happened in the parking lot." Araceli's hand trembled as she told the story.

She hadn't really answered the question about why she'd been in that sketchy neighborhood. Nor had she addressed how she got there. Jessica clearly remembered seeing Araceli's ancient Corolla at her house when she stopped by to question the roommates. But Araceli looked ready to shut down, and Jessica needed to keep her talking.

She tried to be gentle. "Who took you to the warehouse?"

Araceli's eyes grew as big as a trapped animal's. Then she sighed. Closed her eyes. Dropped her head. It looked like surrender.

"I went with Travis. He asked me to wait in the car while he got something for class."

"Was he the one who kidnapped you?" Jessica asked.

"No! I don't know who grabbed me. I was sitting in his truck and two SUVs stormed into the parking lot. There were four guys. They rapped on the window and told me to get out of the truck. It terrified me."

Oh, shit. Jessica could feel the horror in her own veins. She'd seen images like this from across the country. Agents rounded up people like criminals, completely without evidence or trial.

"Please. Tell me what happened. Did you recognize any of them? Were they law enforcement?"

"They just told me to get out of the vehicle. I didn't want to. It seemed safer in the car. I couldn't tell who any of them were. They wore sunglasses, masks, and baseball caps so I couldn't see their faces. Their clothes were black, just like their vehicles."

By this time, not just her hands trembled. Araceli's whole body shook. Jessica skootched the dog over and wrapped an arm around her. "It's okay. You're safe now."

Araceli stayed rigid. "I tried to lock the door, but they opened it before I could. They pulled me out of the car and onto the ground. Then they covered my head. I thought they were ICE, but they didn't say. I've seen the videos of what they do to people."

Jessica wanted to explode with the unfairness of this. Araceli trembled in fear, Jessica in rage. She pushed the story forward. "What happened next?"

"They bound my wrists like they were arresting me. I told them I was here legally. I have a visa. They told me to shut up, said they didn't care." Araceli finally turned to Jessica and looked her straight in the eyes. "They called me a dirty Mexican, a spic. They said I was worse than a, a Black person, but they didn't use that term. Then they shoved me into one of their vehicles."

"Those fucking bastards." Rage engulfed Jessica. She hated that some people judged others by the color of their skin. She'd met a lot more white assholes than any other kind over the years. Shame accompanied the rage. Once, she'd thought the US the greatest country, Texas the greatest state. But these days, both seemed to be more concerned with hate than with improving the lives of the people who lived there.

"What happened next?" Jessica had to keep from spitting the words. She didn't want to scare Araceli, who might not realize her anger pointed at the men who did this, not the victim.

"I thought they would take me to a detention facility. I hoped I'd get a phone call." Araceli moved her eyes from Tela to Jessica. "I would have called you."

Jessica rubbed Araceli's back, matching rhythm with Araceli petting Tela's head. What a brave young woman. Jessica would have cursed the guys out, kicked the seats, caused trouble. But as a white woman, Jessica had a lot less to lose.

"Will you tell me the rest of the story?" she asked.

"We drove forever. I honestly wondered if they had decided to take me to Dallas or San Antonio for processing. I asked where we were going. That earned me an elbow in the side. After that, I kept quiet. That's when I thought they wanted to kill me, not deport me."

Jessica's hand stopped. What a horrible experience. She squeezed Araceli to her, grateful she could. The loneliness of being small in a great big world swirled around her. No matter how tough you thought you were, some things couldn't be overcome.

Araceli took a deep breath, then continued. "The vehicle left the pavement, and still we went on for miles. Then, suddenly, we stopped. The guys in my vehicle got out. They left me alone. That's when I was glad they'd covered my head. I didn't want them to see me cry."

Araceli took breath after raspy breath, obviously trying to calm herself. Tela whined and sat up, crawling into Araceli's lap and licking her face. Jessica kept her arm snug around the woman, letting her know she supported her.

Dizziness pulled at Jessica as she stood on the cliff edge of the rest of the story. And it would not get better. What had those monsters done to her friend?

Araceli took a moment. She hugged the dog close and buried her face in Tela's fur. Then she took a deep breath and seemed to calm herself.

"They pushed me into the sand. Someone kicked me in the butt, right in the crack. I wanted to scream from the pain. I probably did scream."

Araceli inhaled, stared straight at the wall in front of her. "The pillowcase came off my head, and someone kicked sand in my eyes. They said the most horrible things. Called me names. Denigrated my culture and my heritage. My people were here long before the white people. They were the ones who raped and murdered and pillaged. The natives only tried to protect themselves. They were exploited. Terrorized. The way I was."

She turned to look at Jessica. "Then it got worse. They called me slut and a whore. They said I wasn't good enough to be seen with a white man, that I should have never used my dirty cunt to try and tie one down. They knew about Travis." She dropped her head. "Then I felt them grabbing my jeans."

"Oh, Araceli. I'm so sorry. You didn't deserve that." The ache in Jessica grew. Araceli had told her she hadn't been raped. Jessica's mind raced to the clothes Araceli had thrown in the dumpster. They needed to try and retrieve them for evidence.

Araceli shifted from defiant to, perhaps, resigned. And definitely sad. "I felt my stomach rumble. I didn't want them to do that to me. I am a virgin. I couldn't let them hurt me that way. I sat up and tried to back away. The man grabbing my jeans reached for them again and undid the button. Then he grabbed the zipper. It made me so sick that I vomited all over him."

The anguish of hearing the story shifted and a beam of pride broke through. Araceli had to be the bravest woman in the world. Jessica gave her another squeeze, hopefully to let her know that whatever came next, Jessica was here for her.

Araceli sat a little taller, her lips pressed in a grim line. "They said I was disgusting. The one who'd grabbed me was so mad. He ripped off his jacket and his shirt. He was the whitest man I'd ever seen.

"He growled at me, told me, 'You're going to get it now.'

"So, I spread the vomit all over myself. I started shouting incantations in Spanish, hoping they'd think I was a witch. I think one of them called me that. Or maybe it was bitch—there was just so much going on."

"That took guts."

"Well, I'd already puked those out, so I had plenty." Araceli didn't quite giggle, but she showed a hint of a smile. Then, her face dropped. "The one I barfed on said they should kill me."

"That's so terrible. You're safe now." Jessica said as Araceli started to shut down and close into herself.

"I thought I would die." The sentence came out in a whisper. "Someone kicked me in the hip. Then something hit me in the side of the head near my eye and knocked me sideways into the sand. That's when I gave up. I closed my eyes and waited to die. I think I passed out, or slept. I don't know. The next thing I knew, they were gone. I lay in the sand alone, hurt, and ashamed. I did want to die then. But I couldn't leave this earth without my grandmother knowing what had happened. It would have killed her, and I couldn't have that blood on my hands."

"You are incredibly brave. You are a survivor." Jessica wished she could fill Araceli, who looked so deflated, with all the amazement and pride she felt for her. "Do you want to talk to your grandmother?"

"No. Not yet. She always knows when there's something wrong with me. I don't think this is something I can share."

Jessica wanted to press her to tell her story so they could bring these criminals to justice. To get them off the street where they couldn't hurt anyone else. And to protect Araceli and show her that she was safe. Safer. Jessica still wondered whether rogue ICE officers had nabbed her or if copycat criminals had used ICE tactics.

Something didn't fit. ICE aimed to deport immigrants. If they'd profiled Araceli as undocumented, they would have taken her to a detention center to be deported. Instead, these guys took her to the desert, terrorized her, and then left her in the country.

Also, ICE probably wouldn't have known about Travis. Unless Travis had ratted her out? Surely not, but his behavior last night stank of guilt.

The puzzle pieces remained wildly disarrayed, but Jessica swore she'd complete the picture.

"I know how raw you feel, but you have to talk to the authorities about this. These guys must be brought to justice."

Araceli shook her head. "Maybe I should just go home. Life in Mexico was boring, but not dangerous. I've never felt such hatred before."

Shame for how people in the US behaved slammed into Jessica. She'd far rather have Araceli in the US than fifty of the demons who told her to go back to Mexico. When would people here wake up and realize that the US, a country built on immigration, had denied its heritage and become the shithole country? If Araceli left and those guys stayed free, everyone lost.

"I hope you don't go home. I understand why you don't feel welcome. But you are good for this country. I want you here, Robin does, my mom, your roommates, and I'm sure lots of other people. And what these guys did to you was criminal. They need to be prosecuted."

Araceli bent over, wincing slightly, and hugged Tela, perhaps to avoid Jessica's question. When she spoke, her quiet voice barely reached Jessica. "I doubt I'll find justice here."

"Please. It's not just you. Others have been hurt out there." It wasn't fair to use guilt as a weapon, but the crimes happening in the east El Paso desert had gone on too long.

"What do you mean?" Araceli sat up, her face scrunched into a question.

Jessica's reputation for solving local mysteries had brought her in contact with plenty of evil. "A while back, I found two girls, cousins, who'd been kidnapped when they crossed the border with their families. They'd come from Guatemala, and I don't know what would have happened to them if I hadn't come across them that night. They were just eight and ten." Jessica's mind returned to the cabin in the desert and the quiet girls with the big eyes and bravery. She'd promised to help, a promise she had yet to fulfill.

"What happened to them?" Araceli asked.

"They're currently at a detention center in another part of Texas."

"Are they with their families?"

Jessica forced the words out around the rock that had settled in her chest. "Their families were killed shortly after they crossed the border. The girls saw everything. Then the murderers took the girls away." The pain and disgust of the story returned each time Jessica told it, strengthening instead of dissipating.

"No." Araceli's hand went to her throat.

"What if it was the same people who hurt you? What if they're taking other women out to the desert who aren't as resourceful or as lucky as you? Something rotten is out there, and we have to find it." The pleading in Jessica's voice ricocheted through her body. With Araceli's help, she could do something about this scourge. She wanted to run into the desert with a kitchen knife and her newfound skills and chase the demons from their hiding places, cut through their throats and watch their lifeblood drain into the desert sand. The darkness inside her unfurled and fed on the hungry desire.

Tears filled Araceli's eyes. "I don't want to be the one. I don't want to tell my story to strangers. The police, ICE, they are against people like me. I'm sorry if that makes me a bad person."

"You are not the bad person in this situation." Jessica sat back, stroking Tela's fur and trying to find a way forward. "I understand why you're worried about being detained. It's all over the news these days. You could be there for months, or they could deport you to another country. There's no reason to risk that. I have a close friend who is a police officer who you could talk to off the record. He might have some good advice." *For both of us.*

Chapter 7

Araceli excused herself to use the restroom. Jessica moved to the kitchen, hungry after her morning workout, and scrounged for food. She hadn't even asked Araceli if she was hungry. Jessica needed to be a better hostess and not just an investigator.

Opening the fridge, she saw eggs, cheese, and tortillas along with a twelve-pack of beer and a door full of different hot sauces. A bag of salad and a cucumber that had seen better days rounded out the offerings. Time to go to the store.

When Araceli didn't return, Jessica went looking for her. An open door led to an empty bathroom, but the door to the bedroom was closed and Tela wasn't around. Jessica knocked on the door.

"Come in." Disappointment tinged Araceli's voice, as if she didn't want to be found.

Jessica poked her head in the room. Tela sat beside the bed but glanced at Jessica with a dog's version of a worried face.

"Hey, when was the last time you ate?" Jessica asked.

Araceli seemed to consider the question. "I had lunch yesterday."

"It's been more than twenty-four hours. Let me make you something. I don't have much besides eggs, but I'm happy to go to the store. What do you like to eat?"

Araceli sat up. "I hadn't thought about food, but now that you mention it, I'm hungry. Let me help." She rose from the bed gingerly but strode across the room with more energy than Jessica had seen since she'd arrived.

When Araceli opened the refrigerator, she gasped. "Jessica. You don't have any food. How do you live like this?"

"I'm not much of a cook beyond steaks and breakfast burritos. I eat a lot of takeout, and I'm happy to order something. There's a barbeque joint not far away, and since it's El Paso, there's at least one Mexican restaurant on every corner."

Araceli rolled her eyes at Jessica then started opening the cabinets. "Let me make you some eggs, then I'll give you a list for the store."

Jessica sat back while Araceli lit a burner and put a sauté pan on the stove. She seemed at home and happier in the kitchen. The chore of cooking had the opposite effect on Jessica. It was nice to see the appliances being used. Angus cooked, and his mom had taught him some fabulous recipes. She missed that.

Araceli whisked eggs, then opened the fridge door and studied the salsas. She chose a bottle of Tapatio and poured a liberal amount onto the eggs.

"I love to cook." Araceli poured the egg mixture into the pan. "My grandmother always divvied up chores among my cousins and me, and I preferred cooking to cleaning and sewing. I also liked tending the garden."

"I didn't really learn those skills," Jessica said. "Although I don't mind cleaning when I have extra energy. It's something you can really attack."

Two people could have hardly led much different lives. Jessica's parents had left before she learned many of the life skills Araceli had mastered. Since Angus had left, she'd had to do her own laundry, something she despised. Surely, she had better things to do than fold clothes and bedding. If she'd grown up on a farm surrounded by other women, would she be different?

Araceli found a can of black beans in the pantry and cooked them on the stovetop, mashing them with olive oil and salt, then adding black pepper and cumin. Next, she heated tortillas on the open flame of one of the stove burners until they turned golden brown. Jessica usually forgot about hers and had to deal with burned patches.

"It smells incredible in here. Honestly, half the stuff you used, I couldn't have found in this kitchen."

"Maybe I will teach you to cook," Araceli said, a smile on her face. Then, it fell. "Although, I'll probably go home soon."

"Don't. Don't give up. Not yet. At least give it a couple of days. You were so excited about school and the job at the gallery."

Araceli didn't respond. Instead, she filled two plates and handed one to Jessica. The vibrancy she'd had while cooking disappeared. Jessica scanned her face, trying to decide whether fear or sadness had replaced it.

"If you go home, they win."

"I don't feel safe here."

"Would you feel safe if they were behind bars? I understand not wanting to talk to anyone, but I promise, you can trust my police officer friend."

"I don't know."

"Let's invite him over, and you can talk to him off the record. He can give you advice, and you'll make the final decision about what to do with it. I promise he's not ICE, not racist, and doesn't hate Mexicans. If you're uncomfortable with it, let me know, and I'll ask him to leave."

Plopping herself down at the table, Araceli took a bite of the fluffy, orange-tinged eggs. Her eyes closed as she chewed, perhaps a way of keeping Jessica out of her thoughts. Jessica tore off a piece of tortilla and loaded it with beans and eggs, keeping her hands busy so her mouth wouldn't pressure Araceli further. Like a horse waiting at the starting gate, if Araceli said yes, she could spring into action.

"If he comes here, and it's off the record, then I'll talk to him."

Jessica stuffed more food into her mouth to keep herself from leaping up and cheering. They would get the guys who hurt Araceli, and Jessica wouldn't stop until that happened.

Her phone sat like a loaded weapon, waiting for her to pull the trigger. Jessica managed to ignore it until they'd finished breakfast. When Araceli rose to clear the dishes, Jessica told her she'd clean up.

"Go ahead and call the police officer. I can tell that this is killing you."

Jessica snatched her phone off the table. Jaime answered on the third ring. She explained the situation and asked if he could stop by.

"This is a serious crime. She needs to come down to the station. I can meet you there," Jaime said.

"That's not going to happen. She's been through a lot, and frankly, doesn't want to talk to law enforcement at all. Please. I don't want her to feel like she's being victimized further. This needs to be super casual."

Jaime chuckled. "Well, I'm at the gym right now, so this is about as casual as it gets. Let me go home and shower, then I'll be over."

Tela whined near the back door, and Jessica moved to let her out. She stepped outside into the yard where Araceli probably couldn't hear her. "Can you come over now? We've got a window of opportunity where she's willing to talk. I don't want to miss it."

Jaime sighed. "I'm at the gym with Clint. You remember him? My new partner. If I come now, he comes with me."

"I'll make it work. See you soon." She hung up, hoping Araceli would agree.

Jessica wanted to follow up with Travis. She'd hunt him down wherever he hid. Also, she could backtrack from the event hall and attempt to locate the place where they'd terrorized Araceli. The sooner Jaime arrived, the better.

———

Araceli reluctantly agreed to talk to both officers. Fortunately, they arrived before she could change her mind.

Jessica introduced everyone, then took a seat on the couch next to Araceli, who looked incredibly uncomfortable. But with prompting, she retold her story.

Stoic and even-voiced, as if the second telling were easier than the first, Araceli recounted the kidnapping and brutalization in the desert. She didn't break down until she mentioned the names they'd called her. As she repeated the words between sobs, Jessica's anger flared again. Who were these asshats who hated others so much?

This meanness and closed-mindedness had plagued the country for years, but El Paso had borne the brunt of it. A white, gun-toting, MAGA racist had driven to El Paso from hundreds of miles away to murder people in an El Paso Walmart. He didn't care whether his victims were Mexican or American, only that they had brown skin.

The words he'd thought while shooting had likely matched the ones her captors had called Araceli. It wasn't right, and Jessica was going to do something about it.

So much evil had risen in this country. Shootings at schools, churches, and synagogues now happened so often they'd lost their sting. Everyone heard about it and talked about it but couldn't change it. Jessica hated that impotence. Now, she had the chance to combat at least one small part of it. She had to admit, the feeling excited her. She could balance the scales.

It surprised her when Clint rose from his chair and crossed the room to kneel near Araceli, who could no longer talk between the sobs. "I understand how much it hurts to be discriminated against. I don't know exactly what you went through, but I've been through similar. Believe me, this attack feels extremely personal, but they don't know you. They're fighting the idea of people like you, not the person you are inside. Their prejudices are about them, not about you."

The sobbing waned. Araceli peered at Clint. Perhaps she saw the truth in his eyes, because she reached for his hand. "I don't know how to get beyond it. They hate me. They don't want me here."

"I know," Clint said. "And they hurt you. I know." A tear leaked from his eye.

The intensity of their focus on each other astounded Jessica. She glanced across the room. She and Jaime could have been watching through a glass window instead of sitting near them.

"I thought they were going to kill me." Araceli's voice cut through Jessica's heart.

"I know." Clint wrapped her hand with both of his. His cheeks had turned red, and his blue eyes shone with tears.

"What happened to you?" Araceli asked.

Clint bit his bottom lip, as if holding in the truth. Then, his whole body relaxed. "I'm gay," he said. "Some people don't like that."

The admission startled Jessica. She'd only met Clint a few times. She'd never have guessed.

Subtly, Jessica glanced at Jaime, but he didn't look her way. The normally smooth tan of his cheek was mottled and red. Was he willfully ignoring her?

Her attention returned to the other pair in the room when Clint spoke again. "I experienced something eerily similar to what you did, in Arizona, not in Texas. And I was a little older than you are. Please believe me when I tell you this had nothing to do with you as a person. They don't even know you, it's just about what you represent."

Araceli nodded. "That doesn't really make it better. I still have to live with the fact that there are people in my new home that would rather I be in Mexico, or be dead."

"Are you sure you don't need medical attention?" Jaime asked. "We'd be happy to take you to the hospital for a checkup."

"I'm fine. Really. I'm already healing. Being here helps."

"I have a question for you," Jaime said. "Do you think they were all white?"

"I couldn't tell. The guy I threw up on, yes. The others—I tried to get a good look at them, but they had their faces covered. Most of them wore gloves. There was one guy, his hands looked as dark as mine. If I hadn't been so scared, I would have been angry. Our people are the original inhabitants here. A border doesn't make him any better than me."

"Not one of those guys is better than you," Jaime said. "We need to bring them to justice."

"You sound like Jessica," Araceli said.

Jaime chuckled. "I'll take that as a compliment—although she can be a little much sometimes."

Araceli smiled, which gave Jessica's heart a little twinge of relief. Clint rose, squeezed Araceli's hand one last time, and returned to his chair.

"One more question," Jaime said. "You played dead and then they left. How did you find your way out of the desert?"

"It took me a while," Araceli answered. "First, I hid. I couldn't believe they left without killing me. Maybe they thought they had. I know the guy I vomited on wanted to leave. He was pretty grossed out, and I think he was the leader."

"I waited for nightfall before I started walking. I was really sore, and I could feel my face swelling, so I used the nopal sap from the prickly pears to sooth my skin. I had to tear the paddles with my hands."

"She had cactus spines in her hands, the tiny ones." Jessica remembered pulling the barbs from her fingers.

"You need to be seen by a doctor to make sure you're okay. Can I take you to the hospital?" Jaime scooted to the edge of his chair.

"I'm healing. The mental damage is worse than the physical damage." Araceli smirked.

"There are doctors that help with that too," Clint said.

Araceli looked down and shook her head. After a moment, she looked back, her eyes resting on each of them before moving on. "I agreed to talk to you, but please don't ask anything else right now."

"We really appreciate what you've shared. Do you think you could find your way back to where they assaulted you?" Clint asked.

"I don't know. I walked for hours. It was slow. I didn't want to walk on the road in case they came back. I crossed the loose sand."

"That's a pretty hostile area," Jessica said. "I've been through there."

"I appreciate your coming by. And thank you for sharing with me," Araceli said, focusing on Clint. "But I am exhausted right now. Can we stop?"

"Of course." Clint spoke before anyone else had the chance. "Can I reach out to you tomorrow to see how you're doing? And if you decide to press charges, we'll do everything in our power to get these guys locked up."

Araceli nodded. Her lack of enthusiasm told Jessica she'd reached her limit. Maybe later they could explore Google Maps and try to work backwards from the events salon. In the meantime, Jessica wanted to pay a visit to Araceli's boyfriend.

Chapter 8

Jessica knocked on the door of the low-slung house shaded by large trees. Located in El Paso's Upper Valley, the house sat just a few hundred yards from the Rio Grande, close to the New Mexico border. She hadn't found an address for Travis Williams after Araceli's roommate had given her his last name, but she thought she'd found his parents.

A woman with shoulder-length honey-blond hair opened the door. She looked kind, with the crinkly-eyed smile that broadcast safety to puppies and young children.

"Hi, I'm Jessica Watts. Is Travis here?"

"No, he's not. How can I help you?"

"I'm a friend of his girlfriend."

"Girlfriend?" the woman asked.

"Is your son Travis Williams?" Jessica asked.

"Yes." Confusion crossed the woman's features, followed by an exasperated sigh. "He acted so strange when he got up. Perhaps you've got information that can help explain it. He left for school this morning, even though he wasn't supposed to leave for another week. Said there was something he needed to do at the registrar's office Monday morning."

The woman sighed, then stepped back and swung the door open. "I'm Gina. Please, come in. Maybe you can help me get to the bottom of his odd behavior."

Gina's discontent relocated to Jessica as she entered the house. "He left for UTEP this morning?" That made no sense. Was he planning on walking the fifteen miles to the university?

"Oh, no. He's enrolled at Arizona State. He's on his way to Tempe as we speak." Gina led her down a hallway with framed photos of a blond boy in various stages of childhood.

"ASU? I thought he went to UTEP." Everyone Jessica had spoken with said this guy was a UTEP student.

"Not anymore. He went there his first two years to get his grades up and save a little money. I'm an interior decorator, and his dad is out of the picture, so every penny counts. Fortunately, he'll spend his last two years at ASU."

The lying little rat. Travis looked guiltier by the minute. Araceli hadn't blamed him, but he'd led her to where she'd been abducted. An innocent man would have looked for the woman he left in his vehicle. Instead, this guy ran.

"Can I get you anything to drink?" Gina asked as she led Jessica into a casual room with shiplap walls and iron stars. A leather sofa and chairs nestled around a TV and windows facing a tiled courtyard filled with plants. It looked like they'd just filmed an episode of an HGTV show.

"No. I'm fine." Jessica sat in one of the chairs. She vacillated between an extremely direct approach or trying to draw information out of the woman slowly. Jessica doubted the woman would like what she had to say about her son.

As usual, she decided to fuck it and jump in. "My friend has been dating your son all summer."

"I'm sorry. I didn't know. He's twenty-one now, and even though he lived here, he was off doing his own thing most of the time." A worried look crossed Gina's face. "Is she pregnant?"

"Thank god, no." What a disaster that would be. Araceli said she was a virgin, and Jessica believed her. "He convinced my friend, and all of her friends, that he was a student at UTEP. When did he get into ASU?"

"Last spring. He's always wanted to go there. Is there something I can help you with?"

Jessica ignored the question but found it interesting that Travis had lived that lie all summer. Also, the school wasn't exactly an academic powerhouse. It showed real inspiration to want to go to an average college in a city hotter than El Paso.

"Do you know what he was doing yesterday?"

"No. Why do you ask?" Suspicion laced the curiosity in her tone.

Jessica worried that once she accused Travis of something, Gina might close up and refuse to talk to her. She needed to pull the trigger while she still had a chance.

"My friend was with your son yesterday. He told her he needed to go to a warehouse on Paisano. He went inside. While she waited in his car, a gang of masked guys abducted her."

The woman's eyes widened in response. "Is she okay? Was Travis taken too?"

Jessica almost laughed in surprise. Like these stories ever ended with the guy in trouble. This lady seemed pretty naïve, about her son and the world.

"Your son managed to disappear and avoid the trouble. My friend was taken to the desert, beaten, and left to die." The anger spilled from her tongue.

"Oh, no. That's terrible. Is she okay?" Gina clasped her hands together as if she were praying. It was going to take more than prayers to save her son.

"Strangely, your son didn't wonder why his girlfriend had gone missing. He didn't look for her at all. Last night, I called him while trying to find her, and Travis hung up on me. When I called back, he'd turned off his phone." Jessica watched Gina as if she were prey. She wanted to know how Mommy would respond to her son's actions.

"There's got to be some kind of mistake. Travis would never behave this way." The woman sounded panicked. "What did you say your friend's name was? He never mentioned dating anyone. Maybe this is a case of mistaken identity."

"I didn't say her name," Jessica said. "Why don't we call him right now and clear this up?"

Gina paused, as if she finally realized the stakes of taking the next step. "Of course," she finally said, then slipped her cell phone out of her pocket. She hit the green button, then held the phone to her ear.

Jessica heard the ringing, but Travis never answered. He must be running scared.

"He's on the road and probably not in a place where he can take a call. I'll send him a text to call me when he can."

Shit. Now Travis would know she was on his trail. She doubted she could get Gina to hold off talking to her son, but she had to try.

"You know what? My friend doesn't want to talk to him. She doesn't even know I'm here. I wanted to talk to Travis because she's scared to return to campus. If he's in Arizona, this won't be an issue. I'm so glad you shared that information with me."

"I think we need to talk to him. I'm sure he hasn't done anything wrong. Again, it must be a misunderstanding. Travis would never hurt anyone. He's been hanging out with a new crowd this year, but I'm sure they're all good boys."

Jessica skin prickled. "Who has he been hanging out with?"

"Just some kids he met . . . well, somewhere. They're not the usual crowd from high school. I think they all follow that life coach for young men."

"Really? Who's that? Someone in El Paso?" Was there an entire cabal of these men in the city?

"Oh, no. One of those online guys. I can't remember his name."

It would be a pretty serious understatement to say that a few unsavory characters recruited young men online, hoping to change their thinking. Jessica studied Gina. She had to know about this stuff.

"How can I help you resolve this?" Gina asked, her demeanor changed from friendly to suspicious. Time for an exit.

"Honestly. You already have," Jessica said. "Whoever is right or wrong on this, if Travis has left town for the semester, my friend doesn't have to be afraid." She stood. "Do you happen to know the names of any of Travis's friends? I'd love to follow up just in case they know anything."

Gina stood as well. "I'm sorry. I don't. I can ask Travis if you'd like."

So, the game had begun. Gina's cool response had the effect of stacking a brick wall. If Jessica pursued this, Gina would get Travis involved and warn his friends. None of that would be good for Araceli's safety. Jessica might have said too much already.

"Thanks for your time," Jessica said. Then she turned and headed for the door.

Chapter 9

Jessica wandered through the grocery store, certain she'd never find the items on Araceli's list in the mainstream franchise. Before she left that morning, Araceli said she wanted to make mole, the Mexican sauce that included dozens of spices and probably took days to prepare. Jessica hadn't made much progress with Travis's mom, but at least she wouldn't go home empty-handed.

The conversation with Gina kept replaying in her head. She had to tell Araceli her "boyfriend" had lied, about so many things. He hadn't told his parents about her, had lied about being a UTEP student, and had skipped town.

Jessica longed to talk to someone about this. Not just someone—Angus. Which led her to stalking the aisles of the grocery in the same shopping center where he taught kids to play and perform rock music.

She'd driven slowly past his business, peeking in the window. Angus sat at the front desk, checking in a kid carrying an electric guitar, but she didn't think he'd seen her. He'd had a smile on his face. He always did around the kids. Sometimes she wished she had a job that brought her that kind of joy. Not that she didn't love her job, she did. Her boss was awesome, and once Jessica finished law school and passed the bar, Linda had mentioned she'd hire her as an attorney at the firm.

Even so, she'd never grinned the way Angus did when watching the kids on stage or receiving accolades from their proud parents in the audience. He had a special light inside that turned on when helping those kids. His job brought him satisfaction, whereas with her, the need to correct the wrongs of the world weighed on her, propelling her to act.

She glanced down at the list on her phone: three kinds of chiles, almonds, peanuts, Mexican chocolate, and more spices than she knew existed. Jessica scanned the international foods shelves in front of her and saw a jar of prepared mole sauce. Normally, she'd take the easy way out. But when Araceli had cooked her breakfast that morning, she'd almost seemed happy. If making mole from scratch helped her in any way, Jessica would find these ingredients. Hopefully, before they'd both gone old and gray.

"There you are." Angus's familiar voice warmed her skin like sunshine.

"Hey. Fancy seeing you here." She turned to see him just steps away, and her heart sped up a notch.

"I saw you drive by. You were going pretty slow, so I figured you wanted to talk."

"Yeah. I'm subtle that way." She wasn't close to subtle when it came to this man. "I have to do some shopping for Araceli, and I don't have any idea how to find all the ingredients."

She really just wanted to see him, wished she could step closer and inhale his scent. She'd love to tell him about Travis and get his advice on revealing his deception to Araceli. Angus could approach it with kindness, unlike Jessica who just blurted things out. But she'd start with the shopping list.

"She's still staying with you?"

"Yeah. She's been through a lot, and I think she needs some time to heal. It's nice having someone in the house." Jessica gazed up at Angus, wondering how he'd take that last comment. He raised his eyebrows but didn't say anything.

"Anyway, cooking seems to help," Jessica continued. "She gave me this huge shopping list."

Angus took Jessica's phone, their fingers brushing. But he didn't look at her, just studied the screen.

"She wants to make mole? That takes my mom all day. And I don't think you're in the right store."

"I'm sure you're right." But it was exactly the right store, because it had brought them together.

He handed her phone back and slipped his own from his pocket. "Let me get you some help."

"Hey, Mom, I'm here with Jessica. She needs to buy ingredients for mole, and I found her wandering the aisles of Albertsons."

Jessica could hear his mom's hearty laugh come through the phone. It squeezed her heart hard, and she could barely breathe through the pain. She hadn't just lost Angus, she'd lost his whole giant, loving family. Their normalcy. The way they bickered with love, instead of conjuring tears and raised voices the way she and her mom sometimes fought. She wanted to sink to the cold tile floor under the heft of all she'd lost.

"Okay. I'll tell her. Love you too." Angus drew the phone away from his ear, his sparkling eyes focused on her. "She'll meet you at Vista Market in twenty minutes."

"You're kidding. She's dropping everything to help me?"

"Of course, Jessica. She loves you."

The words almost broke her heart. Again. She couldn't stop the tears that flooded her eyes, but she would not let them fall.

Angus must have seen past her bravado. He wrapped her in a hug. Then the tears did fall. She emptied them onto his shirt, finding comfort in the warmth of his arms around her. Inhaling deeply, she reveled in his scent like some kind of wild animal.

Jessica didn't want to let go, but a lady with a remarkably full shopping cart needed to get by. They parted and stepped to the side.

"I'd love to talk to you more about what's happening with Araceli. Do you want to go for a drink later? We could meet somewhere?" She needed so much more of this, of him. It felt like she'd thrown her heart out there with the request.

"There's no way I can meet you in a bar. I think we both know how that would end."

The awkwardness grew between them. Yes, she knew exactly where they'd end up if fueled by tequila and her desire. That's what she wanted. And he'd said no.

"I do like mole." Angus threw the statement out there, giving Jessica a lifeline.

"Of course. If Araceli is up for visitors, would you join us? I can let you know after I talk to her."

"Sounds good. Tell my mom hi."

"I will." She stared at him, her eyes running over the features of his face as if she caressed them with her fingers. "Thanks for calling your mom."

And for coming over here when you saw me drive by. For helping me, even when it hurts. She kept the words back, too much too soon. She didn't want to scare him away by showing him how incredibly much she needed him. She'd never been the needy type, and that had probably attracted him to her in the first place.

"See you soon." She gave him a grin and slid past him and down the aisle, just barely restraining herself from grabbing him by the neck and pulling him in for a kiss, for more, right here in the grocery store aisle.

Soon.

Sharon Delgado stood in the bright sunlight at the entrance to Vista Market, arms crossed and an indiscernible look on her face. Jessica slowed, worried this woman, who had been more of a mom figure than her own mom for half her life, had finally had enough of her.

A few steps away, Sharon rushed at Jessica and wrapped her in an almost violent hug. "Jessica Watts, why haven't you come to see me? It's bad enough that you broke my son's heart, and then I have to go months without a visit?"

Finally, the woman released her, at least partially. She still had her hands wrapped around Jessica's arms and stared at her as if she expected penance.

"I think he broke my heart." Jessica wished the words back, didn't want to complain. Not to this woman who'd shown up to help her, and who clearly wanted her around. She should apologize, not whine, but her mouth and her brain had not connected.

"Oh, honey," Sharon said, hugging her one more time. "You really don't understand anything. He just wants you to take care of yourself."

"I'm working on that," Jessica said, once the woman finally released her. Maybe she'd start seeing Sal twice a week. Anything to move her personal life off this precipice between great and whatever purgatory she'd landed in.

Once in the store, Sharon took Jessica's phone and studied the ingredient list. She moved from aisle to aisle like a homing pigeon, Jessica following in her slipstream.

"This is a complicated recipe," Sharon said as she bustled down a row with crackers and nuts. She reached for a bag of pepitas, roasted and salted pumpkin seeds, on the top shelf, then swung around so fast the bag almost clocked Jessica in the temple.

"Wait. You aren't learning to cook to impress Angus, are you?"

Jessica stared at Sharon as shock pulsed through her body. The thought had never occurred to her. "No. Not at all. A friend wants to cook this. Would he want me to learn to cook?"

"Well, I'm not going to be around forever, and he does love to eat. If you wanted, I could share my recipes."

Fuck. How was she going to get out of this without hurting Sharon's feelings? It's not that she had anything against cooking. But honestly, why bother when picking up something at a restaurant or eating cereal or a piece of fruit tasted better and didn't require any effort?

"Uhm. That might be nice." Part of Jessica wished she could respond with enthusiasm at the request, but she'd rather practice flipping someone on a mat a hundred times before spending an entire day in the kitchen, even with Sharon, one of her favorite people.

"Your face is giving away your enthusiasm." Sharon dropped the pepitas into the shopping cart. The pop of air that released from the plastic bag as it broke cracked like a gunshot.

"I would love to spend time with you, and I probably should learn to cook a few things. But Angus has known me forever, and he's never mentioned wanting me to cook more."

"It wouldn't hurt you to learn a few domestic skills. I know your mom left when you were young, and you kind of had to fend for yourself. But Angus grew up with me. I cook, clean, do the shopping. Rick mows the lawn and changes the oil in the car. We're a pretty traditional family."

Jessica decided not to mention that she enjoyed mowing the lawn. And they both took their cars to a local shop to get the oil changed. "I clean," she said as if laying an offering at the feet of a domestic goddess. Surely people didn't have to live by those old roles anymore.

"Jessica. I know Angus does the laundry."

"But he likes to. And he's better at it than I am."

"It's not like you can't learn. That's just weaponized incompetence." Sharon's hands had moved to her hips and her elbows poked out on either side, making her seem bigger and fiercer than Jessica had ever seen her. She looked like an eagle attacking its prey.

Jessica wanted to take a step back. Or a step back in time. She'd made a mistake coming here with Sharon.

Jessica loved so many things about Angus, but high on that list was how he knew her better than anyone, often better than she knew herself. He'd never try to fit her into the box of what a woman was supposed to be. Instead, he let her chart her own course, even when it got her into trouble. His love was freedom, freedom to become the best version of herself.

Sharon sighed and dropped her arms. "Listen. You're good for Angus, and I know he's not exactly the traditional man either. At least he wasn't in the past. For so many years, he seemed to care more about playing guitar and hanging out with his friends than building a future. But things are changing now. He owns a growing business, not a flailing record store. You two could really build a future together, a family, if you just tried a little harder."

Jessica shut down. She and Angus were already a family, the best family Jessica had ever known. This was just a rough patch, and this conversation would never acknowledge that. Their family didn't fit into a pretty little box like every other one on the block. But that didn't take away its meaning. She didn't want a provider, she wanted a partner.

Someone who understood her drive to balance the injustice in their community, in the world, with small acts that helped those who needed it. Like Araceli.

Jessica steeled herself. Araceli needed these ingredients. Cooking was a form of therapy for her. Learning to cook wouldn't make Jessica a better person, just like earning more money or having a fancy title wouldn't enhance the core of goodness at Angus's heart.

"I hear what you're saying, and I really appreciate your help with the shopping. I love Angus, and I promise I'll do everything in my power to become the person he needs me to be."

Jessica's words would disappoint Sharon, but she had disappointed people before. Somewhere under her rib cage, a knot of confidence formed. She needed to change to get Angus back, but she needed to do it in ways that enhanced, not erased, her. Maybe she would learn to cook, but other improvements needed to happen first.

Chapter 10

Back at the house, Araceli smashed spices between the bottom of Jessica's smallest frying pan and the cutting board. She grunted with the effort, and a sigh that sounded like pure disappointment passed her lips when she looked at her results.

"I can't believe you don't have a mocajete." Araceli stared at Jessica sitting just a few feet away. "You really don't cook, do you?"

Not again. Enough about her lack of kitchen skills. "You know, not every man wants a woman who cooks and cleans for a living." The words came out harsher than she'd meant.

Araceli rolled her eyes at Jessica. "I'm not cooking because I want to attract a man. This dish reminds me of my grandmother. She had a really hard life, and she made something beautiful out of it. I need that kind of inspiration right now."

"I'm sorry. I had someone tell me I should learn to cook to get Angus back." While the actual conversation had differed somewhat, the message remained.

"Huh. It depends. My grandmother was a great cook, but she got left alone to raise three kids. I don't think it's smart to change yourself just to attract or keep a man. You can't trust them." Araceli opened a cabinet and examined a few of the glasses. She found a pint glass and used its bottom edge to crush the spices.

"Speaking of guys," Jessica said. "I went looking for Travis today."

"What?" Araceli froze, the glass hovering in midair.

"I'm worried he's involved in what happened to you. I didn't tell you this yesterday because you seemed so upset, but I got his number from your roommates and called him the night you disappeared. He hung up on me and then wouldn't answer the phone. Plus, it doesn't make sense that he didn't try to find you after you disappeared from his truck."

Araceli's face turned pink and her wide eyes showed a trace of fear. "You shouldn't have done that."

"What? Tried to contact him? If you think you're upset now, wait until you hear what I learned about him."

"You didn't tell me you called him. Did you say your name?"

"Yes. Of course."

"Oh, no. I have to go back to Mexico. I thought staying here would be safe—just in case they decided to go after my family. But now he'll be able to find out where I am." Araceli set the glass down, then pressed her shaking palms into the countertop.

"I don't understand," Jessica said. But she did. She could see the fear in Araceli's eyes. She didn't trust Travis either. "You don't need to worry. He's not even in town. He's not a student at UTEP, either. He goes to Arizona State, and he's already there. I talked to his mom today and she told me."

Jessica worried about Araceli's reaction to the news. Pressing against the countertop didn't keep her arms from shaking, and soon tremors wracked her whole body. Then she sank to the floor.

Jessica jumped off the stool and squatted next to her. "I know he lied, but you need to know what kind of guy he really is. I'm worried that he's involved in your kidnapping. I'm sorry I didn't let you know I talked to him. It didn't occur to me when I picked you up. I just wanted to get you somewhere safe."

"I'm not safe." A tremor wracked Araceli's voice.

"You are. He's hundreds of miles away." Of course, his friends probably stayed behind. "If he had anything to do with this, he should pay."

"Jessica." Araceli's voice barely rose above a whisper. "He was there."

A sliver of ice ran up Jessica's spine. "What do you mean?"

Araceli covered her eyes with her palms, like a child who thought they couldn't be seen if they hid behind their hands. Or as if she wanted to hide her pain and embarrassment from Jessica. But it seeped out from behind her palms and wafted from her body, buffeting Jessica in misery.

"He was one of the men in the desert. They taunted him for dating me because I'm Mexican."

Jessica's gut plunged. This admission changed everything. Travis belonged in jail, immediately. And Araceli, for some reason, didn't want him there. In a moment, the case grew easier and far tougher.

Jessica wanted to leap from the floor, jump in her truck, and follow Travis to Arizona. She'd confront him there, force a confession, turn him in. But that was the old Jessica, the one who took off without a plan. Besides, Araceli needed—something.

She sat bent over, crumpled, in front of Jessica, looking completely broken. Jessica could imagine the humility of betrayal, but Araceli needed to understand she'd done nothing wrong.

Jessica scooted beside her and wrapped an arm around her. "This is all going to be okay. I know it doesn't feel like that right now, but you are going to get through this."

Araceli took one breath, two. Jessica sat as her drive for action leached out of her body and into the floor. For once, patience became her friend, something solid that would help her through this moment—help both of them find a better place.

Eventually, Araceli sat up and looked at Jessica. "I'm so ridiculous, thinking I can come to the US and start my life over. I'm just a paleta from the campo. The first person I trust turns against me and tries to kill me. I don't belong here."

"You have to listen to me. Everyone who hurt you—that's on them. You did nothing wrong." Jessica stared into Araceli's hazel eyes, willing her to believe the words. Araceli wasn't a hick from the countryside, and the abduction and beating could have happened to any woman. Still, the sparkle of happiness that used to reside in Araceli had disappeared.

Jessica had seen the look before: on the Guatemalan cousins, on another young girl betrayed by the pastor she thought she could trust, on women who came into the office, their lives in shambles because of the ill will of others. It infuriated her. And she knew it could be overcome.

"Sometimes, you come across evil people. That's who was in the desert. That's who hurt you. You are not alone. Sometimes, I think I was put on this earth to go after them and to bring their victims justice. Men hurt women. Racism exists. These are things we have to fight. Don't let them win."

A spark of defiance lit in Araceli's eyes. Then Jessica watched it dissolve into smoke.

"I don't think I was made for fighting."

But I was. Jessica tempered the thought. This wasn't about her. Yes, she wanted Araceli's permission to track down every person who assaulted her, but right now Araceli needed to regain her sense of herself as a competent woman.

"Look at all you've accomplished," Jessica said. "You're in college. You have friends. You have a new job that you're proud of and excited about. You can get past this."

Araceli leaned her head back against the cabinets and sighed. Then she pushed herself up from the floor and turned and reached out to Jessica to pull her up.

"I don't know. I can't even envision the future right now. But I can finish making this mole." Araceli dusted herself off. "Are you sure we can't let Tela in?"

Jessica had banished the dog to the backyard earlier when she'd tripped Araceli. The smell of chicken cooking in a pot on the stove had turned the dog into a fiend who refused to leave the kitchen.

"I can let her in, but you know she'll be underfoot."

"Please."

Jessica nodded and walked to the back of the house. Tela stood at the door waiting, and Jessica swore she saw drool dripping from the dog's mouth.

"It's not like I don't feed you." She said the words to the dog's rump as Tela skittered past her and headed to the kitchen. Jessica scanned the backyard. Now that she knew Travis had played a role in the abduction, she worried about having talked to him and his mother. How far would they go to protect him?

She stepped outside and closed the door behind her. Pulling her phone from her pocket, she called Sal.

"Hey, do you know anything about security systems?" she asked after he picked up.

"Of course. What's going on?"

"A friend of mine was kidnapped by her boyfriend and a gang of guys. It was a bad scene." Jessica couldn't think of a way to say more without betraying Araceli's trust. "She's staying with me, and the boyfriend knows I'm on his trail. I'm worried they'll retaliate. And before you ask, I have gone to the police, but she's not ready to press charges yet."

"Give me a couple of hours," Sal said after a pause. Then the line went dead.

Jessica returned to the kitchen, wondering what the hell would happen in a couple of hours. With Sal, you never knew. Hopefully, he'd send her a list of supplies to purchase or the name and number of a security company she could use.

Back inside, Araceli had resumed crushing spices, and Tela sat at her feet, staring at the counter as if she expected half a chicken to drop into her mouth. Jessica gave the dog a treat and then returned to the stool. Maybe now that Araceli had admitted Travis's involvement, she'd be ready to take the next step.

"Why don't we call Jaime and let him know about Travis?" Jessica asked.

The glass in Araceli's hands stilled. "Not yet. I just need a little more time to think things through."

"Can I help?"

Araceli set the glass down and turned to Jessica. "Yes. I don't know if I want to resume my life here or go back to Mexico. I don't even know how to figure it out yet. Both options seem terrible. There's a scar across El Paso now, and I don't know if I'll ever feel safe here again."

Araceli rubbed her arms as if the room had turned cold. It hadn't. In fact, the humidity had risen, signaling an afternoon storm. "The funny thing is, I'm probably safer here than any other place in the US. El Paso is full of Hispanics. Most people look like me. If this could happen here—well who knows what would have happened anywhere else in the country."

"I know," Jessica said. "I'm sorry. It really is only a small percentage of the population that is like that." Unfortunately, they made up a vocal minority.

Araceli held a hand up. "Please don't apologize. It is what it is, and believe me, I understand it now. But I'm also not sure I want to go back to Mexico. I'd be safe there, but my life there was so small. I just want a few days to try and figure things out. Can I stay here?" She fixed Jessica with a stare.

"Of course. Stay as long as you like. It's not like I've got anything going on." Like a husband to come home to. "I really like having you here."

"Thank you."

Jessica heard the relief in the words. She enjoyed having Araceli here. The house no longer echoed with loneliness. But Araceli wouldn't stay long. School began in a week, and she'd need to start classes if she wanted to stay. She had an F-1 visa that required her to be an enrolled student.

"This is in no way a condition of you staying here," Jessica said. "But we need to bring Travis and his friends to justice. They are dangerous, not just to you, but probably to all women and all Hispanics."

Araceli's shoulders drooped as if a heavy blanket, not words, had landed on her shoulders. Even the dog whined. Jessica let the tension build. She wouldn't let this one go.

"They scared me. I don't think I'm ready."

"What if I only followed up with Travis? If I find out who the others are, we can figure out who is dangerous. It will help us protect you and other women out there." The "us" was a stretch. She'd have to get law enforcement involved at some point, but Araceli didn't seem ready for that yet. Still, someone needed to work on this before the case got cold.

"What, exactly, do you want to do?" Araceli asked.

Jessica paused for a minute, then opted for the truth. "I want to pay him a surprise visit at ASU."

Araceli shook her head. "I can't believe he's going there. Everything was a lie."

The slump of Araceli's shoulders annoyed Jessica. Enough of this guy. Araceli was so much better than him. "You should be pissed off about that, not sad. You deserve so much better."

"I do." The sentence lacked any fierceness, but at least it held some conviction. "When do you plan to go?"

"Soon. Tomorrow morning?" Jessica could get a flight out first thing and shouldn't have to spend the night. She probably had enough airline miles for the trip. She'd been saving them for a getaway with Angus. Besides, flying beat the four-hundred-mile drive. Now she just had to figure out how to find this guy on one of America's largest campuses.

"Let me think about it while I finish the mole. I'm not sure I'm ready, but I understand that I can't let others get hurt. Maybe if I go back to Mexico, I won't have to worry what you do. If they hate Mexicans, they probably won't go there."

"I really hope you don't let them chase you away. Do you have photos of Travis and any of his friends on your phone? At the very least, I want to do a little research on him."

Araceli glared at her phone for a minute. "I never met any of his friends. I guess now I know why." She picked up the device, unlocked it, and scrolled to a photo before handing the phone to Jessica. "Here's one. There are couple of others. Please. I don't want to talk about this anymore."

Jessica looked at the photo. She hated his smirk from the moment she laid eyes on the grown-up version of Travis. Pale skin, golden hair, blue eyes. Just a typical guy. Nothing special. But here in El Paso, where over eighty percent of the population was Hispanic, a white guy got a lot more play than he would in a mostly white community. Jessica had never really understood the attraction. But then, she'd met Angus in kindergarten.

She laid the phone back on the counter, then took her laptop to the couch where she could look out the picture window onto the front yard. She'd research this guy the best she could, and hopefully, Araceli would greenlight the trip. The couch also allowed her to play sentry.

She wished now that Travis didn't know she suspected him. He had dangerous friends, and they didn't need to know Araceli's location.

Since she couldn't change her earlier actions, she'd have to keep an eye on things. Maybe her mom could stay with Araceli if she went to Phoenix in the morning.

Jessica texted her boss. *I may need tomorrow off, if that's okay.*

Linda didn't respond immediately, so Jessica opened her laptop. It didn't take long to find Travis's Instagram account. A few photos of kids his age at UTEP, desert four-wheeling, and travel photos. Lucky bastard had visited Europe. Jessica recognized that famous cathedral in Barcelona, the Eiffel Tower, and the giant London Ferris wheel.

Certain he had another account or two that his mom didn't know about, she dug into the accounts he followed. She found it odd that a guy in his early twenties followed Tucker Carlson, but it gave her insight into his politics.

He followed over five hundred accounts and had a couple of hundred followers. He seemed to have plenty of friends from high school and college, and followed sports teams and other innocuous seeming groups. Soon, she just reviewed the blue checkmark accounts he followed, weeding out the noise and trying to figure out who influenced him.

In addition to Tucker, he followed some motivational guy with quotes from Marcus Aurelius—dude must be the "live, laugh, love" guru for teenagers. She noticed a couple of accounts that seemed to focus on men's fashion—although not anything you'd see in El Paso—and fast cars. Also, who the fuck followed Nick Fuentes in an account with their name on it? Nothing screamed racism like that guy. He followed several UFC fighters, which Jessica learned stood for Ultimate Fighting Championship. Was he a fighter or just a fan?

She'd meant to stay away from cases like this, at least until she learned how to better defend herself. It was part of her program to regain Angus's trust. But this was Araceli, a friend. And the smirky little white boy didn't look dangerous.

Enticing smells wafted in from the kitchen, and occasionally, Jessica heard Araceli speaking to Tela. That spoiled rotten beggar. Jessica closed her laptop. She'd had just about enough of Travis. His politics leaned far right, he had a thing for photos of women's boobs, and his "motivational speakers" appeared to be racists and misogynists.

Movement caught her eye, and she turned to see a Jeep pull in the driveway, but not Sal's khaki-colored one. Instead, Keith stepped out of a black Wrangler. He lifted a cardboard box out of the vehicle and then started toward the door.

Chapter 11

This was not cool. Jessica hadn't asked for visitors and didn't know if Araceli would want to see anyone. She opened the door before he could knock or ring the bell and put her hand up to stop him. Then she slipped out and closed the door behind her, hoping Araceli wouldn't hear her.

"What are you doing here?" She barely managed not to add "the hell" to the sentence, but her tone conveyed it anyway.

"Sal said you needed a security system." He raised the box a little higher.

"Yeah. I asked him what kind to get." Not to send a delivery boy over. She crossed her arms.

"This is a starter kit. All wireless. I can install it in about an hour."

"I don't know what to say." She didn't ask for this, but she needed it. She didn't need saving. But Araceli did. "Give me a minute. I have a guest here, and I need to talk to her about this."

Jessica left Keith standing in the yard. Inside, she told Araceli that someone she trusted, her self-defense coach, wanted to install a security system. And he'd sent someone to do it right now.

"Are you okay with that?" Jessica asked.

"With having the house more secure? Absolutely."

"I'll have to bring him in the house." She didn't want to mention Araceli's bruised eye would likely invite questions.

"Do you know the installation person?"

"Yes. I actually sparred with him this weekend. He's also a sheriff's deputy."

"Oh." Araceli's demeanor immediately became more wary.

"He's a good guy. He's helped me out on cases before." Jessica wondered when Keith had moved into her good column. Maybe when he'd helped her overcome her kidnapping. She'd been lost, still wandering the house that had trapped her, even though she'd escaped. He'd shown her aerials of the house on a tablet computer, turning it from monster to structure. He'd probably stepped outside of policy by doing that. And he'd introduced her to Sal, who would make her into a better person.

"You can trust him," she finally said to Araceli. "I do."

"Then let him put in the security system."

As she returned to the door, she wasn't sure which of them had convinced the other to move forward. Fortunately, a security system would help her feel better about leaving Araceli here while she chased Travis to Arizona.

"Come on in," she said as she opened the door.

Keith followed her inside, and she pointed to the table where he could set the box. "Man, it smells great in here," he said.

"I'm making mole," Araceli said. She had her back to them as she stirred a pot on the stove.

As Araceli turned around, Keith's eyebrows rose. "Wow. That's quite a shiner."

"Hi. I'm Araceli." She stuck her hand out and stepped toward Keith, completely ignoring his comment.

"Keith Guerra." He shook her hand, then looked questioningly back at Jessica.

"What do we need to do to get this system installed?" Jessica asked, trying to shut down further questions.

"Um. Let's see."

Jessica could have sworn she saw his cheeks redden as he turned toward the box. He began pulling out smaller boxes, shiny tools, and a couple of cables.

Finally, he stopped and looked around. "Can you give me a tour of the house?"

"Sure."

"I put Tela outside," Araceli said. "In case he's afraid of dogs."

"Tela and I are old friends," Keith said. "She's also probably a decent security system."

"That completely depends." Jessica had seen the dog fiercely protect her with bared teeth and a huge bark. But she had also treated Keith like a friend even when Jessica had doubts. Probably another reason to trust him.

She showed him around the small home, just two bedrooms and two baths, each with windows, as Keith pointed out. When she opened the door to the half-acre backyard, Tela raced toward them.

"Man, this place is fantastic," he said. "You've got a great home."

"Thanks," Jessica said. But Keith had already bounded down the steps to greet Tela. The dog's excitement reminded Jessica of those videos of soldiers returning to their pets. Her dog was truly over the top.

Eventually, Tela and Keith quit playing, and he began installing the system, starting with a doorbell camera in front. Tela watched him work as if she'd like to take up the screwdriver and help.

Jessica wandered into the kitchen, drawn by the incredible aroma. Impossible to describe, it combined the heat of chiles with the earthiness of pure dark chocolate and the spicy hints of a Christmas cookie.

"It smells so amazing in here it's making me hungry," Jessica said. "I'm going to be following you around the kitchen like Tela."

"Or like the way Keith follows you around?"

Taken aback by the question, Jessica stared at Araceli. She must have the wrong idea. "I had to show him the house so he'd know where to put the security devices."

"I saw the way he looked at you."

"No. You didn't. You really didn't. The last time I saw the guy, I kneed him in the balls."

"Jessica!"

"There's only one man on this planet for me, and I'm already married to him."

"Then why isn't he here?"

Well, that was a punch to the gut. And the last thing Jessica wanted to talk about. "Because I'm an asshole, but this is just temporary." It had to be. She'd make sure it was.

"Are you ever going to tell me what happened between you two?"

Jessica surveyed Araceli, the purple bruise below her eye starting to fade, a look of hope in her eyes. For what? A love story? Araceli knew better than anyone how treacherous love could be. Jessica was also battered and bruised, her injuries internal and invisible to the naked eye. "Probably not."

Araceli shook her head, clearly disappointed. "Ask your friend to stay for dinner. The mole will be ready when he's finished."

"What if he's here for another three hours? It's getting late." She wouldn't deny Araceli, even though Jessica had promised to invite Angus. Having both men here would be too much, for her and Araceli.

"We'll eat when he's done," Araceli said.

Jessica turned on the lights in the darkening kitchen. The sun must have slipped behind the mesa, heading off to brighten the other side of the world.

———

Keith happily stayed for dinner. The three of them sat around the table and feasted on tender chicken slathered with the dark brown sauce. Keith and Jessica paired theirs with ice-cold beer, but Araceli opted for water.

"Are you going to tell me how you got the black eye?" Keith asked.

"I don't want to talk about it."

"If you need help, I'm a law enforcement officer."

"Jessica is helping me."

Jessica's skin went hot as their eyes turned toward her. Keith wouldn't like this.

"She's talked to the police. Unofficially." Jessica's answer had the potential to piss off both of them. Araceli didn't want anyone knowing what had happened, but Keith, like any officer, would want a formal report.

"And how involved are you? Unofficially, of course." Keith stared at her with more than curiosity. He almost seemed angry.

"What's it to you?" Why did everything she say sound so prickly?

"I just installed a security system at your house. And I know some of what you've been through. Maybe let the officials handle it."

His response infuriated her. "Like I let them handle the case of the Guatemalan cousins? The ones who lost their families and who remain incarcerated in a detention center?"

Keith's eyes darkened and his forehead wrinkled. She'd hit a nerve.

"I should have believed you that first time," he said. "I still have to live with that one."

"I'm sorry. I appreciate that you installed the security system. I'm just in a mood today."

They finished their meal, then Keith showed Jessica how to monitor and manage the security system. It wouldn't stop anyone determined to get in, but it would warn Jessica of intruders.

Keith offered to have it notify him as well. That was a step too far for Jessica. She couldn't have Angus or her mom attached to it either—they'd worry too much. Maybe she'd ask Sal or Linda as an extra layer of security. She would find someone, the right someone.

"No, thanks, but I appreciate your coming out here and setting everything up. What do I owe you?"

"Nothing."

"That's not right. Who bought all this? What about all the time you spent?"

"You'll have to take it up with Sal. Besides, I got dinner out of it." He gave her a quick grin, then ran a hand through his spiky black hair, suddenly looking nervous. "Speaking of dinner, if you're not busy this weekend, I thought maybe we could grab something to eat."

No. This was the last thing she needed, and a great way to make things even more awkward between them. "No. I'm married."

"But I thought you were separated." His dark eyes reminded her of a puppy who'd been swatted on the rump.

"That's temporary." She hoped. No, she needed to be clearer with this guy. "I did not want him to leave, and I'll do anything to get him back."

Keith shrugged. "Got it. If you ever change your mind, let me know."

Then, thank god, he left. Jessica shut the door behind him, then slumped against it, a mix of feelings running through her. She would call Sal and see if she could pay for the system. She preferred not to owe people. Also, somehow having Keith here made her miss Angus more.

Jessica went inside to help Araceli clean up. She stooped to pet Tela, who also missed Angus.

"Keith really likes you," Araceli said.

"He's just nice. Helpful," Jessica said, wanting the conversation to end.

"Very." Araceli waggled her eyebrows.

"Are you good with me going to Arizona tomorrow?" Jessica asked, forcefully changing the subject.

"You're determined to find Travis?"

"Yes. But I'll be back tomorrow night."

Araceli sighed. "I guess it's okay. At first, I wanted to bury the truth. I still don't want to testify or be involved in any way. But I get it. He's not the guy I thought he was, and that could be dangerous for others."

"I can have my mom come and stay with you tomorrow if you'd like."

"No. I'm calling in sick tomorrow. Stomach virus. I'll stay here with Tela."

"Okay, but no spoiling her," Jessica said, aware that Tela would likely get everything she wanted.

Jessica's phone buzzed, and she pulled it from her back pocket. Angus. She glanced at Araceli. "I think I'll take this in my room."

Seeing his name on the screen sent a wave of vulnerability through her, leaving traces of hope and fear. She sat on the edge of the bed and answered the call.

"Hi." Every fraught emotion found its way into that tiny word.

"Everything okay there?" he asked. "I got your text about postponing dinner, then I saw some big guy hanging out at your house."

That meant he'd driven by. Had he planned on stopping in? Damn Keith. Thoughts whirred faster and faster through her head.

"That was just Keith. He installed a security system." She did her best to sound casual, even though she wanted to crawl through the ether and wrap her arms and legs around him.

"Keith? The sheriff's deputy who arrested you? Sal's nephew?"

"Yeah. You should have dropped by. I could have introduced you two."

"No thanks." Dead air filled the space between them. "So, he's helping you out now?"

Oh shit. Was he jealous?

"No, it's just a onetime thing. I asked Sal about security systems earlier today and for some reason he sent Keith over. It was a complete surprise." She practically stumbled over herself trying to explain.

"Jessica, it's fine. You can do whatever you want." Now he tried to sound casual. It didn't work.

"The only thing I want to do is you."

Neither spoke. Time stretched and curled around them. It felt so good to be honest with him about her feelings. She didn't apologize, didn't say she'd do better, she just let the truth rest between them.

"I love you. I miss you so much," she said.

"I can't do this yet." His soft words remained filled with hurt—the same hurt she'd heard when he left.

But he said "yet" and she'd hang her hopes on those three letters.

Chapter 12

The flight to Phoenix took just over an hour. Thanks to the help of Araceli's roommates and their friends who knew Travis, Jessica now had an address scrawled on a Post-it note. She'd taken the first flight that morning, and if her luck held, she'd be back in the office for a full afternoon of work.

The cheapest rental car at the airport ferried her to Tempe, where she easily located the apartment near a community park a few miles from the school. It must have been built in the sixties or seventies and resembled a cheap two-story motel more than an apartment building. The façade had arches that looked as sturdy as papier-mâché—as if this one nod to Spanish design would give the place class. It didn't.

She strode past a turquoise kidney-shaped pool, then trotted up an exterior staircase to unit 202. The apartment had one window facing the walkway, and she passed it as if she had someplace to be. She couldn't see past the drawn shades and didn't hear anything inside.

She'd come early in hopes of finding him at home. After a long drive yesterday, and perhaps a night of drinking with new friends, she might even find him asleep. She rapped on the door to find out.

When she didn't get a response, she tried again, louder this time. "Hi, this is Susie from next door. Do you smell gas?" Jessica yelled through the closed door. Hopefully, her call wouldn't cause the neighbors to panic. She pounded on the door.

"Just a sec," said an angry voice from inside the apartment.

She crossed her fingers, then the door opened. Travis stared at her, his hair mussed and the whites of his eyes as red as a pot smoker's. Bingo.

Jessica continued the ruse by sniffing the air. "I thought I smelled gas in my apartment. Do you smell anything?"

"What time is it?" he asked, his brain cells clearly not alerted to the danger.

"I think I smell it in here too." Jessica leaned toward him, smelling nothing but the stale odor of a guy who needed to shower.

"Really?"

"Yeah. Let me see if it's coming from your kitchen."

He surprisingly stepped back and let her through the door. The studio apartment held two closed cardboard boxes, a couple of stuffed garbage bags, and a large duffel that had vomited clothes across the floor. She glanced at the bed and saw he hadn't bothered to make it. Instead, a comforter formed a nest on a bare mattress topped by an uncased pillow.

She continued into the so-called kitchen along one wall: just a mini fridge, a couple of cabinets and an old stove with electric burners. What a dumbass.

"Do you smell anything?" he asked.

"It must be a false alarm. I'm Susie," she said, offering him her hand and pitching her voice higher than normal. At least he didn't sleep in the nude. He wore a pair of boxers and a T-shirt that proclaimed that "The Matrix was a documentary." Whatever.

He'd followed her into the room, and the front door had swung most of the way closed. She needed to make her move quickly.

"Are you a student at ASU?" he asked.

"No." Jessica leaned back against the kitchen counter and crossed her arms. "I'm a friend of Araceli Gamboa's."

His face changed from sleepy-eyed to fully awake and riddled with fear. "You're the one who called me."

"Yes. You really should have talked to me then. Instead, you've ruined your life." Jessica could see his mind working, probably trying to figure out how to get out of this situation. Finally, something like regret appeared in his eyes.

"Is she alright?"

Jessica took her time answering. He clearly knew nothing, giving her the chance to protect Araceli's whereabouts and scare the crap out of him.

"You think she's alive?" Jessica asked, angry. Araceli might not have survived. She certainly feared she wouldn't but had proven resourceful enough to stop her enemies and find her way out of the desert. This little rat should pay for that.

Travis's face fell at her words. "You need to leave."

"Only if you're going with me, and we head to the police station."

"Susie. Go home. You have no idea what you're involved in. Don't contact me again—for both our sakes." His voice sounded completely defeated.

"I don't think you understand," Jessica said. "You kidnapped and assaulted a woman in the desert. You are looking at some extensive jail time."

He sharpened at her words. "So she's not dead. That's good. If she's smart, she'll go home and never set foot in El Paso again. I escaped. She needs to also. Tell her that. I do like her. She's a nice girl."

What was with this guy? Jessica's fury threatened to overwhelm her. She'd love to put some of her new moves into action and hurt this guy the way he'd hurt her friend. She wouldn't. It would jeopardize the case against him and get her into trouble, but the desire for physical justice tempted her.

"I don't think you're listening," she said. "You're either going with me to the police station or I'm calling them to come pick you up. Your choice."

"It's not going to go down like that." Travis crossed the room and sat on the mattress. "The people who took Araceli are fearless. She's lucky she survived. If they find out you or I are going to the police, they'll come after us. We won't be as fortunate as she was." He peered up at her, his blue eyes bright.

"You were one of those guys. You're not making any sense. Explain it to me like I'm five." Jessica's frustration grew, but she held on to her calm with white-knuckled fingers.

"I know these guys, but I'm not really one of them. They're ruthless. They've told me about some of the things they've done. That's why I came here. I've got to get away from them or they're going to ruin my life."

"You should have thought about that before you tried to ruin Araceli's life. End it. You will pay for what you've done, and you've told me zero about why you shouldn't be in jail."

Travis stood. "Get out."

"Fuck no. What are you going to do? Call the cops? That's what I want."

He rushed her, arms out, like he wanted to hug her. He was about her height, about Sal's, only Sal had more grace and thought three moves ahead. This guy seemed to think he could overpower her. She stepped toward him quickly, then kneed him in the groin. As he dropped to the floor, she hit him in the side of the neck with the edge of her hand.

He cried out, in pain from her knee and then in indignation after the second blow. Jessica danced out of his reach, but the way he lay crumpled on the floor told her he wouldn't put up much more of a fight.

"What the hell is wrong with you?" he asked once he could talk.

"You." The word came out too loud, and she barely controlled her fury. "You tried to kill my friend, and now you're acting like you're not responsible. Like I should give up and go home because you're afraid of your friends."

He sat up, hands cupping his balls. "If you were smart, you'd be afraid of them too. If they find out Araceli's still alive, they will kill her, so you need to get her out of El Paso. If I show up at a police station, they will find a way to kill me. And believe me, if they know about you, you're dead too."

Jessica couldn't tell if he actually feared his friends, or if this was a tactic to avoid jail. Either way, she needed to figure out how to move forward. Of course, if Araceli wouldn't press charges, none of this mattered, but she could deal with that part next.

"Listen," he said. "I feel really bad about Araceli. I never wanted her to get hurt, but when these guys found out I was dating a Mexican, they went ballistic. They were mad at me too." He lifted his hands as if in surrender, then dropped them to the edge of his T-shirt and pulled it over his head. A foot-wide trail of purple, green, and yellow bruises wound around half his torso.

"What the fuck," Jessica said. "These guys need to be in jail. Why do you put up with this stuff? And why did you throw Araceli under the bus?"

He shook his head. "One of them saw me with her. That's when they came for me. They told me to go along with their plan or else. Nothing I did would have saved her."

"So you caved and set her up? You drove her to their designated location and then joined them in the beating? You are not innocent." Jessica spat the words at him. He might be injured, but that just proved he knew what they'd do to Araceli. He defined aiding and abetting.

"I couldn't have saved her." Travis yelled the words.

"You could have gone to the police, you dumb fuck! You didn't have to just go along with it. What is wrong with you?" Her anger spilled into the room. This guy wouldn't do the easiest thing to get the upper hand—involve law enforcement. He'd rather go along with his bros than protect his girlfriend. Travis needed to turn in his man card.

"Susie. Let me explain it to you one more time. They kill people. They brag about killing people. They like killing people."

Jessica shook her head. At the same time, dots connected. People who killed. People who took Araceli to the desert east of El Paso. Someone killed the families of the Guatemalan girls in the no man's land on the outskirts of town. It couldn't be coincidence. But none of that explained why the jerk in front of her refused to do the right thing.

"That's why you go to the police. Don't you think people who kill other people belong in jail?" Jessica asked.

"I think the cops are on their side. At least some of them. The only way to survive is to run."

"Your bravery astonishes me." She hoped to use the words as an axe to fell him. But he didn't react. "Let's go. You have a date with the Tempe Police Department. If you won't go willingly, I think I've shown that I'm stronger than you." She probably wasn't, but she'd taken him down once, and hopefully, he'd believe she'd do it again.

"I'm not going anywhere. Do whatever you want. Hit me. Kick me in the balls. It's better than how they'd treat me. I'm telling you, I'm here to escape them, and this might not be far enough away." He leaned back and spread his legs, making himself completely vulnerable to her.

"Look, if you're not willing to go after these guys, I am. Just give me their names and I'll take care of it. Although, once they're behind bars, I'm coming after you." Perhaps this offer would finally get them somewhere.

Travis laughed at her. "You really have no idea what you're up against. You can talk tough all you want, but I'm not going with you. You can try and have the cops come here and arrest me, but I bet they won't. If Araceli was pressing charges, you would have arrived with the cops, but you didn't."

Jessica glared at him, but he stared right back. The earth tilted as the balance of power shifted. She had nothing. He wouldn't even give up their names. She refused to leave with nothing.

She surveyed the room, saw a phone charging on the nightstand, trotted across the room and grabbed it. Returning to the stovetop, she turned on a burner and set the phone on it.

"This is going to smell worse than a gas leak," she said.

"You are fucking crazy. Give me my phone."

Jessica ignored his demand. "Tell me their names. Tell me where to find them. Tell me anything valuable and you save your phone. Otherwise, you're going to have a destroyed phone and a ruined cooktop."

Jessica leaned back against the counter and crossed her arms again, smiling this time. The electric burner would take a while to heat up. She didn't know how long it would take to destroy the phone, but the smell of burning plastic hit almost immediately.

She saw the moment Travis thought about rushing her again and lifted an eyebrow. He must have realized he couldn't outfight her. That had to be a devastating blow to someone who liked to hit women. The chemical smell worsened and Jessica's eyes began to sting. But she didn't move. She didn't care if the whole apartment burned down. She wouldn't leave without getting some kind of information from him.

Finally, Travis broke. "His name is Jace, and he hangs out at a bar called Crazy Cat on the east side of El Paso."

Jessica turned the burner off but left the phone there. "Thanks for the info. By the way, I'll be back for you, and don't think you can run. I'll follow you to the ends of the earth if I have to."

She walked out the door without looking back. She had a bar to find.

Chapter 13

Jessica arrived at the office before two. It took the plane ride home for her energy to ebb after meeting with Travis. His comment that the men who abducted Araceli had killed before stuck with her the most. If truthful, they might kill again, endangering Araceli. As much as Jessica didn't want her to leave El Paso, Araceli's safety came first.

The other intriguing thought revolved around who else they might have killed. How many people? The region had seen its share of gruesome murders. While El Paso remained one of the safest cities in the United States, during the drug wars, Juarez had spent time as the world's most dangerous city.

Even before that, women disappeared in Juarez in frightening numbers. Rumors about serial killers and corrupt police officers wound their way through the region's lore. Beyond those stories, outside the cities' borders, tales of migrants whispered through the wind. People had made their way to this land looking for ways to improve their lot in the world long before the country's founding. The southern border had always served as a place to cross the Rio Grande, a river that now divided the US and Mexico. The southernmost pass through the Rocky Mountains, El Paso served as a crossroads between those traveling east or west and the old royal road between Mexico City and Santa Fe, built when Spain ruled the land.

The journey through harsh deserts filled with predators started tough and became more difficult when human desires entered the equation. The drive to survive competed against the thirst to profit off others. The passion to save your family versus the fear of people from a different place with a different skin color.

Unfortunately, the competing desires ended in death far too often. At times, the desert and lack of preparation took their toll. Other times, murder was the culprit. A buzzing beneath her skin told Jessica that if she found the mysterious and fearsome Jace, she'd close in on the truth of the migrant killings.

Jessica looked up the Crazy Cat bar, surprised she hadn't heard of it. After all, she knew her bars. Online, it looked familiar. Perhaps it was the dollar shot night, or the excess of cleavage and cowboy hats in the online photos. She'd fit right in.

She had less luck trying to find a Jace in El Paso. Her search results returned an appliance company, a child, and a student on a high school soccer team that lost the private school city championship.

Digging a little deeper, she learned that the soccer match had taken place five years earlier. That could be her guy. The school had a reputation for enrolling rich kids and fuckups. When she crossmatched the name Jace with the school, she found a couple more references and a last name, Jeffries.

An alarm triggered. She knew that name. Well-known in politics and Texas money circles, Tim Jeffries had started a megachurch called The Way. Jessica had come across a preacher associated with the organization when she'd tried to help a friend's daughter. That had led to finding the Guatemalan girls in the desert, and to the preacher's death.

But the preacher just worked for the church. Jeffries had started it, but he lived in Lubbock, hundreds of miles away. Probably no connection. It was a common enough name.

Only it wasn't. In fact, she couldn't find any Jeffries in El Paso's white pages.

Her thoughts kept returning to the case until Linda finally walked through the door. In her sixties, Linda had lived in El Paso her entire life except for college and law school. If anyone knew of a Jeffries family in town, she would.

"Glad to have you back," Linda said, dropping into the chair facing Jessica's desk. "I thought you were going to be out all day."

"Finished early. How was court?"

"The case should go to the jury tomorrow. Thanks to your work uncovering all of Mr. Black's extracurricular activities, I'm pretty certain we'll win."

"No problem. Everyone in the commercial real estate community here knew that guy was a scumbag. Getting a few of them to share info was easy." Jessica's years in the industry helped, although most jurors would have had trouble providing the guy his requested alimony, especially from his wealthy and extremely sweet wife. Jessica usually hated the sadness and acrimony of divorce cases, but she took pride in their work on this one.

"Hey, do you know anyone in town with the last name Jeffries?"

"Is that why you missed today? I smell another side case." Linda's eyebrows rose in interest.

"Perhaps. I can't really talk about it yet because one of the people involved isn't ready to disclose anything. But I did come across a Jace Jeffries whom I'm trying to learn more about."

Linda's forehead wrinkled in thought. "I don't know anyone in town with that name. The only Jeffries I can think of are the oil barons, but they're way east of here in Dell City."

Jessica had passed by Dell City on her way to Carlsbad Caverns. It sat on the edge of a huge salt basin, the remains of an ancient sea. It was a wild area, with Texas's tallest mountain rising on the far side of the flats. She'd never stopped in Dell City and couldn't imagine many did.

"What's their story?" Jessica asked.

"They've been in Texas forever. Made a fortune in oil. Lately, they've made a second fortune in renewable energy, mostly wind. The community also sits on top of a huge aquifer, and those water rights are valuable."

"And they live in Dell City? There can't be more than a couple of hundred people there."

"I doubt they live there anymore, but I'm sure the family homestead is still there. There's a bunch of agricultural land in the area because of the water, and I wouldn't be surprised if they owned most of it."

"But you don't think they live here?" Jessica asked.

"I don't think so, although I'm not sure. Just because I haven't run across them, doesn't mean they aren't here."

But it kind of did. El Paso might have 700,000 people, but the rich stuck together, especially the white ones. Jessica didn't believe in coincidences. It took money to go to private school, and the Jeffries family from Dell City had plenty of that.

Another question still poked at Jessica. "Do you think they're related to Tim Jeffries, the guy from Lubbock who started The Way?"

"Definitely. There were two brothers of that generation, Tim and Russell. Their grandfather and father were the first waves of money, but the Jeffries brothers inherited everything. I think Russell still runs the company. Tim spends his time converting people, trying to take women back half a century, and buying politicians."

"Huh. I wonder if there's a connection." Already, Jessica's fingers itched to find out if one of the Jeffries brothers had a son named Jace.

"Jessica, this is a powerful family. Be careful."

Three nights later, she sat on a barstool at Crazy Cat. For the third night in a row, she nursed a beer, hoping she'd get lucky, and not in the go-home-with-some-guy sense.

She'd done her research on Jace Jeffries, Russell's son and a former Radford student who had attended the University of Texas for two years. He didn't have much of a presence online, at least not that she could find, although he might use an alias.

Jessica had walked a thin line over the past few days. Normally, a full day of work and then hanging out in a bar searching for someone who abducted and beat women would have maxed her out. But she had also spent as much time with Araceli as possible.

The woman existed in a no-man's-land, never leaving the house except to play with the dog in the back yard. Jessica had spent a couple of hundred dollars on groceries, and always came home to incredible, freshly prepared meals. While Araceli's bruises had faded, her fear hadn't diminished. In fact, it shone, multifaceted, as she worried about her abductors finding her, whether she'd be fired from her job, and if she should remain in the US, go home, or find some new place to start a life.

Jessica had coffee with her every morning, came home for lunch, and talked with her until she left for the bar each night. Araceli seemed stuck in a holding pattern. Not wanting to press charges, return to work, or leave the house. She didn't want to make any decision at all. Unfortunately, she could only call in sick for so long, and fall semester started in a week.

The first night, Araceli had pleaded with Jessica not to go to the bar. Jessica explained that she had a responsibility to find out if the people who'd hurt her also killed the Guatemalan immigrants. She also swore she'd be careful, and finally Araceli acquiesced.

Jessica had also begun teaching Araceli self-defense moves, hoping it would instill confidence in her, thus depleting the oxygen that sparked fear. Araceli had struggled with applying strength to her moves, even though Jessica repeatedly told her not to worry about punching, kicking, or blocking with too much force. Her words had yet to make a difference, but Araceli kept trying.

Jessica searched for the key that would unlock Araceli's anger at what had happened to her. Perhaps if she found it, Araceli would want revenge and simultaneously refuse to be scared out of the city and the life she clearly desired.

Jessica swung back her beer, taking a giant gulp as if trying to quench her frustration. The sour lager didn't work and didn't even taste good. Plus, she needed to slow down to make it to her outer limit of one in the morning without risking driving home drunk.

For three nights, she'd sat at the bar or a high-top table, trying to befriend the staff. While the women servers and male bartenders wore smiles, none seemed friendly. Jessica hadn't bothered asking about Jace. Regulars filled this bar, and the servers wouldn't risk their sure tips by feeding information to a stranger. Jessica respected that. The required female outfits of tiny shorts, tube tops, and knee-high boots, not so much.

Jessica had found a couple of photos of Jace online. In both shots, freckles covered his face, even his lips. His red-brown hair fell onto his forehead in what he probably thought a style, although to Jessica, it looked like he'd slept on his face for a week.

She'd also looked up photos of Jace's father and uncle, controllers of the family fortune. Both men shared Jace's coloring, dark auburn hair and slime-green eyes, but the older men looked ruddy and tough. Jace looked like a faded copy of the originals. The older men appeared at the head of boardroom tables, speaking in front of large crowds, or on horseback. True Texans. In Jace's graduation photo, and even in the one on a soccer field, his pale skin and oversized red ears suggested he belonged in a dark basement playing video games and listening for trouble like a bat.

She'd searched for Jace's mom online as well. Unfortunately, Russell Jeffries had a series of wives—four that Jessica found—and few family photos online. She discovered photos of each of the wives at gala events during their Jeffries marriage, and given the years of the photos, each successive woman was smaller and blonder than the one before her. In the end, Jessica couldn't be certain whether wife three or four had birthed Jace, although wife four looked suspiciously young to have a twenty-five-year-old son.

Many people Jessica knew posted family photos online incessantly, as if they'd forget who their kids were if they couldn't check their photos on Facebook. The Jeffries family avoided the camera. Perhaps when you had a lot to lose, you made sure no one knew about it.

The bar door opened, and a throng of loud young men came in, laughing and punching each other in the shoulders. Two large Hispanic guys entered first, flanked by a pale, beefy man with a brown buzz cut and a freckled kid with bright red hair. In the center of them all was Jace.

They paused for a moment and Jace looked around the bar warily. His eyes widened when he caught Jessica staring at him. She slowly warmed up her biggest smile. He held her gaze for a long second, then turned and followed the others to a table near the patio.

When she turned back to the bar, her skin prickled as if someone stared at her back. It would be obvious to the men if she got up and moved to a table where she could study and overhear them. But drunks became oblivious to the obvious, so Jessica put a plan into motion and raised a finger to the server.

"I'm tired of beer," Jessica said in her whiniest voice when the tube-top-clad server approached. "Do you have any fun drink specials like margaritas or palomas?"

The server managed to smile while still looking completely bored. "Our drink special this week is called El Macho. It's tequila, cucumber, and cardamom syrup."

It seemed a fancy drink for such a divey place. She also couldn't remember what cardamom tasted like, but thought it was a spice used in Indian cooking. Whatever it was, it would do the job.

"I'll have that." She gave the woman a smile she hoped looked friendly and conspiratorial. "By the way, do you know any of those guys who just walked in? A couple of them are gorgeous."

Jessica turned her head back to the table of men, but none of them looked her way. When she returned her gaze to the waitress, the woman's smile had disappeared. "Nope," she said, then walked away.

Travis said these guys came here all the time. The server didn't seem like a new hire. Why would she lie about knowing them? Jessica surveyed the bar while waiting for her drink. Most of the crowd clumped into groups. A couple of loners sat at the bar, both older and relaxing into their seats like the barstool was home. Three bartenders and half a dozen female servers staffed the business, far more than at most establishments. Their attentiveness to other customers but not to Jessica meant this was enemy territory. They'd take her money, but their loyalty remained with the regulars. She'd need to stay wary.

Her drink arrived in a blue-rimmed, stemmed margarita glass. Its wide, festive bowl provided the prop she needed. She poured half of it into her plastic water cup which she hid behind her beer bottle.

She lifted her lips to the rim of the glass and let the cool liquid flow down her throat. The delicious elixir combined the brightness of lime and cucumber with the earthy hint of cardamom. A small part of her wanted to slam the drink back and let it take the heaviness and responsibility away. But no, she had to be careful, only pretend to be drunk, watch every eye and every move.

Since learning self-defense, she'd changed. Her eyes analyzed every movement, and her body prepared to respond. Where once she'd moved through the world with complete abandon, now, she checked in with her suspicions when she entered a new environment. Someday, maybe, the quick survey of every place she entered would be automatic, unconscious. But not yet. It had become an extra step that slowed her down and burdened her with apprehension.

But today, it would serve her well. She pulled cherry-colored lipstick from her bag and swiped it across her lips, then took a few small sips to spread the color around the rim. Drunks were sloppy drinkers. She adjusted her bra and shirt to maximize cleavage and tucked a strand of long dark-brown hair behind her ear. The move opened up her face and usually had great results.

Jessica took her time closing in on her mark. She sauntered to the patio door and stood a moment as if deciding whether to go out there or not. When she turned back around, one of the Hispanic guys had his eyes on her. She boldly met his gaze and gave him a smile, then glanced at the floor, suddenly demure.

Instead of returning to her original table, she chose one catty-corner from theirs. She altered her original plan of trying to hit on Jace to see if she could take advantage of the one who kept looking her way.

Jessica flagged down the server and ordered another drink, having dumped the remainder of hers in an empty planter near the patio door. Normally, drinking did not turn her rowdy, but today, her job required something different. She gushed over the woman who brought the cocktail, fortunately a different server from the original, thanking her profusely. She didn't sit on the stool at her high-top, but remained standing, moving her position, adjusting her clothes, and spinning her glass. When the light green liquid spilled onto the table, she giggled.

She saw the guy who'd eyed her talk to his friends and nod her way. When they looked, she dropped her head to take a sip but then looked up at them through her eyelashes. The move had worked before.

Jace spoke first. "Hey there, slutty."

Jessica raised her head in shock. Had he really said that? The comment deserved a slap, or at least a view of her backside as she walked out the door. But she had to stay in character.

"How are you fellas doing tonight?" She'd even managed an East Texas accent.

"I haven't seen you here before." Jace's flat voice didn't carry a bit of flirtation. She peeked at the guy who'd originally looked at her, but he moved his eyes to Jace. The others seemed to defer to him.

"I just moved here a couple of months ago. My name is Sandra. Who are you all?" *Smile. Flirt. Take a sip of your drink.*

"Why did you come to a bar alone?"

Jessica struggled to keep the smile on her face. Every cell in her body wanted to flip him the bird and respond with a short "thirst." But that wouldn't get her closer to him.

"Well, I was thirsty and thought I'd come out and try to make some friends. I don't really know anyone here and this town can get pretty lonely." She pouted her lips and batted her baby blues at him. Most guys would be drooling over her by this time, but not Jace. Maybe he had no game—one of those guys who spent more time commenting on social media than interacting with others.

"You look like you've had plenty of *friends* in your lifetime," Jace said with a sneer and a dismissive tone.

"What does that mean?" Jessica kept the east Texas accent but lost the groveling. This guy was an ass.

"You look like you've got a high body count."

Ice plunged down Jessica's spine making her brittle. He wasn't wrong, she'd slept around a lot. Because she wanted to. Who the hell was this nasty-looking dude to judge her?

She stepped out from behind the table and looked him up and down. "At least one of us is capable of getting some action."

He didn't seem to notice the loss of the accent. Instead, his cheeks went red and his eyes flashed in anger. Jessica watched the shock pass through Jace's friends. This guy must not get called out a lot.

He came out from his table and squared off against her. Fuck. She didn't want to fight. Not in here, and not against all five of them. Would he really hit a woman in a place with so many witnesses? She didn't know, but she wouldn't stand down.

"I can get anything I want." He sneered through his lame comeback.

"Yeah? Well maybe your friends here will take care of you, but you ain't getting nothing from me." She knew the blow would hit. She recognized that special combination of insecurity and anger that some guys wore like a too-tight pair of jeans. Typically, she'd stay far away from someone like him, but she needed to get closer and flattering him had clearly failed.

His fists closed, then pumped. He really did want to punch her. Jessica shifted her weight to the balls of her feet, ready to duck or block, even though he remained more than an arm's length away.

"Someone needs to teach you a lesson." His nose wrinkled, probably in disgust, but it gave him the look of a drowned opossum.

Jessica kept herself from rolling her eyes. He was about her height and had the physique of a video gamer. Unless he had some surprising moves, she could probably take him.

Why did Travis fear Jace so much he left town? Yes, he was a bully, but Jessica bet without his posse, his spine folded up like a card table. She decided to go for the ego.

"I'm sure a couple of these guys could teach me something," she said, swinging her voice back to flirtatious and cast her eyes on the two hottest guys in his crowd. Then, she looked Jace dead in the eyes. "But I doubt you have anything to teach me."

Watching his face and neck go red filled her with power. She preferred confrontation to a pleasant but weak façade.

"How about you go on a little ride with us?" Jace choked out the words around what must have been a fist of rage buried in his throat.

"Fuck no. I've heard what you do to girls in the desert." The comment crossed a line, but Jessica no longer cared. This guy probably tortured kittens as a child, trying to make up for his own inadequacies.

The comment had a chilling effect on all the guys. They looked at each other nervously, then trained their eyes on Jace, waiting for his command.

When Jace made his decision, his shoulders relaxed and he looked around at his crew and smiled. "We'll be waiting for you outside. I think you'll do whatever we ask you to do, especially after you meet my other little friend."

Jace's right hand slipped behind his back. When it came back, it cradled a snub-nosed revolver. He briefly opened his palm, and she glimpsed the matte gray metal with a darker barrel and handle. Its lack of shine gave it a mean look.

Fucking Texas and its concealed carry laws. Probably half the customers here carried weapons.

Jace put the gun behind his back. Jessica assumed he'd tucked it into the back of his jeans.

"I've got a friend for you too," Jessica said. She would not put herself in the position of facing these guys in a dark parking lot, with or without weapons. She might have learned to fight, but five to one was not in her favor. Plus, unlike Wonder Woman, she couldn't stop bullets. Instead, she quickly reached behind her, grabbed her new drink, and threw its contents at Jace.

"Damn it!" The icy liquid covered his face and chest. Jessica had never been so grateful for big-bowled margarita glasses.

The shock wore off quickly, and he closed the space between them. He raised a fist, then his eyes scanned the bar, realizing where he was. He ended up wrapping his arm around her and pulling her into his sticky, cold chest. She let him. Wrapped an arm around him.

The noise level around them exploded as several servers came running over and asked what was wrong. One of them said the sheriffs were on their way. Jessica briefly wondered why they'd called the sheriffs since the bar was well inside the city limits. Most would have called the police.

Jace held her hard against his scrawny chest. He smelled stale and sour, like he needed better deodorant. The cucumber/lime/cardamom didn't cover his stink.

"I'm coming for you," he whispered into her hair.

"You don't stand a chance. Let me go or I'll start screaming." She punctuated her comment by slamming a booted heel onto his sneaker.

He grunted and jerked forward in pain. She used the opportunity to slip his gun from his jeans while simultaneously inhaling and preparing to scream.

He released her, holding up his hands and backing away.

Jessica spun away from him, her hands at her stomach. "I think I'm going to be sick."

She bent over, then grabbed her bag and dropped the gun into it. She stood, legitimately shaking from her audacity. And the fear that she'd be found out.

One of the servers, the one who'd been rude to Jessica, offered Jace bar towels to clean himself up. "Are you okay? Is there anything I can do to help?" She pouted and batted her eyes just the way Jessica had earlier.

A bartender big enough to double as a bouncer approached Jessica. "You can leave now or wait for the sheriff to sort everything out." He glowered at her but didn't look mean.

"Fine. Escort me to the door, and I'll leave." Jessica spoke low, hoping to limit the number of people who overheard her.

The bartender understood, or at least Jessica thought he did. He grabbed her by the upper arm and pulled her toward the entrance. He even shoved her out the door and stood there with his arms crossed, in case she tried to get back in.

"Thanks," she said as some of the tension left her body. She grabbed the keys from her bag, praying she wouldn't somehow cause the gun to go off in the process.

"You're not welcome back here. And stay away from those guys. They are very bad news."

She gave him a nod, then raced to her truck. She needed to get away before the others came out and followed her, or worse, caught her. Hopping in, she left the parking lot as fast as possible, causing the old tires to screech on the pavement.

She got hold of herself after that. The sheriff's deputies were en route, and the last thing she needed was to be pulled over for erratic driving and be caught with a stolen weapon.

She'd taken it when she feared Jace would use it on her. She would not be the next woman he took to the desert.

Of course, now that she had the gun, she had to figure out what to do with it. Tonight would not be her last run-in with Jace Jeffries.

Chapter 14

J essica didn't take the freeway home. Instead, she drove through neighborhoods and side streets to ensure no one followed her. It would take her well over an hour to get back, but she needed the time to figure out the night's repercussions and what she'd do next.

After twenty minutes of driving with no headlights following, her blood pressure calmed. She wound through the streets heading toward the star high on the mountain. Huge bulbs made up the five-pointed shape that had adorned the landscape ever since she could remember. She imagined it like a lighthouse on the coast, a beacon showing the way home. She really needed that right now.

Jace wouldn't be able to figure out who she was and thus couldn't find his way back to Araceli. That's why she'd used the alias instead of her real name. But Jessica hadn't achieved her goal. Instead, his bad manners and her hotheadedness had escalated into a fight. But she still needed information from him.

Seeing him, however, had made her cautious. Something was wrong with him. He acted like a bully, but without the meatheads backing him, he'd probably be the coward, not the tormentor. Was that what it meant to be really rich? You could turn yourself from wuss to thug by passing a little cash around?

If she could just get him alone, she'd love to force a confession from him. The way he reacted when she brought up women in the desert surely meant he'd kidnapped and assaulted Araceli. Had he also killed immigrants in the desert? Did he run a sex trafficking ring? Because what else would he have wanted with prepubescent Guatemalan girls?

Her mind sank into a sickening morass of what might be happening just outside the city limits.

Jessica needed to talk to someone. Sal came to mind, but he might go off guns blazing, or bring his knife, which could be just as deadly. She'd seen him kill a rattlesnake with it from yards away. Linda, one of the smartest women she knew, would try to protect Jessica. Besides, she shouldn't pull her job into her more dangerous escapades. At her last job that had happened, and Jessica had to leave the firm.

Underneath all those thoughts, her heart told her she wanted to talk to Angus. She'd missed having him as a sounding board, even if she hadn't always taken his advice. He understood the emotion behind why she needed to act. When she buried her feelings, he showed how much he cared. And he'd always cared for her.

She took the road around the edge of the mountains and pulled into the Scenic Drive parking lot. There, she could see over El Paso's downtown and across the sparkling lights into Juarez. The undeveloped mountains in Mexico showed black against the carpet of lights, a no-man's-land like a black hole in the landscape.

Terrible things probably happened there, just outside the city, like they did in her town. She had a responsibility to stop it. A summer night several years ago, she'd crossed the bridge from Juarez into El Paso, having barely escaped a burning mansion and an evil man. She'd decided then to use what was left of her life for good. She'd make something out of her second chance.

She'd also called Angus that night. She'd asked him for help. Then, she'd asked him to marry her, because he gave her life meaning. He was her star on the darkest of nights.

Jessica pulled out her phone and called him. She may have messed things up between them, but his was still the only voice she needed to hear.

"Hey, is everything okay?" he asked.

She regretted how many times she'd heard that question from him. He always worried about her, usually for good reason.

"I'm fine. Araceli's fine. But I've got a problem I can't sort out."

He didn't respond and the night grew colder. She'd called to burden him with yet another problem. She hadn't looked at it that way, but he probably did. It sucked to need someone as badly as she needed him.

She'd just stood up to six guys in a bar, and now she puddled at his lack of response. If he'd just let her, she could bare her soul to him and he'd keep her safe.

"Do you want to talk about it?" he said.

"Yes. Please. I'm on Scenic Drive. We could meet at the X." Her favorite dive bar split the miles between them. "Or I could go someplace closer to you."

"Jessica. I can't meet you in a bar. Neither of us has enough willpower for that to end platonically."

Jessica snickered. Yeah, they'd probably end up in bed together. "Would that be all bad?"

"Do you really want to risk our long-term prospects for a single night of fun? I don't know how to move forward with our relationship, in fact I'm still figuring out if I want to. I know we're good in bed, it's everything else I worry about. I think we need to keep things chill."

"If we've got a chance at long-term prospects, I'll do anything. Even keep from throwing myself at you." She tried to keep her tone light, but she meant every word.

"We could hike up to the C like we did that one New Year's Eve," Angus said. "You're pretty close to the trailhead."

Jessica smiled at the memory. El Paso's mountains cut through the city like a knife, and they'd watched fireworks on the city's east and west sides and in Juarez, while sharing a bottle of champagne.

"That's a great idea, but unfortunately, I'm dressed for a bar. These boots aren't making it up that mountain."

"Fine. Meet me at Whataburger, but you're buying me onion rings."

"Be there in fifteen minutes. Thanks."

When Jessica pulled into the Whataburger parking lot, Angus already occupied a booth. The fluorescent lights shone on him like a Hopper painting of a New York diner. Thankfully, the fast-food chain never closed, making it a haven for late-night drinkers after the bars shut down.

Two drinks and an order of onion rings already sat on the table. Jessica slipped into the booth. "Hey, I was supposed to buy those."

All it took was his smile, and the worry and tension from the night's happenings released her. She settled into the hard plastic booth like she'd returned after a long time away.

"I got here first," he said. "So, tell me what has you all keyed up." He reached across the table and grabbed her hand, a move from the past. He looked at his fingers as if they had betrayed him, but she gave his hand a squeeze.

"Thanks. Long story short, Araceli admitted that her boyfriend was at the assault. I talked to the guy, and he said someone named Jace was behind it. The boyfriend also mentioned the bar where Jace hangs out. I met him, and things did not go well."

"That's surprising. Usually, bars are your home turf." Angus gave her a half smile this time and grabbed an onion ring.

"True. This one is different. I've never met a bar with such an uptight staff. I mean, they're in tube tops and all, but not friendly. At least not to me. It seemed like a locals-only place." Perhaps the rude server fancied herself Jace's girlfriend.

"What happened with this guy that didn't go well?" Angus immediately pierced the heart of the matter.

"Well, it started out with him saying I was slutty, and that I must have a high body count." That one still pissed her off.

Angus's eyebrows disappeared behind a shock of brown hair. "Wow. Sounds like you found an incel. I didn't know those guys ever left the house."

"I don't get it," Jessica said. "Guys like that want to sleep with women, but they don't want women to have ever slept with anyone else. The math doesn't work." Although, she wasn't sure Jace wanted to sleep with anyone. He came across as more of a torture-and-kill kind of guy.

"It's easy to hate what you can't have. I, myself, don't mind a more experienced woman." His teasing smirk returned.

She was glad he'd made the events of the evening a little lighter. "Hey—you were my first."

"Yeah, but after me, your body count really went up." The corners of his eyes crinkled at the teasing.

"Does that bother you?" She swerved the conversation into uncomfortable territory.

Angus ran a hand through his hair, and his brow creased in thought. "It bothered me that you punished yourself that way. But the guys didn't bother me. We weren't together then, plus you never brought any of them home or saw them more than once as far as I know. Hard to be jealous of a ghost."

"I woke up eventually. Since then, it's only been you." Her heart wanted to split in two all over again.

He gave her hand a quick squeeze then moved his back to his side of the table. "So how did you leave things with this guy? Something must have happened if you called me."

Where on earth could she start? "He thought I should go outside with him and his thugs. And he showed me his gun, like that was supposed to make me want to go with him."

Angus's eyes widened in alarm. She hated that she could take him from teasing to worried in seconds.

"We were in a bar full of people, and as long as I stayed where the people were, I felt pretty safe. So, I threw my drink on him and stole his gun." She spoke quickly, hoping they'd move on to other topics before he realized the magnitude of her rash behavior.

"Fuck. This isn't fun anymore." Angus stared at her a long moment. The disappointment on his face seared her with embarrassment. "You're here, so you obviously survived."

Poor Angus. If he only knew what she wanted to talk to him about. He would soon enough. "Yeah. A bartender escorted me out. Saved my bacon. I made sure I wasn't followed, and I used a fake name at the bar."

"Well, there's that." His demeanor didn't improve.

"Between talking to Araceli's boyfriend and my conversation with Jace at the bar, I'm pretty sure Araceli's not his first victim. He and his crew may be involved in the immigrant murders. Like what happened with the Guatemalan girls."

She watched the struggle inside him, the same one that haunted her. When bad things happened in the neighborhood, someone needed to stop them so they wouldn't spread.

"Didn't you think the sheriff's department was tied up in that?" Angus asked.

Jessica bit her lip. She hated being the bearer of bad news. "When we had the fight in the bar, the bartender said he'd called the sheriffs. The bar was inside the city limits."

The onion rings cooled between them. She wanted to squeeze into his side of the booth, curl into his chest, and have him hold her. She had the strength to follow this through, but just a few minutes of safety and shared misery would help. Once, it would have happened, but not tonight.

"I understand that you have to do something about that. But you need to involve someone else this time. You can't be the Lone Ranger on this one."

She nodded. That'd be great, but she didn't have a team. Sal had helped once, but she'd put him at risk that time. It was bad enough that she wanted to run into the darkness and bring these guys to justice, endangering someone else terrified her.

"What about the big guy who was at the house?" Angus asked.

Caught in her thoughts, it took Jessica a moment to realize who he meant. "Keith? The sheriff's deputy?"

"Yeah. I thought you trusted him after he picked you up when you escaped from Juarez. Plus, he hooked you up with Sal, and now he's hanging around the house and everything."

"Angus Delgado, are you jealous? He wasn't hanging around the house. He was installing a security system. I didn't even know he was coming over. Sal sent him."

"I'm not jealous, Jess. I'm just trying to keep you alive."

She crossed her arms and stared him down. He always carried the burden of her safety. She rarely felt that weight. But that didn't mean he wasn't jealous.

"He does seem like the kind of guy you'd end up with. Burly, gun toting, probably loves to fight."

The memory of Keith fighting her, flipping her to the ground and hovering over her flashed through her mind. The sting of Angus's accuracy made her suddenly hot with shame.

But then she looked at Angus. Saw the kindness in his eyes that made kids believe in themselves. Saw the lean fingers that pulled music out of guitars and pleasure out of her body. She saw him at every age—kindergarten, college, today. He'd always been the rock that kept her steady, the friend who cared how she felt, the person she shared her dreams with. And he'd shared his right back.

"You're the only one I want to be with. I want a man who brings music into the world and teaches children to do the same. I want someone who cares about his family, laughs at his mom's bad jokes, and goes to concerts with his dad. I want the guy who cared about me even after I punched him in kindergarten and who's been there for me every day since."

She uncrossed her arms and reached for an onion ring. "Besides. Sal had me fight him the other day. He tripped me so I kneed him in the balls."

Angus chuckled. "Jesus. You really know how to make friends."

He took a sip of his drink. Jessica munched on her snack, and the tension dissipated. For the first time since he left, the air between them relaxed into the old rhythms of two friends who would always love each other.

"You know I don't buy into any of that he-man bullshit," Jessica said. "I think your job is honorable. I love that you cook. When your mom met me at the grocery store, she said you'd probably take me back if I learned to cook like her."

"Please don't. I do not want to be married to my mother." He ate his own onion ring, then wiped his hands. "You should call him to help you with this one. Keith. Or call Jaime. You said the bar was in the city limits."

"You're right." He was. Jace had his thugs, and for all she knew, she'd only met some of them. "Although I think I need to get rid of the gun first. Jaime and Keith are kind of sticklers for things like stolen property, and Keith's already arrested me once."

"You still have the gun?" He rolled his eyes and shook his head. "What are you going to do about that?"

"I don't know. I've been trying to figure it out. Maybe I can ask Linda tomorrow. She'd have to keep it confidential, but then I'd have to tell her about the case."

"Tell her. She's an attorney and an ex-cop. She'll know what to do."

"I always worry that I'm going to get fired. I hated what happened when I worked with Alma. My work on an outside case got her in a lot of trouble at her firm."

"First, I don't think Linda will fire you. She loves you. Second, who cares if you get fired. Stay alive. Don't get arrested. Keep Araceli safe. Those are the things that matter. You can get another job. This is exactly why I left. You have to avoid unnecessary risk. I can't stand that you don't understand how precious your life is." He shook his head slowly, his eyes filled with frustration.

She'd done it again, ruined a promising conversation. "I promise. I will ask Linda what to do about the gun tomorrow. I'll also get her take on whether I should tell Jaime or Keith about what happened at the bar. Maybe Jaime since he's already met with Araceli about her abduction. I will let Araceli know as well. She really doesn't want to be involved, but hopefully I can convince her to formally speak with the authorities."

Jessica stopped talking. She had hope in her heart and a plan to move forward. The worry she'd carried driving through the streets of El Paso and looking out over the cities had vanished. That's what plans did. They took away the uncertainty.

"Thank you," she said. "It really helped to talk through everything with you. I see what I need to do now."

"I'm not really sure how I helped."

"You're like half my brain and all of my heart. You really do make everything better."

His eyes still carried a hint of sadness, but one side of his lips tweaked up in a grin. "Maybe next time, call during the day instead of the middle of the night. It might do us both some good."

"Yeah. Speaking of—we should probably get home." She slid out of the booth and offered her hand to help him out. Not that he needed it, she just wanted to touch him.

He took it and pulled her into a hug as soon as he was up. "You take care of yourself."

"I will." She hugged him tight then stepped away. "Love you," she said, then turned away. She didn't want to pressure him to say it back.

"Yeah, you too." His voice carried exasperation wrapped in a smile.

She didn't turn but could picture him shaking his head. It didn't matter. She could tell he meant it.

Chapter 15

By the time Jessica arrived at work the next morning, Linda had already left for court. She hated getting in late, but sleep hadn't come easily. Before leaving the house, she checked in with Araceli. Her black eye had faded to lavender and puce. Tela had completely abandoned her owner and slept alongside the guest room bed. Best dog ever.

Jessica hadn't talked to Araceli about meeting Jace or about the gun now hidden in her closet. Hopefully, Linda would return to the office for lunch and Jessica could brainstorm with her about what to do with the weapon.

She dove into her job, using coffee to stave off exhaustion. Soon, the lack of sleep and overabundance of caffeine had her fingers shaking and her blood coursing rapidly through her veins as if she'd fed her body cocaine instead of java. She took a couple of aspirin for a latent headache. If she didn't eat soon, her stomach would rebel. But first, she needed to power through the morning's tasks.

The phone rang. "Linda Reed Law."

"Jessica Watts." Her once rushing blood froze in her veins as she matched the voice to Jace's face. How could he have found her? And so fast.

Her next thought flew to Araceli. If he'd found Jessica, he could easily get her address. Her gut clenched in fear that her determination to find Araceli's abusers had put the woman in even greater danger.

"How can I help you?" She managed to get the words out, but they didn't contain the nonchalance she'd hoped for. She could almost smell her fear, and he could certainly hear it.

"I think you have something of mine." He sounded so much more evil than he looked.

"Who is this?" No reason to walk into a trap. Not that he hadn't already locked her in a cell just by finding her.

"Don't play games with me. I'm the guy from the bar last night. One of my guys saw you take my gun."

Jessica fought to quell her shaking hands and calm her voice. She would find a way out of this and get Araceli to safety. "What's your name? I don't think we were introduced."

"The important thing is that I know who you are, and you do not want to piss me off."

Jessica took a breath, the initial adrenaline rush subsiding. What a blowhard. Why didn't he just get to the point? "Whatever. I'm at work. How can I help you?"

"You need to meet me right now and return my gun."

"Given the way you threatened me last night, why would I meet you anywhere? Besides, I don't have your gun." She didn't have it on her, anyway.

"Well, I guess me and the guys will have to pay you a visit tonight."

Fuck. That was the very last thing she wanted They absolutely had to stay away from her home. "Fine. I'll be there with my police friends."

"Are they going to protect you every night for the rest of your life? Do you think you'll be safe driving around town? Will your family be safe? It's so easy to find out about people in El Paso. Where they go, who they love. Trust me, it will be a lot easier if you meet me alone today."

She'd really done it this time. This guy was a sick fucker, and she had no doubt he'd follow through on the threats. She only wished he had called on her cell phone instead of the landline so she could record him. That way she could probably get a restraining order, not that those provided complete protection.

With no other way out, she had to respond. "What did you have in mind?"

"That's better. Meet me at my house. It's about forty miles east of downtown."

No wonder she hadn't found an address for him. He lived way out in the middle of nowhere. She couldn't meet him there, not if she wanted to come back alive. But she'd love the data for when he needed to be arrested someday. "What's your address?"

"Tell your boss you're taking the rest of the day off. It's a ways out here. Take Montana Avenue about twenty miles beyond the loop road, then turn right on Lisa Avenue just past the top of the pass. Make the next right, then you'll dead end at the house."

Jessica looked up the location on her computer. This place was truly in the middle of nowhere, miles beyond where they'd beaten Araceli. "There's no way I'm going out there. I have to work. Besides, I'm not stupid enough to walk into that kind of trap. If you really want to meet, I can make it to any Starbucks in El Paso. You know, someplace with people around."

"You don't have any leverage here. Either you do what I say, or I do what I want."

An idea occurred to Jessica as he spoke. She pulled out her phone and hit record, then put it on speakerphone.

"Dude, if I go out there, there is nothing to stop you from raping and murdering me. I won't do it."

"Then I'll meet you at your house tonight."

"You realize you sound like a psycho killer, right? Why don't you stop by my office if you're coming to El Paso anyway? I wouldn't feel safe going to see you unless I brought a brigade of law enforcement officers with me, and even then, you and your buddies might start a firefight in the desert." She had to keep talking, to keep him away from her home. Yes, she could get Araceli out of there, but then she would feel hunted, maybe forever. And Jessica sure didn't relish the idea of this monster keeping an eye on her. "You've got to give me something I can work with."

Silence. Jessica spoke into the void. "How did you find me anyway? I didn't give you my name."

"Did you think it was smart to stalk me, night after night, paying for drinks in the same bar? Asking about me?"

Jessica sorted the words in her brain, searching for the thread. *Paying for drinks.* She'd paid with her phone. Which had her credit card information, including her name. How could she have been so stupid? She couldn't believe someone at the bar shared her information with him. That had to be illegal. But it had happened.

"Return my gun today, and I promise you'll be fine, but only if you come alone. Otherwise, you're gonna get a little taste of me." The disgusting words blasted through the phone. Then silence as the line went dead.

Revulsion coursed through her.

What the hell was she supposed to do? The last thing she wanted was to meet this guy on his turf. But she also had to protect Araceli and didn't want him anywhere near her house.

She left a note for Linda saying that she had an emergency and to call as soon as she was back in the office. Then, Jessica headed for her truck.

During the drive home, she tried to get her thoughts in order. She must protect Araceli and keep that creep away from her home. And her family. Her mom lived alone in a pecan grove, and while she had two dogs for protection, this guy had a gang of thugs.

How could she get Jace Jeffries locked away forever? Whether he went to jail for accosting Araceli or for the other crimes Jessica suspected him of committing, or something else entirely, someone who threatened her the way he did needed to be put away. He was a menace to society.

She also had to get rid of his gun. Taking it had seemed smart at the time. Well, not smart, really. More of a way to get back at him for threatening her, and of course, keep him from using it.

But meeting him on his turf took danger to a whole new level. Did he just want his gun back? No, he wanted to teach her a lesson.

And what did she have for leverage? Not much. His address. His phone number. His gun.

If she asked anyone she knew, Jaime, Keith, Angus, they'd tell her not to meet him. But Jace had promised they'd meet, leaving only the location and time up to her.

Her stomach roiled. No good choices. But letting him come to her home was off the table. She'd go to him, but she'd also find a way to stay safe.

By the time she pulled into her driveway, she hadn't solidified her next steps, or what she'd tell Araceli. As usual, she'd wing it.

She opened the door to Araceli and Tela curled on the couch together. Araceli had an open magazine in her hands, and Tela lay beside her, with the sleepy look of a dog who had just woken.

"Hey, you two. I don't have time to stay for lunch today. I just need to grab something and get back to the office."

Araceli swung her legs off the couch. "Can I make you a sandwich to go?"

"No. Don't get up. I'll be in and out in a flash." Jessica practically sprinted to the bedroom, and she heard Araceli rise behind her.

The gun waited for her on the top shelf of her closet. She'd wrapped it in a towel and put it in a grocery bag. She snatched the bag from the shelf. Now she just had to make it out the door without questions.

She went on the offensive. "Have you decided about starting school next week?" Jessica asked Araceli as she walked into the kitchen.

"No. I don't know." Araceli had opened a loaf of bread, but twisted it closed again at the question. "I wish there were a third option."

"Like what?" Jessica scooted through the kitchen, listening, while still focused on the front door and escape.

"If I only knew. I don't want to go anywhere else in the US. It would only be worse outside of El Paso. But I still want to get my degree." Araceli's unhappiness with the choices showed on her face.

"What about somewhere else in Latin America? Or Spain?"

"Sure." Araceli chuckled.

Jessica had almost made it to the door. "Someone I used to work with in Mexico relocated to Spain. They have some kind of program. You should look into it."

She opened the door and glanced back at Araceli. "We can talk more when I get back. Thanks for keeping Tela company."

The moment she left, she had the urge to turn around, go back into her home, and huddle down and wait for the storm to pass. But it wouldn't. It would show up on the doorstep unless she did something.

The last time she'd run toward a dangerous situation, she hadn't known a criminal waited at the destination. She'd taken Sal with her, and only luck got them out alive. She hadn't quite forgiven herself for putting him in that situation, even though he'd volunteered. She didn't want another person's life on her conscience.

But this time, she knew who awaited her. He wanted her in his home, so very far from anyone who could help. How would she survive this encounter?

As the highway wound through the city, she formed a plan. She had part of the recorded phone call from Jace. Fortunately, Texas was a one-party consent state, making the recording legal.

Jace had said to show up alone, or else. Given where he lived, he'd probably see multiple vehicles coming from miles away. What if she showed up alone, but reinforcements followed close behind? She'd have to find a way to stall him. She could talk a good game and already knew how to get under his skin. If he confessed, they could take him straight to jail. If he didn't, hopefully the threat of law enforcement would keep him away from her house. It wasn't a perfect plan, but if she got the timing right it might work.

When she pulled off Interstate 10 and onto the ring road, she stopped to fill the truck's tank. No reason to run out of gas in an empty desert. She forwarded the recording to Keith's cell phone along with a pin drop sharing Jace's location. She'd have preferred to contact Jaime, but Jace's home lay far outside the city limits and the police department's jurisdiction. It might even sit outside the county limits, although she hadn't checked.

Her next turn took her onto the US highway that shot northeast past where she'd picked up Araceli and then beyond where they'd assaulted her. The road continued, past the boulders of Hueco Tanks State Park, and Dominion, the ranch where an evil preacher had abducted young women. Who knew what other horrors had occurred in this land of sand, creosote, and cactus?

She traveled roughly the course of the Butterfield Stagecoach that had brought mail across the country before trains and automobiles. This harsh desert had seen many things. Native Americans survived the ruthless climate, finding hidden springs to help them in a land of little water. Missionaries brought religion and disease, nations brought war, yet the people still scraped by out here, some surviving, others dying due to thirst, poisonous reptiles, or their fellow man.

A long line of tragedy preceded her, yet she couldn't help loving the desert. She fit in this hard, tough land. Today it would test her again.

Compelled to take action, she would also call in reinforcements. It straddled some kind of middle line between who she was and who she strived to be. She couldn't fool herself. The people who wanted her to take fewer risks would scoff at this plan.

If she didn't hear from Keith soon, she would pull over and wait for his call. One way or another, she'd deal with Jace before the day wore out.

She'd rather confront him out here in the desert than allow him to threaten her home. Araceli and Tela waited there. She would protect them. Angus belonged there. She wanted to protect him too, but he thought he needed protection from who she was—this creature of the desert bent on justice at her own expense.

She thrived on the hunt. Fear became an aphrodisiac followed by the sweet relief of justice. It had worked that way, so far. Each time, she'd eventually ended up on the winning side of the battle. She had to believe that would happen again.

The phone rang. She glanced at the screen. Keith. Finally.

"What the heck did you just send me?" Keith asked without so much as a quick hello.

"Jace Jeffries threatened me this morning. He's a local thug. Well, kind of local. His place is about twenty miles east of the loop road on US 62." The road stretched before her, and she had miles to go. As long as her cell phone service held out, she could update him.

"Please tell me you're not on your way out there." Frustration pierced his voice, and she could tell he already knew the answer. "Is he what happened to Araceli's eye?"

"Yes, but she won't file a report. He and a group of friends kidnapped her and beat her."

"Stop right now and turn around." Keith's voice bellowed through the phone. "Let law enforcement handle this."

Man, Jessica hated being told what to do. "I do want your help, but he threatened to come to my home this evening if I didn't meet him alone. I can't have that. He has no idea Araceli is still alive, but she probably won't stay that way if he finds her. He told me not to arrive with law enforcement, but he didn't say you couldn't follow."

"Shit, Jessica. Someone needs to be there to protect you. Hang on a sec." Murmuring reached her as he spoke with someone else.

"Are you still driving?" Keith's forceful voice filled the truck cab. "I'm on my way. If you're not going to turn around, then pull over so we can talk about this. For all you know, you're walking into a trap."

"Of course it's a trap. For fuck's sake, he made that very clear." Jessica took a breath, and her exasperation dissipated. She forced her fingers to loosen their grip on the wheel. She'd just dumped all of this on him, she'd probably have responded the same.

Jessica started over. "Sorry. I appreciate your willingness to help. I've had a couple of go-rounds with this guy. He won't be satisfied until I show up, and I absolutely have to keep him away from my home."

"You're not prepared for this. Stop the car. I can be there in twenty minutes. Maybe less. I can get other deputies out there also."

Great. Exactly what she wanted. She did have to show up alone, but she could stall him until the sheriff's arrived. Keith wouldn't like it, but it was the best way to protect her home. "He told me to show up alone. I can do that if I know the cavalry is on its way."

"Damn it, Jessica."

She wondered how much it cost him to curse. He hadn't done that before. Ahead of her the road wound up a low pass of rocky hills dotted with desert sage. On the far side of the rise, she'd leave the main road and travel toward the house she'd seen on the maps program. The home where she'd meet him topped the rise, looking back over the vast wasteland toward El Paso.

"I'm getting close," she said into the phone. "Maybe five more miles."

No response.

She glanced at the phone resting in the console. The call had ended. She'd likely driven beyond cell phone range. Empty desert surrounded her. Just past the top of the rise, a gravel road extended on either side of the highway. Jessica turned right.

Chapter 16

S he saw a sign that said "Summit Way" and turned right again. In another mile, maybe two, she'd reach her destination. The truck rolled to a stop and Jessica turned off the engine.

She opened the door and stepped onto the road. Closing her eyes, she breathed deeply a few times then stretched her arms over her head. Sal had taught her a series of stretches to complete before each lesson.

The tugging on her muscles and deep breaths slowed her thumping heart and cleared her head. Whatever would happen would happen. She'd keep her wits about her. Hopefully she could string him along until reinforcements arrived. Like a cat with a lizard, this guy wanted to play with his prey first. Last night at the bar, he'd proven how he toyed with people, or women. He tried to bring her down with shame. That emotion didn't work on Jessica.

If his goal was to kill her the moment she stepped out of the truck, then he'd probably succeed. But if that was his goal, he could have assassinated her anywhere. He wouldn't have needed to bring her out here or call her at all. He wanted something else.

Of course, she had a goal too. This guy liked to talk, and she'd prod him for a confession about Araceli and anything else he cared to admit.

She took a final breath and pulled herself back into the truck. One last bend in the road and the house emerged fifty yards away. Made of stucco, it almost faded into the desert, its paint just a few shades darker than the surrounding rock.

She parked ten yards away. To the right, the hills fell away to a view of the vast desert beyond. The Franklin Mountains, the heart of El Paso, rose on the horizon. Ahead, the door of the house stood open, a gaping hole beckoning her forward.

She hit the "record" button on her phone, then stepped out of the truck and slid the device into her back pocket. The grocery bag with the towel-wrapped gun lay on the passenger seat's floorboard. She'd leave it there. No reason to give him one more weapon—arriving as prey would be enough.

She tried to let her anger take hold. It provided great cover for fear. But her constant companion in tough situations had abandoned her. Instead, she smelled herby sage, felt the warm sun on her back and the breeze stirring her hair, whispering of a coming monsoon.

The home's gaping maw scarred the beautiful surroundings. Recent rains had decorated the sage with purple flowers and turned the spiny arms of the ocotillo deep green with soft leaves. She'd have so much to enjoy here if she turned and tramped through the hills instead of continuing toward the viper's pit.

Five feet from the door, she stopped. The difference between the bright sun where she stood and the house's dark entry played tricks with her eyes. Shadowy things seemed to lurk just beyond the few feet of visible dark hardwood floor. She didn't want to go farther.

"Hey. Are you here?" she called. No one answered.

She waited a long minute for Jace to respond. Still nothing.

"I'm not going in there. You could justify shooting me because of illegal entry." Or trespassing, or whatever. It wouldn't take much for a jury to acquit a property owner for shooting someone. Not out here.

She considered leaving, even turned around and looked at her truck, the sole visible vehicle. There must be more parking or a garage around back.

"Come inside." Jace's voice clutched at her confidence.

"I'd prefer to do our business out here."

"You need to learn to mind when someone tells you what to do. No wonder you hang out in bars alone."

Jessica smiled as a spark of anger ignited. She'd focused on the door instead of the jackass behind it. The memory of how he'd talked to her at the bar added fuel to her flame, and she even thought she caught the scent of cardamom on the wind. This guy had beaten and humiliated and tried to rape Araceli. Fire transformed, making her powerful and fully in her element. Maybe she wouldn't survive, but if not, she'd do her best to take this asshole with her.

"Man, I bet you never get laid. You really need to work on your game." She hoped he could see the grin on her face. It would infuriate him.

"Where's my gun?" Anger pierced his voice.

"What do you need a gun for? Do you use it to shoot people in the desert? Immigrants?"

A pause. Hopefully, the questions had him on edge.

"You mean illegal aliens? People who don't belong in this country?" If sound had a sneer, he'd just used it.

"Careful, your racism is showing. Most people use undocumented individuals these days."

"Fucking woke feminist. They don't belong here. Just like women who don't obey. Now get your ass in here."

So much to address in so few words. "First, they belong here as much as your relatives did, probably more. You do know that back in the day, people didn't just show up with a visa. They came, got off the boat, and were processed. Not put in jail. As for that 'obey' bullshit, you're the one who invited me here."

Jace appeared in the doorway. "Come inside. We need to talk."

He stood in shadow, but everything about him read tense. Good. She stepped toward the door, pleased that she'd burned some time. She needed to keep him talking until the sheriffs arrived. It helped that she could set him off so easily.

Her body hummed with anticipation. Anger fed her darkness, but she had a new weapon. If she had to, she could fight. A part of her wanted to test her skills by adding a physical encounter to the verbal gunslinging. She'd never share that feeling. If someone as screwed up as Jace thought she wasn't ladylike, what would Angus think if he could see inside her thoughts?

She focused on the doorway and removed Angus from her mind. He didn't belong here. Her next steps led to a battle arena, away from love. Love would be her reward for winning.

Jace stepped further back into the darkness and gestured for her to enter. She'd have preferred to keep him in front of her where she could watch him. He probably had the same thought. She hesitated, but didn't see a gun on him, although she couldn't see his back.

"Would you mind turning around and showing me you're unarmed?" Might as well ask.

He looked at her with a snarl on his face, then slowly turned and lifted his shirt. No gun. It wasn't safety, but it was something.

Normally, she'd have spent a moment in the entry letting her eyes adjust from the harsh sunlight. Instead, she stepped quickly into a wide living room with low furniture and lower lighting. She caught a rim of light around drawn shades on the far wall. The place probably had a spectacular view, but Jace kept it as dark as a basement. As far as she could tell, they were alone.

At the sound of his footsteps behind her, she spun around. He stopped quickly. She backed up an additional step to keep him out of arm's reach. The glint in his eye told her the retreat pleased him.

"You didn't do what I asked. You were supposed to bring my gun. Why did you come all this way?"

The way he leered at her made her want to spit at him. As if she'd ever consider sleeping with someone so vile. "I'm here because I want to know more about you and what you do out here."

"That's not our deal."

"It is if you want your gun back."

"Sit." He gestured toward a blocky, saddle-tan leather sofa.

She skirted a square coffee table made of ebony wood. Books about history and the Old West topped the table, all artfully arranged as if left by a designer. She settled onto the buttery sofa, as far from him as possible. Not that he wouldn't close in to intimidate her.

But he didn't. He chose a space perpendicular to her. Maybe he didn't trust her either.

Jessica quickly scanned the room. A wet bar. Paintings of horses, mountains, and deer on the walls. More furniture over by the darkened window. Thirty people or more would fit easily in the large room. What was this place? The outside looked like a house, but this felt more like a club, one of those stodgy old places where men smoked cigars.

"Do you live here?" she asked.

"Yes. I run the ranch." He crossed one leg over the other, ankle to knee, and widened his arms as if trying to make himself larger.

Funny how he didn't mention the ranch belonged to his dad. She noted the potential sore spot.

"What on earth do you ranch out here? It doesn't look like a good spot for cattle." Not that she knew that much about it, but she hadn't seen any grass, and centuries of flash floods had cut steep arroyos through the hills. It seemed like a dangerous place for livestock.

"What do you care?" he asked, suddenly angry again.

"Just curious," she said, looking for signs that he'd grown bored of their conversation.

"Why were you stalking me? You'd been going to the bar for days."

"Just a couple of days. I heard a rumor that you know what's happening in the desert out here. People getting hurt, dying."

"This is dangerous country."

She let the silence stretch. His foot pumped back and forth, possibly nerves. His jaw worked as if he wanted to talk, but he clamped his mouth shut before the words could escape. She stared at him, even though she wanted to look for weapons. This guy seemed warped. He planned on hurting her, but he didn't seem to know how to get to the next step. And he lived in this strange place that didn't feel like a normal home. No family photos. Nothing out of place. The western décor screamed quality without personality.

"So this is your parents' place?" she finally asked. She remembered his father's trail of wives. She still didn't know which one he belonged to.

His nostrils flared. "It's my place. My parents live in La Jolla."

Jessica immediately thought of Dick and Robin Saunders. Isn't that where they'd moved. Was it a coincidence or something more? If the ex-mayor and her mother's gallery owner were mixed up with the Jeffries, that would have far-reaching implications.

Jace must have realized how he sounded—like he had to compensate for leeching off his family. "Where's my gun?"

Back to this. "You tell me about the killings, and I'll tell you about your gun."

"You're not in charge here."

"Oh, did your parents leave you in charge?" She purposely provoked him. Keith would arrive soon, and she had nothing to show for her journey. Time to find out what he really knew.

He stood, quicker than a cat. She jumped up as well. She had to stay in an equal position. It gave her the best fighting chance.

"You're a fucking bitch. A stupid one too. You shouldn't bring up things you don't know about. It's a good way to get hurt." He stood, arms held away from his body. He seemed to want to make himself bigger, but what an odd way to do it, like something from a cartoon. Or a video game.

"Have you ever hurt anyone, Jace? Like women or immigrants?" She kept her voice calm and left her arms by her side, hoping he'd stick with words.

"You really don't want to know. Like they say in the movies, 'if I tell you, I have to kill you.'"

He was playing some fucking game and had cast himself as the hero. She'd had enough. "Tell me about the immigrants who get shot in the desert. Do you slaughter innocent people?" She loosely crossed her arms, getting them close to fighting position in case she set him off. She'd definitely set herself off. This fucking bastard was dangerous, although she wasn't sure he had the balls to pull the trigger.

Jace mirrored her, crossing his own arms and seeming more at ease. "If they're here illegally, they're breaking the law and deserve to be punished. That's like taking out the trash."

It took every fiber of restraint she possessed not to strike first. Eighty percent of El Pasoans were Hispanic, brown-skinned, and they'd lived here centuries before the privileged whites arrived. "I'm in law school.

Coming into the country illegally is a civil offense. It's not a death sentence. And they are people who are just as good as you, maybe better."

"It should be a death sentence. Sometimes ranchers have to take the law into their own hands to protect themselves and their property. I say if they cross our land, it's fair game. Just like you, trespassing on my land." His voice lowered an octave. "You stupid femoid."

"I don't even know what that means. And you invited me here. And immigrants aren't game, they're human beings." She wanted to scratch this guy's eyes out and knee him in the balls. What a horrible human.

"They're not nearly as valuable as game. They're just target practice." He leered at her, a smile turning up the corners of his lips. "Now the women, they're game." With that, he pounced toward Jessica.

She stepped to the side, glad he had to negotiate the corner of the table. But he was fast. Clear of the table, he lunged at her and she swerved again. She couldn't tell if he wanted to hit her or grab her. His hands flailed and she batted one away as she turned.

"What are you doing?" She tried to pitch her voice high, like a scared woman. "I told people I was coming out here. They'll find you."

He faced her with conceit etched across his face. "As you said earlier, I'll just tell them you were trespassing. Now, I'm going to teach you a lesson."

Jessica backed toward the door, trying to escape the dark room and get him outside. But her heel caught on the corner of a table and she tripped.

It was all he needed. He grabbed her arm and pulled her toward him before she could get her balance.

She used the momentum to drive forward, butting him in the chest with her head. She needed to think three steps ahead, but instead, her mind stalled as his iron grasp squeezed her arm. His hands seemed so much stronger than the rest of him.

He had her twisted around in no time and pulled her against him. She faced away from him, with his arm locked across her chest.

"Why did you think you could run?" he whispered in her ear.

Her mind unlocked and her body followed. She brought her boot heel down on his foot, just like she had in the bar. He grunted an exhale and pitched forward. She met his falling head with her own, slamming the back of her skull into his face.

"Bitch!" he shouted. But he released her and she darted for the door.

Again, he was too fast. She'd made it three steps before he tripped her from behind. She slammed into the wood floor, her breath shooting from her body. She rolled over, but he was on top of her before she could rise. His fist came screaming toward her. She partially blocked it with a forearm but only slowed its path to her cheek.

The blow stunned her. She'd enjoyed hitting others, and Sal had sparred back. But he'd never hit her like this. The pain enraged her.

Jace swung at her again. He fought like a gorilla, swinging his arm out wide. She easily blocked it with her forearm, then slammed the heel of her other hand into his chin. Before he could recover, she attacked again. She grabbed the arm he'd tried to hit her with, set her feet, and with all her strength, bucked up and to the side.

It worked! His body jerked off her, and she scrambled away and regained her feet. He started to struggle up. She might have run for it, but he blocked the way to the door. Almost without thinking, she stepped forward and buried her boot in his gut.

"Stop!" he yelled.

But she couldn't. Stopping now meant giving him a chance to find a weapon and possibly hunt her down before she could escape. She dropped to one knee, using the momentum to power her as she struck him with the edge of her hand where his jaw, ear, and neck met. Sal had told her about this spot, had her practice this hit.

Jace went completely still. She'd knocked him out. Funny how she thought triumph would follow this achievement. Instead, remorse pricked at her. In practice, elation followed good hits. Today, only relief and a certain disgust.

She shook her head and rose. The cavalry should arrive at any moment, but she needed to leave, to get far away from this hellhole and figure out if her visit had accomplished anything at all.

"You fight well." The unfamiliar raspy voice came from the depths of the house behind her.

A wave of adrenaline crashed through her system, threatened to smash her to the ground. She slowly turned. This had to be it. A weapon. Death.

A man watched her from a shadowy hallway. Had he been there the whole time? She looked at his hands. No gun. At least not one visible.

"I don't need a weapon. I am the weapon."

Fuck. He sounded like the bad guy in every movie. Benicio del Toro. Javier Bardem. She couldn't see his features other than he was short and Hispanic.

If she weren't so damn tired, maybe she'd have another fight in her. But this guy looked like a coiled rope and seemed far more dangerous than Jace. She glanced behind her to make sure he remained immobile.

"Who are you?" she asked.

"Where did you hear about the killings?" He completely ignored her question.

"Which ones?" Jessica asked. It seemed there were plenty to choose from. Immigrants. Women. Perhaps others.

"Any of them."

"People talk. Some people survive." Her thoughts went to Araceli. And the Guatemalan cousins.

"You're the one who found the immigrant girls."

Jessica hated that he put the puzzle pieces together so quickly. "What do you know about that?"

"There are many ways for the white man to make money out here." He stepped out of the shadows. Shorter than her, he looked twenty times as strong. Ropes of muscle ran down his neck and hit broad shoulders. His arms bulged, but in that cut way without any fat. Deep lines furrowed his forehead and ran down his face. Slits for eyes showed cold dark pupils. Jessica had never seen anyone more threatening.

She wanted to run, tried telling her legs to move. But her brain decided to use her mouth instead. "You're not white. Why are you here?'"

"I'm just a lowly manager. Pendejos like that one's daddy own the place." He nodded at Jace, still unconscious on the floor. "Who sent you?"

"No one," Jessica admitted. "I came on my own. But the sheriffs will be here soon."

He shook his head, seemingly disappointed. "Who taught you to fight? That last strike was impressive."

Was she supposed to be proud? "Just a friend. Can I leave?" No reason not to ask. He didn't seem to be in a hurry, but right now she didn't know how Keith, or anyone else, would react to finding Jace passed out and this guy—well, whatever this guy was doing.

"Friends are temporary. Someone who called me a friend tried that same maneuver on me once." He stared at Jessica, a questioning look on his face. "He hit just like that."

Jessica had nothing left to say. Hopefully he'd let her go, but if he didn't, each minute she stayed was a minute closer to rescue. She wouldn't leave with him. No matter what.

"Go. Don't ever come back. And if you want to live, stop looking for trouble."

She almost wanted to tell him he sounded like her husband. For once, she kept her mouth shut. She turned around, expecting to feel a knife or gun at her back. As she strode quickly out the door, she passed Jace, still silent on the floor. The sight of his chest rising and falling brought relief that she hadn't killed him.

Jessica didn't turn around until she'd opened the truck door, using it as a shield from anything that might venture from that house. She spied the gun on the floor and grabbed it, bag and all. She walked behind the truck to the edge of the hill. There she held the gun with the towel and tossed it down the slope. It wasn't exactly well, hidden, but you'd have to look for it. If Jace ever called her again, she could prove she'd returned it.

Back in the truck, she started the engine, then spun the wheel hard left and hit the gas. A rooster-tail of gravel streamed behind her as she

U-turned and left that mausoleum of a house and the strange men it held.

Chapter 17

Jessica sped down the gravel as quickly as the road allowed. The truck skidded around a blind curve that would put solid rock between her and the evil behind her. She hit the brakes and pulled to the right as another vehicle barreled up the road.

Keith had finally arrived. Relief swelled like a bubble, then popped. It was a sheriff's deputy vehicle, but the driver had gray-blond hair instead of black. And ice-blue eyes.

Jessica's foot hit the gas before she fully registered Deputy Mayfield behind the wheel. She'd last seen him shaking hands with Dick Saunders outside of the gallery. She trusted him less than anyone in a sheriff's vehicle except for the sheriff himself. Her heart raced faster than the tires spun. His SUV continued to churn up dust, and she couldn't tell if he'd turned around to follow her or continued to the house.

Finally, she reached the turnoff where private drive met public road. Just a quarter mile more and she'd be on the highway, just another traveler in an ocean of sand.

Ahead of her, a black-and-white sheriff's deputy vehicle turned off the highway. Nerves prickled her skin. Friend or foe? As the SUV neared, she spied Keith's spiky black hair.

Jessica slowed the truck. Friend, probably. But why had Mayfield shown up first?

Keith pulled beside her, his window rolling down. She braked fully, rolled hers down as well.

"What happened? Are you okay?"

"Yes." Physically. "Jace and I had a fight."

She remembered her phone, still recording from her back pocket. "Then some other guy showed up, or maybe he was there all along. Really scary dude. I think bad things happen there, maybe related to the immigrant killings."

"I'm so relieved you made it out okay."

"The scary guy let me go. I saw Deputy Mayfield driving up after I left. I thought it'd be you." Why had she said that? It sounded like she needed him. Maybe she had. Her thoughts about the day still skittered about in her head, needing sorting.

"Huh. He must have been out this way. I put out a department-wide call for anyone nearby to respond." He ran his hand through his hair, a worried look on his face. "I was afraid I wouldn't get here fast enough."

"Thank you for responding." Gratitude—that she wasn't all alone, that she'd made it out alive—flowed through her. Maybe they'd have enough evidence to start a full-blown investigation. Heck, if Araceli agreed to testify, that alone could lock away Jace and his minions. If the case went well. They didn't always.

"Well, I better get up there to help since I called the case in." He looked forward, started to roll up his window, and then turned back to her. "I'm really glad you're okay."

"Yeah. Me too." She smiled. He'd proved to be someone she could rely on. She could use more of that in her life. "Thanks for coming."

An hour later, Jessica had made it back to the office. She cleaned herself up in the bathroom, then removed the note from Linda's desk. Her boss obviously hadn't returned from court. Jessica's cell phone rang from the reception area, and she trotted back to get it.

Keith. She couldn't wait to hear what had happened after she left. She answered and said a quick hello.

"Jessica." Keith's voice sounded strained. "Where are you?"

"I'm at work. Why?"

"When I got to the house, Deputy Mayfield had been shot. He's dead."

"What?" The words didn't process. It couldn't be. She'd just seen him. The raspy voice and fighter's build came back to her. It must have been him. "Did you get him, the scary guy? Is he in custody?" She hoped so. Otherwise, a murderer was on the loose—one who knew who she was.

"There was no one else there. You were the last person to see him."

Oh, shit. "It wasn't me. I swear."

"I don't think you did it. Remember, I saw you right after. And we found a gun. We're processing it for fingerprints."

Jessica's bones turned liquid and she sank into her chair. "Where was the gun?"

"I can't discuss the details of the case with you. I've already said too much."

"If it looked like it had been tossed off the side of the hill, then my fingerprints will be all over it."

"Shit."

Jessica could picture him shaking his head, the disappointment etched across his face. "It's okay. I recorded my visit. Everything will be fine." She hoped.

"Listen. There's a deputy coming to pick you up and bring you in for questioning. That's why I needed to know where you were. I've already sent them the address, and they should be there in a few minutes. Go with them, Jessica. Don't run."

"I'm not guilty. Why would I run?" she snapped. "I've got to go. See you at the station."

She hung up and quickly emailed the audio recording to herself. They'd probably confiscate her phone, and while she trusted Keith, he wouldn't control the investigation. For the second time, gratitude pulled her toward him. He didn't have to call, probably shouldn't have. But he did.

This time she texted Linda instead of leaving a note on her desk. *Busy morning. Went after a criminal. After I left a deputy was killed at the site. Going to sheriff's for questioning. Sorry.* So much to explain in so few words.

She glanced up as a sheriff's department vehicle rolled to a stop. She typed one more text, to Araceli. *I'll be late tonight. Don't wait up.* Then she dropped her phone into her backpack and met the officer at the door.

———

Hours later, Jessica told her story to deputies Ruiz and Rodriguez for the hundredth time. Rodriguez, the woman, played the bad cop, while Ruiz tried to befriend her. Her story never changed. It couldn't. It was the truth. The audio recording should have cleared her immediately.

Jessica had just returned from a bathroom break. Both deputies sat at the table.

"It's been three hours," Jessica said. "When do I get to leave?"

"When we hear the truth," Rodriguez said. "You can't kill one of us and get away with it. And that bruise on your face tells us you were involved."

"I didn't kill anyone. I've explained the bruise. You have the recording," she said for the thousandth time.

"Then why are your prints on the murder weapon?"

"I'm guessing that wasn't the murder weapon. Has forensics given you their analysis?" This conversation had gone round and round for far too long.

"I gave you my recording." It took every ounce of her self-control not to shout. "Haven't you listened to it yet? I left before Deputy Mayfield got there. Two other people were at the scene before I left. Where are they?"

"No one else was there when our deputies arrived."

When Keith arrived. He had believed her. He would listen to the recording. She just had to survive this.

Suddenly the door opened and Linda stepped through. "Why the hell are you in here answering questions without waiting for legal counsel?" Linda's anger practically set the room on fire.

"Because I'm innocent and I have a recording to prove it. I want them to find whoever killed Deputy Mayfield."

"Stop talking." Linda's glare slashed through Jessica.

She'd really screwed up. Shit, she knew better than this. But she thought she could easily prove she hadn't killed anyone.

Linda turned to the deputies. "Unless you're arresting her, we're leaving."

Rodriguez started to talk, but Linda raised a hand to stop her. "She won't leave the county."

Linda glared at Jessica one more time, then left the room. Jessica followed.

Despite towering over her, Jessica could barely keep up as Linda stormed out of the headquarters and into the parking lot. Her boss didn't say a word until she'd driven her Porsche off the lot and to a nearby shopping center while Jessica sat silently in the passenger seat.

Linda parked in a quiet corner, made even more incognito by the now dark sky. Then she turned and glowered at Jessica.

"What the holy hell? You are going to be the world's shittiest attorney. You don't talk to the people who arrest you without your attorney present. How do you not know that? Have I taught you nothing?" Linda's nostrils flared.

Jessica faced a fire-breathing dragon. "You're right."

"They wanted to arrest you. Also, you know I don't take my phone into court. You have to call and have someone get me."

"I know. They came so quick." Mere minutes had passed between when she'd found out about the murder and when the officer had shown up. And she hadn't been thinking.

"You've got to do better," Linda said. "Now, I assume you haven't eaten anything. Can I take you to dinner so you can tell me everything that happened?"

"Let's get takeout and go back to the office. I've got a recording on my laptop you need to hear."

———

Jessica paused the recording. She'd already told Linda everything that had happened that day, and the days prior, including the pieces Araceli didn't want anyone to know. Jessica could apologize for that, and it would be a lot easier in person than from a jail cell.

"I can't wait for Sal to hear this," Linda said, smiling. Her demeanor had changed after hearing the video. Incontrovertible evidence. "You kicked that guy's ass."

"Yeah. Sal's a good teacher. Although I don't know if anyone could outfight that second guy."

"I really wonder about him. He didn't have much time to get Jace out of there, kill a deputy, and then escape. Maybe there were more people in the house than you saw."

"It's possible. I had no idea he was there until he emerged from the shadows. He's really frightening. Also, I still don't quite understand how Jace, his friends I saw at the bar, and his parents play into all of this."

Linda gazed into the distance. "There's definitely a puzzle there." She turned to Jessica. "But that's not our issue to solve. Our job is to make sure you're not a suspect in the case. The recording should do that, especially since you left it on until after you spoke with Keith."

"Yeah. That was mostly luck. I had to get out of there as fast as possible, and I'd already spent time throwing the gun away."

"I'm still not sure that was a good idea. Actually, taking it was the bad idea. Whatever possessed you?"

"Trust me, if you met Jace, you'd take his weapon away also." Jessica yawned. This day had lasted forever.

"You look exhausted. Let's call it a night and regroup in the morning."

"Thanks. And I'm really sorry for not bringing you in earlier. I realize how big a screwup that was." Jessica would probably fire someone who made a mistake like that, Hopefully, Linda was bigger-hearted.

"Jessica, you can't be a cowboy all the time. There are rules we follow for a reason. They're there to protect us and our clients."

"I know. I really do."

She had to stop letting down the people on her side. Angus had learned to live with her endangering herself, until he couldn't anymore. She'd heard the disappointment in Keith's voice when he'd told her she'd be picked up for questioning. And now she'd have to go home and tell Araceli about everything that had happened today.

And, of course, Jace, the guy who'd hurt Araceli, had disappeared.

Chapter 18

The aroma of coffee woke Jessica. She would need it after yesterday's ordeal. Araceli must be in the kitchen already. Time to come clean.

The scene Jessica walked into comforted her. The dog gobbled kibble, bread browned in the toaster oven, and Araceli stirred a batch of scrambled eggs. Jessica grabbed a mug and filled it with coffee.

Araceli's eyes went big when she looked at Jessica. "What happened to your eye?"

"I'll tell you about it if you'll share some of those eggs with me. The place is definitely more of a home with you in it than when I lived by myself."

"Well, since I can't really go anywhere, I have to find ways to keep myself busy," Araceli said, slicing off part of the aloe plant for Jessica to use on the fading bruise under her eye.

Jessica hadn't expected the hint of resentment. But what had she expected? That Araceli would be happy here until she took her next step? Jessica would have gone stir-crazy days ago.

"I totally get it. Have you decided what you want to do next?"

Araceli sighed, the exasperation buffeting air particles about the room. "I guess I have to go back home. I can't imagine another way for this to work out. Robin comes back from La Jolla tomorrow, so I'll tell her in person I can't take the job. Is it okay if I invite her here?"

"Sure, but what if we get these guys put away?"

Araceli turned off the stove just as the toaster dinged. She turned to Jessica. "We don't even know who they are. And it's not like Travis will stay in Arizona forever. He'll come home for Thanksgiving and

Christmas. Am I supposed to check his schedule and hide while he's in town?"

Finally, Araceli's anger had arrived. Jessica had waited for this, because it would likely lead to her wanting to fight. Unless she gave up and went home, leaving her dreams shredded on the wrong side of the border. Araceli made this city better. Jessica would trade her for Travis and Jace every day of the week.

"You shouldn't have to hide," Jessica said, returning to the question. "I found Travis's friends. They are not good people and belong behind bars."

The plate Araceli held in her hand clattered to the countertop. "Have you talked to them?"

"Yes. I've mostly talked to Jace Jeffries, the ringleader."

"Does he know about me?"

"No. He doesn't know you survived or that you're here. But I think he's involved in killing immigrants." Jessica watched the emotions cross Araceli's face. Fear. Anger. Sadness.

"Of course he is. I heard what he said about my kind. I need to go home."

"No. He needs to be in jail."

Araceli didn't look at Jessica as she loaded two plates with food. She took them to the table and sat with her back to Jessica.

Jessica took her place at the table, wondering how to make this better. Araceli had the right to do whatever she wanted, but it should be a choice, not a running away. Maybe choices became impossible after experiencing so much hate and trauma.

"The sheriffs are looking into it. After I left my—meeting—with Jace yesterday, a deputy was killed."

The terror returned to Araceli's eyes as she gasped. "Oh, no. It wasn't Keith, was it?"

"No. He found the deputy who was shot."

"That must have been terrible for him."

"I guess. I only spoke with him briefly." Jessica suddenly wanted to call Keith and find out if he was okay. She'd relied on him over and over again yesterday, and he'd shown up, called in reinforcements, followed her to Jace's house, reassured her after she'd escaped, and then called to warn her. He'd shown up for her, and she needed to do the same for him. "I need to find out how he's doing."

Jessica looked at Araceli. Her bruise had faded to an ugly yellow, and bringing up death had returned the fear to her eyes. Dreams could only flourish in safety. That had to be the priority. "If you want to go home, whatever you decide, I'll help. I want to be there for you, now and in the future."

"They'll kill anyone." Araceli's words barely passed a whisper.

They ate the rest of their meal in silence. Araceli disappeared into her bedroom while Jessica cleaned up. The homey atmosphere had vanished, and Jessica didn't know how to make it better. Even finding Mayfield's killer wouldn't help unless Jace had pulled the trigger. But Jace was some type of man-boy probably overly influenced by the rancid men podcasters who hated women. The scary guy didn't seem like the type who enjoyed beating up women in the desert. He seemed the type to control armies.

———

It didn't surprise Jessica that Linda waited for her in the conference room when she arrived at work. Although, she hadn't expected to see Sal.

"How is Keith?" Jessica wouldn't even bother with hello before asking the question she most wanted answered. She'd texted him from home but had heard nothing.

"Yesterday was hard for him." Sal's steady eyes watched her. "It's not easy finding a dead colleague. Or knowing a friend was the last person there. He worried that you'd barely escaped, and he had no idea what had happened to Mayfield or how much danger he was in. When he called it in, he was commanded to leave Mayfield there and retreat until reinforcements arrived. I think that was the hardest part of all."

She could imagine. Keith was all cop, would want to hunt down the killer and chase justice. But Jace and the other man would have shot him just as easily as they'd probably taken out Mayfield. She wished she could talk to Keith. Help him the way he'd helped her after she'd escaped being kidnapped and held hostage.

Linda broke into the conversation. "I'd like for Sal to hear the recording you made."

"Of course." Jessica brought her laptop to the table and set it up. "I started recording before I left my truck and didn't remember to turn it off until after I'd talked to Keith. I met him down near the highway."

Sal nodded and she hit play. It made her stomach roil listening to it today. Yesterday, the recording had been a lifeline, or a get-out-of-jail-free card. Today, she realized the danger she'd put herself in. If the scary guy had wanted to kill her, he could have easily done so.

She noticed Sal shift, become more alert, when he heard her speaking with the man whose name she still didn't know. It had shocked her to see him, to first hear that distinctive voice. Perhaps his voice had the same effect on Sal.

When the recording ended, the room remained silent for a long moment. Jessica wondered if asking Keith for help had resulted in Mayfield's death. She would have survived anyway. Had she caused this?

Sal's voice broke the silence. "This is bad."

So few words, yet the gravity behind them seemed to pull Jessica into a hurricane. She stared at him, waiting for an explanation of the next very bad thing.

"I know him," Sal said. "And I hoped I would never hear that voice again."

A chill threaded its way through every cell in Jessica's body. Sal didn't fear anyone. She'd seen him kill a rattlesnake. He'd taught her how to fight. Keith had mentioned his tours in the Army and long service as a sheriff's deputy.

"What did he look like?" Sal asked, piercing Jessica with his stare.

"Short. Bald. Hispanic. Cut. Huge arms. Dry, rocky voice."

"What else?"

The man had just appeared in the hallway. Or maybe he'd been there the whole time. "Silent."

"His name is Andres Sepulveda. We served together in the Army." The wrinkles on Sal's face sank deeper, and his troubled onyx eyes, so like Keith's, looked tired.

Linda laid a hand on his arm. "You need to tell us everything. For Jessica and for Keith."

He nodded. "I know. It's a long story and covers a lot of years."

"Anyone want coffee?" Jessica asked.

"Please," Linda said as Sal nodded.

Jessica escaped to the kitchen. The pressure of the room overwhelmed her. Her stomach skated down a sand dune. She couldn't stop Sal's story, but she'd be worse off at the other end of it. The guy already scared Jessica, and if even Sal feared him, the future looked grim.

She poured out the remnants of the coffee someone had made earlier and started a fresh pot. She rummaged around the kitchen looking for who knows what, then stopped and bent over the counter, both hands on the cool tile. She inhaled deeply, once, twice, three times.

This should have been cut-and-dried, an easy case. Figure out who hurt Araceli and put them in jail. Instead, the case had grown the tentacles of an octopus, reaching out to Arizona, killing Deputy Mayfield, and now, somehow, involving Sal.

She stood back up, got ahold of herself. She'd walk back into that room and face whatever surprises came her way. She wanted to turn back time, focus on learning to fight and getting her husband back. Instead, at every turn, this case grew more complex and more dangerous. A murdered deputy.

She pulled three mugs from a cabinet. The coffeepot hadn't finished brewing, but she no longer cared. Funny how pouring coffee, then walking into a room she'd passed through hundreds of times, now felt like an act that would change everything.

She did it anyway. Passed out the mugs then took her seat and asked Sal to start.

He told them he and Andres had met in the Army at eighteen. "We were both from El Paso but met at Fort Benning, Georgia. Ranger training school."

Jessica didn't know much about the Army Rangers beyond their special forces reputation, akin to the Navy SEALs. El Paso had one of the country's largest Army bases, Fort Bliss, and plenty of retirees. You couldn't help running across veterans and hearing the stories. It was part of the fabric of the city, baked into the desert sun.

"It was the seventies. Bruce Lee was king, our hero, so we learned to fight. We had a sanctioned fight club. Both of us became skilled, could beat anybody, except each other. We walked away from our battles bloodied, and always thinking about how to gain the advantage. We took pride in our work, formed a kinship. We were like brothers."

"Friends are temporary." Jessica repeated the words Andres had spoken on the recording. "He asked me about my last strike on Jace. He wanted to know who taught me. He knows it was you." Alarm thumped through her, in time with her heart.

"It is possible. We haven't seen each other in many years," Sal said. "Things did not end well between us."

Jessica saw the strain on his face, heard it in his voice. "What happened?"

"Andres always looked for angles, ways to get ahead. The Army didn't satisfy him. I doubt anything ever has. In every branch of the service, there's a black market. Things can be bartered for, traded, or even stolen. Eventually, money changes hands, lots of it."

"What kinds of things?" Linda asked.

"Weapons. People. Other things too. Supplies. PX inventory. Vehicle parts."

"Sounds like the dark web," Jessica said. She'd never put a lot of trust in government institutions. Still, it hurt to find out how much worse they were than she'd imagined.

"There was definitely no web back then, but greed always finds its way into human endeavors. I found out what he was doing and reported him."

Linda nodded. "Of course you did."

She didn't say with nearly the sarcasm Jessica would have used. Linda and Jessica each combined toughness and a desire to uphold the law. Linda bent toward the law. Jessica craved justice more than she wanted to follow rules.

"I imagine he was pissed," Jessica said, sarcasm dripping from her voice.

"Furious. A week later, he accused me of beating a local woman. He got the police involved, and the Army threatened to court-martial me. It almost worked. The woman said a Hispanic man jumped her, and she picked me out of a lineup."

"How did you get out of it?" Linda asked with concern.

"His voice." Jessica responded. They didn't look alike, at least not as older men. But back then, a white woman might not have discerned one Hispanic from another when they had similar heights and probably had the same haircut. Hell, thousands of men in El Paso would fit their description, then and now. But Jessica would never forget that voice as long as she lived.

"Yes," Sal said. His brows arched in surprise. "I told my commander I thought Andres had done it. He believed me because Andres never stayed out of trouble. I suggested letting the woman listen to our voices."

"Bad conduct discharge?" Linda asked.

"Yes. And later, criminal prosecution. He spent some time in prison. Probably picked up a few skills there."

"Holy shit." Jessica couldn't hold in the comment. This sounded like a lifelong feud.

"Did you stay in touch?" Linda asked.

"No. By the time he finished his sentence, I worked at the sheriff's department. I never heard from him again, although I occasionally heard about him. I'm not sure he was ever on the right side of the law again, but he was smart enough not to get caught."

Jessica thought back to their conversation. "He said he was a manager at the Jeffries place, but he didn't seem to like them. Said something about the white man finding ways to make money."

"I heard that on the recording. That's when I knew it was him. He hated the Army because the white men seemed to have an easier path to promotion. But that's how our country is. The sheriff's department was no different. The system is set against people of color. Although less so here than many places."

Linda huffed. "Try being a woman."

"Yeah. The good-old-boy system is part of the landscape as well," Jessica said. "Not to mention, women have to worry about their safety here—just like everywhere." Visions of Araceli's bruised face emerged.

"I understand that. Really. But dealing with Andres is a whole new problem." Sal looked worried, an expression she hadn't seen on him before today.

"I doubt Jace regained consciousness before he and Andres disappeared," Jessica said. "If so, he'd have been pretty woozy. Also, I don't know how many other people were there. I didn't see anyone else. And there must be a back exit. Otherwise, Keith would have seen them leave."

"Hopefully, the sheriffs will make quick progress on this one," Linda said. "Until then, you'll remain in their sights. I'm sure they'll call soon for another interview."

"Doesn't the recording clear me?" Jessica asked in frustration. "There are other things I need to take care of today."

"Like what?" Linda asked.

"I'm worried that this guy knows who I am and that I've looked into the killings in the desert. If he comes after me, well, I have more than myself to protect right now. I need my security system set up to go to a second phone. Keith offered, but . . ." She let the sentence hang. No need to mention that her estranged husband might be jealous.

"Use me." Linda responded immediately.

"Both of us," Sal said.

Multiple people meant more protection. Jessica nodded and handed her new phone to Sal who set everything up. What else could she do? The sheriffs didn't need help solving Mayfield's murder. Unless Araceli testified against Jace, the sheriffs wouldn't punish him or his accomplices.

Jessica still wanted those bastards punished, but the danger seemed greater now that a career criminal who seemed especially menacing complicated the case. Perhaps her next move should be to help Araceli figure out her next step. Jessica doubted that El Paso remained a safe option.

Chapter 19

Jessica took an early lunch to accomplish two things. She needed to tell Angus what had happened before he found out from other sources. The deputy's murder had been in the morning's news, although her name had yet to be mentioned. She also had to warn Araceli, a woman already living in fear, about the new development.

She waited for Angus at JJ's, one of his favorite restaurants. She'd already ordered two gordita plates. Their order here never varied from the masa pockets stuffed with green chile and sauteed ground beef topped with lettuce, cheddar, and a wickedly hot salsa.

Angus walked in the door the moment the server placed the plates in front of Jessica. She'd chosen a booth in the corner. The main lunch crowd hadn't arrived yet, and no one would overhear.

He slid into the booth and thanked her for the food. "What's up? You said it was important."

Jessica grimaced. "It's bad," she said. Angus raised his eyebrows and waited silently.

"Have you heard the news about the deputy who was shot?" she asked.

Angus blew out a sigh. Jessica hated the things she did to this man. Should she not have followed up? Given up on retribution for Araceli? Not tried to make their community safer?

"I was at the location where he was killed. I left before he arrived, and I have a recording proving that. But the sheriff's department has interviewed me, and I don't know if I can keep my name out of the press." Her teeth dug painfully into her bottom lip as she waited for a response.

"I don't give a damn about the press. Are you in danger?" Concern flowed from him and blanketed her.

"I don't know. Maybe," she admitted. "I'm going to talk to Araceli about it after lunch. She's already talking about going home. I'm not sure what she'll decide."

"Maybe she could stay with Robin. You'd have to be nuts to attack the ex-mayor's home."

It was an interesting idea. "I'll ask her about it."

"What about you?"

She wanted to hold on to his empathy, wrap herself in it. It felt a lot like love. How had she let this relationship slip away? Irony. By getting herself into situations exactly like this one.

"The new security system at the house is really good." She had nothing else to offer, it seemed the best of her limited options.

"That's not enough." He sighed again. Ran a hand through his hair. "You can stay with me."

The offer pulled at her heart, bringing unbidden tears to her eyes. She wanted nothing more, but this seemed like it would pull their relationship backwards instead of pushing it forward. She wanted to tell him that but found herself unable to speak.

"Oh, Jess. What am I supposed to do with you?" He laid his hands on the table, palms up. She placed her hands in his, savoring his warmth. "I still love you, you know. I'm not sure that will ever stop. I don't know what the future holds for us, but if you're in danger, I'll be there for you. Not that you need my help."

"But I do. I do need your help," she whispered.

He shook his head. "I'm not like Sal or Keith. I've never used a gun, can't throw a knife, would probably get my ass kicked taking on a skilled fighter. The world you've entered is more dangerous than I'm capable of dealing with."

"I don't need you for protection. I need your love. I need your belief in a world that's better than the one I see." She realized the truth of the words as she spoke. "Your world is filled with kids who play music, lifelong friends, and families who love each other. When I'm with you, that joyous world is part of my existence."

Jessica became aware of how little she had to offer in return. It sliced through her heart like a scythe, leaving her breathless. He'd always been too good for her, but she hadn't understood the vastness of the difference.

Angus chuckled. "That's not how it feels from this side. I'm not powerful enough or skilled enough to be the man you need. There are many better candidates. Guys who could protect you. Maybe if I were like that, I wouldn't be so terrified of you dying." He squeezed her hands so hard it hurt.

Jessica welcomed the pain. It kept her tied to him. She didn't know how to bridge the gulf between her world and his.

He must have seen the troubled look on her face or intuited her emotions the way he had in the past. "I'm glad you're out there fighting the bad guys and making the world better, or at least our corner of it. I'm just not a guy who can do that. And when you bring it home, like after your kidnapping, I don't have the resources to help you."

Memories of the lost days after the kidnapping flooded her. He took care of her when she could hardly leave the bed, wrapped himself around her and filled her with his good energy until she felt whole. No one else could have healed her so quickly.

"You're the reason I'm whole again. You poured your goodness into me and made the world a better place. One where I wasn't afraid. You are the balance to all the bad in my world."

"How?" he asked.

The question shattered her heart. How could he not know everything he meant to her? "You give me something to fight for. Kids who want to create art. Grandparents who share their stories. Friends who invite fifty people over for their kid's first birthday, where the grill is on all day, kegs are tapped, and a hundred people show up and stay all day and half the night to celebrate the child, life, and each other. Yours is the world I want to live in, the one I have to protect. I'll walk into any desert, track down any villain, as long as I get to come home to you and everything you represent."

The words were too big for a Mexican diner in a strip shopping center at eleven o'clock in the morning. They should have been proclaimed on a moonlit mountaintop where stardust swirled around them. Instead, they sat, hands clasped above plastic plates laden with food growing cold. Maybe this was how heroes' journeys and passionate romances played out in real life.

They were two people whose love was bigger than their surroundings. They each wanted to make the world better, one by imbuing the world with song and cheer, the other by slaying dragons. Two halves of a coin, his side shiny and bright and hers made of darkness and danger.

Evil existed, and it required people to beat it back and keep it from consuming the brightness and virtue on the other side. For the first time, she saw clearly how their outlooks, their drive, fit together in the world the way their bodies fit together in their bed.

"You are the other half," she said. "You are the sunlight that makes midnight bearable."

He gazed down at the table, his cheeks going red. "The world doesn't work that way. We got everything backwards. You're fearless. You bring down criminals, put yourself in perilous situations to protect people weaker than you. I teach kids music. There's no comparison. Don't you ever want to run with your own pack? Be around people who are as fierce as you are?"

She tugged on his hands, made him look at her. How could he think that? "That's not what I want. Without you, I'd forget what I fought for and lose myself in the depths of human depravity. I can fight the darkness because I'm made of it. At least part of me is. Without you to show me what's good, to believe that it's inside of me as well, I'd go all the way over."

She'd tried to explain, but the dour look on his face told her he didn't understand. "What is it?"

"I love what I do, but it's not in the same league as what you do. You're a protector. Just like Jaime and Sal and Keith. There's fight in you, but you've always used it to help others."

"And you're a teacher. Just as important. More important. You create the light we protect. And you left out Linda. This isn't a gender thing. Believe me, I've heard more ridiculous gender beliefs over the past week than I'd ever wanted to. Can we stop trying to fit people into boxes and just let them be who they are? Do you think less of me because I want to trek into the desert and fight for justice instead of doing whatever 'normal' women do?"

"No. I respect the hell out of that. Although, I hate how careless you are with your life."

"I understand that. I'm working on it. I promise. But you need to understand how much I respect what you do. I've seen you stand on a stage with music pouring out of your fingers, your lungs, it seems like your very pores. And you take that passion and pass it on to future generations. My mom paints incredible scenes that break my heart every time I look at them. I don't have this ability to throw good into the world, create it out of nothing. So I work in the dark, trying to make space for everyone else to bring the light."

She paused and took a breath. A tear dripped down her cheek. She'd peeled back her skin and opened her heart. She'd exposed her flaws, her inability to measure up to those around her. Not because she was a woman. But because her talent lay in hunting down the despicable so others could shine.

"You're afraid I'll get hurt out there or won't come home. I don't think I can completely take that risk away, although I'm trying to lessen it. But I will always do everything I can to come back to you, because without you, my life is hollow. You bring the joy that makes the brutality worth it."

He no longer looked at the table but fixed her with his eyes. "I'm terrified of losing you for selfish reasons. As much as I admire how you battle evil, I'm not sure I'm ready to live with that again. But this talk helps."

A spark of hope lit in her chest. They loved each other too much to not end up together. He made her whole, and maybe she helped him some as well. "If you use your special brand of teaching to bring joy to kids, I'll use my trademark bitchiness to fell the forces of evil. Together, we'll create a world worth living in."

"I like that idea."

"Me too. And thanks for offering me a place to stay. I'll let you know what Araceli wants to do."

She couldn't take her eyes off him, even though he released her hands. They'd stepped into a new version of themselves. She hadn't looked at him as a hero before. Maybe she'd known him for too long and had become too familiar. If she met him today for the first time, what would she think?

He smiled at her, the corners of his lips curling up in that way that hammered dimples into his cheeks. She'd fall for him all over again. He might deserve more than she could give, but that didn't mean she wouldn't fight for him.

———

When Jessica arrived home, she found Araceli and Tela in the backyard. Araceli heaved a tennis ball, and the dog faithfully retrieved it.

"You know, she'll do that all day," Jessica said.

"Or until the ball gets too slobbery for me to touch." Araceli said with a smile.

Jessica called Tela and took her turn throwing the ball. She'd do anything to delay the conversation they needed to have.

"You look worried," Araceli said. "Or more worried than usual. And that's saying something. You really need a less stressful career."

Interesting observation given her recent discussion with Angus. But she wasn't here to talk about career choices.

"This morning, I learned that the guy I saw at Jace's house yesterday is a career criminal and all-around bad guy. He may have shot that deputy.

And he knows who I am. I think we need to find you a safer place to stay."

Araceli dropped to the steps of the deck. Tela bounced over and tried to lick her face and sit in her lap. Despite the way Araceli petted the dog, Jessica saw the tension in her jaw. Of course the news had upset her. Maybe it would help her decide what came next. Unfortunately, Jessica expected her to return to Mexico.

"I've been thinking a lot about my choices. I'm not ready to give up and go home. But I don't want to stay in El Paso either. I need one of those big traffic signs with the blinking arrow to show me where to go." Her voice ached with sadness.

"If you need more time, maybe you could stay with Robin."

"I decided not to ask her. I haven't forgotten the terrible things Dick said to my family when he found out we were related to Robin and thought we wanted their money. Of course, with this new information, things look different. It might be okay if he's still in La Jolla. Let's see." Araceli pulled her new phone from her pocket and placed the call on speakerphone.

"Hey, Ari," Robin said as she answered. "I'm glad you called. I've got some updates."

"It's good to talk to you, and Jessica is here also. I have a favor to ask. Are you and Dick back from La Jolla?"

"That's what I wanted to talk to you about. We've decided to stay out here." A whirlwind of words spewed from the phone. "We've rented a furnished apartment, and I'll just be back for a few days to put the house on the market. Also, and I'm really sorry about this because I know I just promoted you, but we're closing the gallery. Now, what did you want to ask me?"

A bubble of time formed while both women processed the information. Shocked, Jessica stared at Araceli, who wore a wide-eyed look of surprise.

Finally, Araceli moved her eyes to the phone. "Um, nothing."

"I hope you'll help me pack up the gallery," Robin said.

"I don't think I can do that." Araceli ended the call then looked at Jessica. "What is that about?"

"I have no idea. I wonder if she's talked to my mother?" And what an odd coincidence, this move made suddenly more urgent after Deputy Mayfield's death. She wanted to explore that thought and call her mother to see what information she had, but her phone rang.

Linda's face lit the screen. Jessica answered with a hello.

"The sheriff wants to see you."

"I was really hoping I wouldn't have to sit through more hours of interrogation today. I've already told them everything I know."

"This isn't the deputies. The sheriff, Lee Burns, wants to interview you."

Shit. During Jessica's last interaction with the man, she'd practically accused him of being a murderer. It wasn't long after Keith had arrested her and refused to investigate a concern of hers—at the sheriff's orders. An order that had hurt the Guatemalan cousins. Now she'd have to face him.

"Will you be there with me?"

"You bet. Come by the office and pick me up. We'll head out together."

Jessica pressed end. She and Araceli hadn't finished their conversation. Hopefully she'd understand.

"I've got to return to the sheriff's office for more questions. Can we continue this tonight?"

A pensive look crossed Araceli's face, then she seemed to make a decision. "Yes. I think it's time to call my family."

"I think that's a good idea. Remember, you did nothing wrong."

Jessica reached out a hand to help her stand. She paused for a moment and let Araceli get her balance, then Jessica pulled her into a hug.

Jessica, as a rule, didn't hug people. She'd always considered herself far too prickly for that. Better to imitate a cactus in the desert, showing your spines and thick skin, rather than risk exposing your mushy interior.

But the will of her body overcame her mind's resistance. She wanted connection with this woman, needed to let her know how important and brave and strong she was.

Araceli hugged back. Jessica's defenses tried to pull her back, create some space, but then she relaxed and let the energy flow between them. Maybe, sometimes, you could let people see how much you cared about them.

Chapter 20

essica and Linda strolled down the bland hallway of headquarters. Beige walls, industrial carpet, nothing intimidating except the ability to lock people up.

"Let me do most of the talking," Linda said. "You can answer his direct questions about the events of that day, but I'll stop you if I think there's trouble."

If only Linda could do all the talking. "No problem."

They'd discussed why the sheriff himself wanted to interview her. Highly unusual didn't begin to explain it. Still, a deputy had died. The media covered the story like a hungry dog, and it had to be a hit to staff morale. Jessica would have preferred to be anywhere else.

The receptionist led them into what looked more like a boardroom than the interrogation room where they'd questioned Jessica yesterday. A sweating pitcher of ice water and stack of cups sat on a finely grained table. Linda and Jessica sat next to each other facing the door and waiting for trouble.

Sheriff Burns made them wait fifteen minutes. Perhaps he considered it a power move. The waiting bored Jessica, but she wouldn't show it.

Finally, the rat-faced man strode into the room. She shook his hand, staring straight into his shifty brown eyes. He squeezed her hand hard, then let go quickly. That might be a power move as well. Maybe he needed to intimidate people because of his small stature and thin, wiry frame.

"Thank you for coming in today. It's great to see you again, Linda. I wish we were meeting under different circumstances."

"I'm sorry about the death of your deputy," Linda said. "How can we help you?"

"It's a real loss, a terrible thing for the department." He sat at the head of the table. "George was a friend as well as a colleague."

His sorrow surprised Jessica, and she chastised herself for thinking the worst of this man. It would be devastating to lose someone with whom you worked closely. She wanted to acknowledge his grief but kept silent, knowing that anything she said could be used against her.

"Thank you for sharing your audio recording with our department, but I have a few follow-up questions." His tone changed into something probing.

It immediately put Jessica on edge. She glanced at Linda, who nodded, first at Jessica and then at Lee.

"I saw from the report that you said you incapacitated Jace Jeffries. How were you able to do this? I've met that young man, and frankly, my money would have been on him."

Jessica glanced at Linda who nodded slightly, giving Jessica the okay to answer. The question offended her. Why wouldn't she be able to take him? "He wasn't a great fighter."

"And you are?"

"I've taken self-defense classes. I held my own against him."

"Well, I guess we have to assume so since there's no video."

What an ass. How good a sheriff was he if he held such prejudices? Jessica glimpsed Linda's hand between them making a "calm down" gesture. Jessica took a breath.

Linda was right. He was trying to get under her skin. And she'd fallen for it. She needed to up her game. He hadn't asked a specific question, so she kept quiet.

"I'm curious about the man you said watched you from the shadows." The sheriff's tone was a little more conciliatory this time.

Again, no question. Jessica laced her fingers and stared at him, waiting for a true question. She relaxed and began to enjoy their little cat and mouse repartee.

"Do you know his name?" Lee asked.

This time Linda glanced at Jessica and gave her head a quick shake. Jessica kept quiet.

Linda turned to the sheriff. "We believe the man's name is Andres Sepulveda. A friend of mine—well, you know Sal Guerra, he worked here. He recognized his voice. They served in the military together."

Jessica studied the sheriff's face. At the mention of Sepulveda's name, a tremor passed over it, like the shadow of a crow flying overhead. The frown line in his forehead deepened.

Surely the sheriff knew a former deputy and a local crook. Still, something had briefly changed his demeanor at the mention of the men.

"Would you describe this man for me?" Lee asked.

Jessica went through the same description she'd given Sal and Linda, the exact one she'd given the deputies in this very building. As she spoke, Lee's eyes lost their focus, as if he hadn't merely listened to the words but had turned them into an image.

"And as far as you know, he was the only other person in the house apart from you and Jace?" he asked.

"He and Jace were the only ones I saw, but I didn't tour the property. I also didn't see any vehicles out front, beyond my truck."

"And you said he just let you go? Did he follow you outside?"

"No. I left quickly and didn't look back."

"Did he scare you?" the sheriff asked.

Jessica sat back at the question, surprised by its directness. "Yes. He was frightening."

Lee nodded. Then he leaned forward as if closing in for the kill. "If he scared you, why did you take the time to remove the gun from your truck and throw it down the hill?"

It was a good question. It had taken time to do that, time when she feared he'd come after her. But a different fear had driven her to get rid of the gun. "I knew the sheriffs were on their way, and I didn't want them to find Jace's gun on me."

At the time, stolen property had seemed problematic. Now, after the death of Mayfield, it had become a minor infraction.

"Tell me how and why you had Mr. Jeffries's gun?"

Jessica glanced at Linda again. She'd given this information before. It had to be in his report.

Linda nodded at her to continue.

"I'd been at a bar the previous night and ran across Jace and some of his friends. They were real jerks. Called me names, insinuated that I was a slut because I was in a bar by myself. It got a little heated and at one point he showed me his gun, threatened me with it. Later, he grabbed me, and I slipped the weapon out of his waistband without him knowing. I didn't want to give him the chance to act on his threat."

"That's a pro move. How did you manage that?" Lee asked.

She wanted to tell him she had skills, but that wouldn't help her get out of this room. "I'm not sure how sober he was. After all, he flashed his gun in a bar."

"And why were you in a bar all alone and so far from your home?"

"I needed a drink." She cocked an eyebrow in challenge.

"We talked to the staff. They hadn't seen you there before, and then you showed up several days in a row. Care to elaborate on why you chose that establishment?"

Jessica braced herself. She hadn't told the deputies about what had happened to Araceli or why she'd been on the hunt for Jace. Fortunately, they hadn't asked questions that would have forced her to reveal anything Araceli wouldn't want out there. Her luck had just run out.

"I recently separated from my husband. I didn't want to risk running across him, so I chose a whole different side of town." It wasn't exactly a lie. Not exactly the truth either.

Linda gave her a cold stare. Jessica smiled back.

"One of the waitresses said you asked specifically about Mr. Jeffries." Lee leaned back in his chair and crossed his arms. He clearly thought he'd caught Jessica out.

"I did ask about him after he and his friends came in the door. He's not handsome, but he's charismatic. I thought maybe I'd make a new friend." She stared at the sheriff, daring him to challenge her or call her the kind of names Jace had.

"What possessed you to meet Mr. Jeffries at his house? You'd already had a serious altercation with him. That seems like a foolhardy risk."

"He said if I didn't return his gun, he'd hunt down me and those I love. It didn't feel like much of a choice. And I did call law enforcement for help."

"Yes. You called Deputy Keith Guerra. Isn't he Sal's nephew?" He directed the question to Linda.

"Yes." She offered nothing more.

He changed tack. "Are you sure you hadn't met that Sepulveda fellow before?"

"No. I'd never seen him before." Jessica went on alert. Where was this leading?

"You asked about Mr. Jeffries at the bar, stole his gun, and then ended up at his house. Maybe you were working with Sepulveda all along. It sounds a little like a setup. Maybe you two wanted to blame Mayfield's murder on Jeffries. Is Sepulveda the reason your marriage broke up?"

Shock surged through Jessica like an electric current. "Why the hell would I want to kill Mayfield? How would I even know he'd be there?"

At the same time, Linda slammed her briefcase on the table. "That's enough. You have no basis to make that accusation."

"I'm just trying to explore all the possibilities. I want to know absolutely everything both of you know about this Sepulveda character."

Linda held up her hand to stop Jessica from talking. "We've told you everything we know except that he enlisted in the Army and was a Ranger. We're handing you his name on a platter. Now it's time for you to do a little detective work. Unless you have any relevant questions for my client, we'll be leaving."

What a badass. Jessica loved her boss.

"I'm done. Make sure your client stays in town." He stood up and reached out to shake Linda's hand. When she didn't take it, he shrugged and left the room.

"Jerk," Jessica said.

"Don't talk in here." Linda rose and walked out the door.

They headed straight for Jessica's truck. Adrenaline made it hard not to hit the gas and peel out of the parking lot, but Jessica just managed to hold on to her cool.

"You were great in there," Jessica said. "Thanks. I'm so glad you were with me."

"You weren't too bad yourself, although it's usually best not to obfuscate your motives to law enforcement."

"Well, if they find Jace, it will all come out. Araceli will probably return to Mexico soon. If I can give her a couple more days of privacy, it will help."

Jessica lowered the dial on the air conditioner. In their hurry to get away, they hadn't properly aired out the truck, which had heated to mid-oven range in the hot summer sun. The air coming from the vents seemed hotter than the outside temperature.

"Sorry about the A/C," Jessica said. "Sometimes it takes a while to cool down."

"From the hot seat to the hotter seat," Linda joked.

With higher temps yet to come. With Jace and Andres on the loose, things likely wouldn't cool down anytime soon.

When Jessica returned home, the stifling weather still hadn't broken. Usually at this time of year, a monsoon rain would blow through in the early evening. The heavy bursts of driving rain caused problems like humidity and floods but brought relief from the heat.

The monsoons had yet to start, but the trademark humidity had arrived anyway. She happily left the hot cab of the truck and entered the air-conditioned house.

"It's too hot to cook," Araceli said from the couch.

Even the dog looked hot. The house used swamp coolers, a desert specialty where air moved through moist pads on the cooler's sides before circulating through the house like a regular air conditioner. They worked great in the dry desert air, less so in heavy humidity.

Jessica lifted a plastic grocery bag to show Araceli. "Great minds think alike. When I was at Vista Market getting things for your mole, I saw all the great prepared produce they had."

She moved to the table and pulled out cup after cup. "Cucumber spears with lime and chile. Spicy mango. Watermelon chunks. Fresh fruit Mexican popsicles in half a dozen flavors."

The happy look on Araceli's face buoyed Jessica's spirits. Each day she seemed slightly less traumatized, and Jessica hoped she'd make a full recovery.

"You're the best," Araceli said, bounding for the table.

They gorged themselves on cold fruit. After the sun finally set behind the mesa, they relaxed on the back deck. Thanks to the damp air, the August temperature didn't drop the way it would have normally, but at least without the searing sun, outside became bearable.

"Tell me what your family said." Jessica's curiosity had poked at her all evening, but she didn't want Araceli to feel unwelcome.

"It went better than I thought. I didn't tell them everything, just that some men had attacked me for being Mexican. After the shooting here and the way this country is behaving, that was plenty for them to beg me to leave."

"You're lucky you have family that cares so much about you, but I'm sorry you have to go back to the farm when you wanted so much more out of life."

"Actually, I may not be back there for long. One of my aunts went to the Universidad Autónoma de Guadalajara, and she's contacting the school to see if I can enroll. It's an excellent university."

"Wow." A third option had appeared that might be better than the first two. "I've heard Guadalajara is beautiful."

Araceli's smile glowed in the fading light. "It is beautiful. I went there with her once. They have gorgeous green parks, amazing colonial buildings, and it's a big city where there's always lots to do."

"It sounds like a great option." Jessica's emotions wavered. It thrilled her to see Araceli happy, but she'd miss her and remained furious that the US had ceased to welcome this talented woman.

"I've thought a lot about my place in the world lately. There are many wonderful universities in Mexico and across Latin America. And my aunt told me that Spanish universities welcome Mexicans. My family, probably most in Mexico, always looked north, to the US, for opportunities. I grew up thinking of it as the best option, but there are so many places that are just as good or better."

"That's for sure," Jessica said.

The world had opened to Araceli. Jessica had never experienced that, had never thought beyond the desert around her. Whether driven by lack of opportunity or a dearth of vision, her sights only stretched as far as the nearest horizon. That seemed pretty damn far away, here where you could see forever. But a bigger world existed beyond this town, this country.

She guessed that's what people would learn in the coming years if the US remained inhospitable to others. A country built on immigration would lose its engine as opportunities fled. Unfortunately, the country faced another major shift as men like Jace and his buddies listened to assholes on podcasts instead of getting out in the world and interacting with other humans. Maybe Jace was a symbol for the nation's state of mind. His sadistic behavior didn't help him. The entire country sending asshole signals meant talent would go elsewhere.

Wasn't that the opposite of the country's ideals? Her white ass had landed in the southwest desert because this looked like the land of opportunity to her grandparents. What would happen when nobody new wanted to come to this aging, racist, gun-happy place?

Tela whined, bringing Jessica out of her thoughts. She reached down and grabbed the tennis ball, then flung it across the yard.

"How can I help?" Jessica asked.

"Let me stay another night or two, then come visit me in Guadalajara."

"Absolutely." She should be able to keep the young woman safe for a couple of days, especially with her fancy new security system.

Chapter 21

A screaming alarm woke Jessica. Her head swirled with confusion. It was dark out, the deep dark of the hours past midnight. She had a security system, but the alarm beeped instead of sounding like a siren.

A loud pounding came from the front door. "Is anyone home?"

Jessica pulled a T-shirt over her tank top and grabbed her jeans on the way to the door. She saw Araceli's bedroom light turn on. In the main room, Tela stood at alert, watching the front door and trembling.

Jessica looked through the peephole, praying she wouldn't see Jace or Andres. Instead, she saw a fireman. An orange glow lit the air behind him. She pulled open the door.

"What the fuck! That's my truck!"

Flames engulfed her white truck, more of an old friend than transportation. She started down the steps, but the fireman stopped her.

"Don't go down there," he said, wrapping an arm around her. "Sparks are flying everywhere, and if the flames hit the tank, it might explode. We'll have the fire out in a few minutes."

"What happened?" How? Who?

"Ready," came a call from one of the other firefighters. He stood near the big red truck with its lights pulsing.

"Ma'am. You are the vehicle's owner, correct?" the closest fireman asked.

"Yes." Shock poured through her.

"Okay. I'd like you to step back inside for a minute. We're going to put this fire out, and then I'll be back to talk with you."

Jessica retreated and stared out the plate glass window overlooking the front yard. Two cop cars pulled up, and then the firemen let loose with two different hoses, one spraying water and the other some kind of white foam.

They extinguished the flames quickly but continued drenching the truck for what seemed far too long. Anything the fire didn't destroy, the layer of chemicals probably would.

The second the firefighters turned off the hoses, two police officers came to the door. Tela had disappeared, and Jessica guessed Araceli had coaxed her into her room. Araceli had to be terrified.

Jessica opened the front door before the officers knocked. She invited them in and prepared for yet another interrogation.

She asked for a minute to use the restroom and get some shoes. When they agreed, she checked on Araceli.

Jessica found Tela sitting on Araceli's bed with her. Araceli's wide hazel eyes teemed with fear.

"What happened?" Araceli asked.

"Someone set my truck on fire." Jessica hated saying the words. Hated admitting someone had attacked her on her home turf and didn't want to think about what this meant for her future, not to mention Araceli's.

"It was them, wasn't it? Travis's friends?"

"We don't know for sure, but that would be my bet. We've got to get you out of here tomorrow. Or today, since I assume it's morning. I'd offer to take you to the ranch, but the truck is out of commission." Not to mention a crime scene. Plus, Linda had told the sheriff she wouldn't leave town.

"I'll call my uncle. He'll come get me."

"That's good. And I'm really sorry about this. By the way, I'm going to see if the cops will post someone outside the house for the rest of the night. What time is it anyway?"

Araceli pulled her phone from the nightstand. "2:28."

"Seems about right. Bars close at two, and nobody sober would do something this stupid."

"What if they had come inside?"

"This was just for show. They're trying to send a message, although all they're really doing is broadcasting that they're idiots." At least Jessica hoped so.

Jessica hoped her words calmed Araceli. In fact, they were lucky the criminals had targeted the truck instead of them. Although, it sure didn't feel lucky.

"I've got to talk to the police officers. I assume you'll stay in here so you don't have to answer questions?"

Araceli nodded and Jessica left. In her room, she stuck her feet in a pair of old sneakers and grabbed her phone from the nightstand. No calls, not that any of her friends knew about what had happened.

Passing through the kitchen on the way to talk to the officers, she stopped to put on a pot of coffee. They seemed patient, and she supposed they'd like the java as much as she would.

The officers had settled into chairs in the living room. Jessica decided on the sofa and glanced outside on her way over. A spotlight lit the remains of her truck. The vehicle's skeleton had turned sooty gray. She shoved down the memories of the many good times the truck had witnessed so she wouldn't cry.

Firemen wandered around the yard, and a few neighbors had gathered in the street. It resembled a wake, and Jessica wished she were out there paying her respects. Instead, she turned and faced the officers.

The questions were expected. Had she set her truck on fire? When did she last use the vehicle? Did she think someone had done this on purpose?

Another knock at the door, then Angus entered.

Jessica looked at him barreling into the house and her exhaustion gave way to love. Here he was at the exact moment she needed him most.

"What happened?" he asked, beelining toward her.

"Excuse me," one of the officers said. "Who are you?"

"He's my husband." Pride filled her voice. She introduced Angus to the officers.

The officer's suddenly stiff body language put Jessica on high alert. She patted the couch next to her, and Angus sat.

"How did you find out?" she asked.

"Bart from next door called me. He's the one who called the fire department. Good thing he has a bad prostate and has to pee five times a night."

She widened her eyes at Angus. Way too much information. She had met Bart a few times. Tela loved to run the fence between their houses with his Australian Shepherd racing her on the other side. She barely remembered his name, and he definitely didn't have her number. Angus had befriended all the neighbors. She needed that in her life.

"We need to get back to questions," one of the officers said. "Where were you tonight, Mr. Delgado?"

Jessica and Angus eyed each other. Nothing like airing dirty laundry. She could tell he realized the questioning was about to get a lot more difficult.

"I was staying at a friend's house," Angus responded.

"We're currently separated," Jessica said. Shit. Linda was going to kick her ass for talking to these guys without having her attorney present.

She texted Linda. *Someone burned my truck. Cops here questioning me.*

"What are you doing?" one of the cops asked, suspicion lacing his voice.

"Texting my attorney."

"Why do you think you need an attorney? Are you guilty of something?"

Jessica sighed, trying to release the tension that flooded her body like lighter fluid at the question. Why did everyone presume her guilty? The rude question and attitude threatened like a lit match, but she had to stay calm.

"I work for attorney Linda Reed. Former cop. She'll be furious with me if I answer your questions without her."

"Never heard of her," the cop said.

Jessica's phone rang. This cop was going to wish he'd never said that. Jessica put Linda on speakerphone.

"Hey, Linda."

"Where are you?"

"I'm at my house. The firefighters woke me up. My truck was in flames. Now officers . . ." Jessica looked at the two officers and read their name badges. Man, she really was tired, she'd heard their names at least twice. ". . . Flores and Anderson are questioning me. And Angus is here."

"Angus?" Linda asked, the curiosity oozing through the phone.

"Hello, ma'am," Angus said.

"We are in the middle of an investigation and need to continue our questioning," Officer Anderson said, his frustration obvious.

"If you want answers tonight, you'll wait until I get there. Twenty minutes." Linda said in her bitchy lawyer voice.

"Twenty minutes! We haven't Mirandized her. We're not arresting her. We're just trying to find out what happened to the truck." Anderson's cheeks had gone red, and the stain crawled up to his buzz cut.

"That's my only offer. Take it or leave it." Linda was not messing around. When no one responded, Linda said, "See you soon," and ended the call.

"Would you all like some coffee?" Jessica asked.

Chapter 22

Linda strode through the door with Sal on her heels. He must have stayed at her house last night. Jessica cocked an eyebrow at her boss, who ignored her. Jessica had never seen Linda like this. Her face was shiny with a thick layer of moisturizer, and she'd pulled her blond mane into a ponytail.

A Texas woman through and through, Linda never went anywhere without a full face of makeup and perfectly coiffed hair. Usually, a power suit accompanied the look. She actually looked younger without the makeup, not that Jessica would ever tell her that. Dark jeans and a chambray shirt completed the casual look, but her manner was all business.

Linda introduced herself to the two officers. Sal approached Jessica, asked her to open her phone, and took it from her. He retreated to the kitchen while working on the device. Jessica wanted to protest, but Linda turned to them.

"It's nice to see you," she said to Angus. "I hope your being here is good news." She raised an eyebrow at Jessica, then told her to scoot so she could sit down.

Jessica wanted to squeeze Angus's hand to tell him everything would be okay, despite Linda and the cops putting him on the spot, but it was all too awkward.

"You can continue your questioning now." Linda eyed the officers.

"Ms. Watts, do you have any idea who set your vehicle on fire, or why?"

All hell would break loose when she said Jace Jeffries's name. Somehow, they hadn't connected her with the Mayfield killing, but they certainly would have heard about it. The press had kept her name out of the news while the investigation continued, but the fact that she'd been at that scene, the home of the person she'd bet had set the fire outside, would kick things up to a whole new level.

"I think I can answer your questions." Sal walked over to Officer Flores and held Jessica's phone in front of him.

"What's going on?" Jessica asked.

"I pulled the recording from your security camera. The entire crime is on video."

Officer Flores took the phone and showed it to her colleague. Then she brought it to Jessica.

"Do you know who this is?" Flores asked.

She did. She'd fought the lanky body who on the phone screen poured gasoline onto her truck. She recognized how he moved and could picture his freckled skin and dull green eyes. "That's Jace Jeffries."

Anderson, the male officer, addressed Angus. "Well, I guess this gets you off the hook. It normally doesn't work out this way with estranged marriages."

Jessica glanced at Angus, saw his jaw clench in anger. She did take his hand then and gave it a squeeze.

"Thanks for being here," she said.

As questions continued, Jessica's eyes grew heavy and she caught herself nodding off. Linda must have noticed, because she asked if they could wrap it up or continue at a later time.

"That's fine," Officer Flores said. "I'll need to take the phone for processing."

"No," Jessica said before checking herself. She'd just purchased the new phone after having left her other one with the sheriffs. But explaining that would take longer than she had. They'd link this crime to Mayfield's death soon enough. Right now, she just wanted a couple of hours of sleep.

"Sorry. You can have the phone. I'm afraid this guy will return, and he won't stop with the truck this time. How do I stay protected?"

"You have a good security system," Anderson said. "And we can have a patrol car circle by every once in a while."

It wasn't much, but she'd take what she could get.

As soon as the officers left, Sal approached Jessica. "I'm worried about your safety. I'd like Keith to stay here until they pick up Jeffries."

"I can stay," Angus said.

"No offense," Sal said, "but Keith is a trained law enforcement officer and carries a gun."

A long, taut moment stretched across the room. Angus pulled his hand from Jessica's. She didn't want him leaving hurt. Or leaving at all. And she couldn't imagine anything more awkward and bad for her marriage than Keith staying here. Jessica opened her mouth to voice her feelings.

Linda spoke first. "Angus. Man up and sleep with your wife in your marital bed. Keith can stay in the guest bedroom."

Linda had suggested something more awkward than just Keith staying here. And the guest bedroom already had an occupant. Jessica shook her head. How did this damn day keep getting worse? Angus's tension came at her in waves.

"Listen. I'm too tired to decide any of this right now. Sal, thanks for finding that video on my phone. I'm really glad you had that system installed. I don't need Keith to stay here. The night's almost over."

Jessica turned her attention to her boss. "Linda. Thank you for coming down here in the middle of the night. I appreciate your willingness to protect me. Can we all get a few hours of sleep and talk again later?"

"That's fine," Linda said. "But we need to tell the police everything."

"I know. I'll call Jaime and let him know what's happening. Meet in the office at ten?" Jessica asked. "You don't have court today, and I'm pretty sure your next meeting isn't until tomorrow."

Linda agreed, and then she and Sal left. Angus tried to go with them, but Jessica held him back. "It meant the world to me that you showed up tonight. I'm sorry about what Sal said, that wasn't fair. And there is absolutely nothing I'd rather have than you staying here with me."

"He's right," Angus said, disgust coloring his words.

"Angus. Stop it. You left me. You are the only man for me. I would like you to stay, tonight and every night. Not because you want to protect me, but because you love me."

He stepped onto the front landing and surveyed the burned truck. A battle seemed to rage inside him. She couldn't help staring at his back, the shaggy hair she missed, the broad shoulders tapering to a slim waist, that ass. She had to hold her hands against her body to keep from reaching for him. And what if she did?

He had a magnetic pull. Mere inches before her fingers touched him, he turned around. "Is it okay if I sleep on the couch tonight?"

"Seriously?" she asked. The front of him was just as hot, and she could feel the blood rush to all the places she wanted him to touch.

"Yeah. I'll just grab a blanket and a pillow." He brushed by her, searing her skin every place he touched. She followed.

She stood in the bedroom doorway while he pulled bedding from the closet shelf. Months. He'd left months ago, and she'd been celibate ever since. Now he stood in their bedroom, three feet from the bed she wanted to push him onto, where she could strip his clothes and ravage every part of him.

He turned. "Jess. You can't look at me like that." He looked helpless.

"Like what?" Her voice came out husky, like she'd walked through the desert for hours with no water. Parched, just like she felt.

"Please," he whispered.

Just one spark would have ignited the room, causing a fire ten times more powerful than the one that destroyed her truck. The tension between them became a physical thing, a cocktail that burned through her veins and made her tremble with desire.

"Please," she whispered.

They stood at an impasse. Jessica ached with desire and the storm brewing in Angus's eyes turned the thermostat higher.

Finally, he threw the bedding to the floor. "I'm going to regret this."

He surged toward her, ripping off his shirt and unzipping his jeans. She shed her clothes so fast they might have been singed from her body.

"I'm so worried about you. So angry," he said.

Those emotions lit his eyes. And desire. He locked the door, then pressed her against the wall, practically shoving his body into hers. She moaned into the heat of it. He kissed her savagely. Need overtook every other emotion.

Angus lifted her against the wall, and she wrapped her arms and legs around him, sank onto him and cried out as her world exploded. He pushed his rage, his fear, his desire into her again and again, and she selfishly took it all until every synapse in her body overloaded and threw her into ecstasy.

Angus shuddered against her and she held onto him tightly and vowed to never let him go. Their ragged breathing matched, and she couldn't tell where one sweat slick body ended and the other began.

He kissed her once, so gently that the world that had come apart with their passion pulled itself back together. Her feet dropped to the floor and their bodies parted in sweetness and loss.

"I'm going to shower," he said, leaving her completely satisfied yet still wondering about the future.

He slept on the couch. She'd expected to stay awake, pining for him, so close yet so far from her. Instead, her eyes closed to visions of fires and charred landscapes.

Chapter 23

The next morning passed in a rush. Araceli had called her uncle before Jessica awoke. He'd already started north to fetch her and return her to Mexico. She'd called her roommates and let them know her plans.

Since Jessica had to leave for the office, Angus offered to stay at the house until the uncle arrived. Jessica wanted to hug him for his kindness but didn't since she might not be able to let go. She took his lead and acted like nothing had happened, no earth-shattering sex. She couldn't wait to get him alone, talk through it, and if she had her way, repeat it. But not in front of Araceli, and not when she had so many things to do this morning.

She called Jaime as soon as she got to the office. She told him everything: Araceli's departure, finding Travis and then Jace, stealing Jace's gun then going to his house. She recounted seeing Mayfield before his death, and finally, the immolation of her truck and the video showing Jace Jeffries as perpetrator.

Concern tinted Jaime's voice as he told her he'd follow up and get back in touch when he had new information. A little of the tension from the past days seeped away with Jaime in her corner.

Finally, she called the insurance company. The measly amount she'd get for her truck wouldn't buy a new one, but she'd find something that worked.

By four that afternoon, she still hadn't decided what to do that night. Jaime offered to call once they'd located Jace and had him in custody, but she hadn't heard from him yet. Jace just might be depraved enough to come for her again, even though he'd already destroyed her vehicle.

Sal had offered her a room in his house because he didn't think she should stay in hers. Jaime had offered the same. She hadn't talked to Angus since he'd called to let her know that Araceli had left and he'd locked up the house.

Angus wouldn't get off work until nine that night, and Jessica couldn't decide between the patience of waiting for a call and the gratification of showing up at his business. She figured if he hadn't called by eight thirty, she'd stop by before he went home.

Linda stopped by her desk at four and said she was taking off early to catch up on sleep. She looked exhausted, giving Jessica pangs of guilt.

"Thanks so much for all your help these last few days. I'd don't know how to repay you," Jessica said.

"You definitely keep life interesting. Which is good. Things had been getting a little staid around here before you came along. Be careful today. This guy is still on the loose, and we already know he's dangerous."

"Thanks, I will be," Jessica promised.

Finally, quiet surrounded her. She worked on a few remaining tasks for the firm, then checked out used car websites looking for her next ride.

She barely saw the movement outside before the office door opened. Andres walked in. Jessica froze in panic. Everyone had worried so much about someone finding her at her home, yet he'd shown up here. At a place without security cameras.

"Hello, Jessica." He took a seat in front of her desk.

Jessica struggled to keep her voice calm, even though she wanted to run from the room screaming in terror. "What are you doing here?"

"The police just picked up Jace. They got a tip that he was staying in room 1508 at the Paso del Norte hotel."

"That's oddly specific." She glanced around, not seeing any weapons. She should have planned for this. Talking was the only option. "How can I help you?"

He laughed, the sound even scratchier than his speaking voice. "That's exactly why I'm here. I need your help and would like to reach an agreement with you."

The hairs on her arms stood at attention, accompanied by a prickly feeling of dread. "What do you mean?"

"Jace's arrest is an opportunity for me. I'd like to know what happened between you two, and I need you to testify against him."

Jessica's panic eased a notch. "He burned my truck. Ruined it. I'll happily testify about that. In fact, I've already filed a police report that includes video evidence."

Andres's face clouded. "Destroying property is not enough. His father will get him out of that in no time. What happened before that? Something made you steal his gun."

This man wanted something Jessica couldn't provide. "He was just rude to me in a bar. He showed me the gun as a threat, but in Texas that will get you a congratulations instead of a prison sentence. I took it so he couldn't use it against me."

Andre's lip turned up in a stray-dog snarl. "There's more. You talked about him hurting women in the desert. I heard you at the house. I want names given to the police."

"He hurt a friend of mine, but that's not my story to tell. Besides, she left town, and she won't be back."

Of course that wasn't the whole story. Jace belonged in jail. Jessica suspected he'd brutalized more women than Araceli. And she believed he had some kind of involvement with the migrant deaths in the same general area. But she couldn't prove any of it, much less testify about it. Plus, Andres might be involved as well.

She looked at his cold eyes, and he stared back, waiting. "When I was at the house, you asked me what I knew about immigrants being killed in the desert. I think he might be involved in that."

"That topic is off limits." He spoke without emotion, like he'd mentioned the weather or stock prices.

"Well then, I'm not sure how I can help you."

"Get your friend back here. Make her testify against Jace. Are any of those other little perverts he knows messed up in that?"

Wow, this guy liked Jace about as much as she did. "Yes. They were."

"You see, that's good. A gang of young men hurting women. If the police look into his computer files and social media accounts, they'll find out what a deviant he really is. He posts all kinds of horrible things about women."

"That I believe. I ran into a little of that at the bar." Strangely, the conversation seemed almost normal. Two people chatting about a guy they didn't like. Although, she might like Andres even less than Jace if she knew more about him.

"You can help," Andres said. "He and his friends call themselves alpha males. It's ridiculous since they just spout what other so-called alpha males say online. It's quite the little cult. He has no idea what a real man is. I'd sure like him to figure that out in prison."

"Shit. You really don't like him. Don't you work for him?"

Andres's face went cold. "I work for the prima donna's asshole father."

He leaned forward, and Jessica could smell his breath. Surprisingly, she caught a whiff of minty gum. Jessica forced herself not to lean away from him. She couldn't show fear, regardless of how it had taken hold of her.

"You will help me. Start by getting your friend to testify against him. Mr. Jeffries, the dad, has too many friends in law enforcement for the property destruction charge to result in jail time. But if women are scared of a gang of young men taking them to the desert to brutalize and kill them, then we give the prosecutors something they can't ignore."

"I told you, my friend is gone. She won't testify. But it sounds like you know of other women he's hurt or killed." Instead of finding a way to get Andres out of her office, she'd become drawn into his story.

"I hope they can find more about them on his computer. Until then, if you don't get your friend to testify, I will. Let's do this the easy way."

"No." The word spilled from her lips without thought. None needed. She would never give this guy Araceli. Although maybe she could be an excuse to get this guy out of her office. Jessica sighed. "I'll talk to her and see what I can do."

"You will help me. I've learned a lot about you. You've come a long way since your daddy was convicted. Don't let all that effort go to waste."

A prick of anger came to life in her spine. She hated when people tried to pin her dad's crimes on her. "I don't like to be threatened. Why is this so important to you anyway? Are you really that concerned with Jace being an alpha male or whatever?"

"I don't give a rat's ass about Jace. He's just a means to an end. It's old man Jeffries and his friends that I want." Andres shook his head, then stared at Jessica. "This is the land of my people. Guys like Jeffries stole it from us, pocketed its value, and took our dignity. It's time to take it back."

Another puzzle piece fell into place. Jace had probably learned his racism from his father. A man who relied on Hispanics for the success of his company. The same hatred that fueled Jace's attack against Araceli probably caused the father to disrespect his employees in a thousand small ways.

"So, old man Jeffries is as racist as his kid?" she asked.

"Worse. He couldn't make a dime without my help. It's time he learned that." His voice grew even raspier, like it could shave tailings from the air itself.

"I understand. I'm just not sure I can help."

"You think you understand? Don't patronize me, white girl. Find the women he hurt and bring me their names." He didn't have to voice "or else." His tone made it clear.

Jessica stilled in the impossible situation. What did this guy really want? Land? Power? The dots didn't connect. "No. I'm not a part of your battle."

"Oh, but you are. You made yourself a part of it the minute you showed up and kicked apart my plan."

"I don't know what . . ." but she did know. "Mayfield."

"Jace killed him." Andres narrowed his eyes as he spoke.

"Jace was unconscious on the floor."

"Jace killed him. Unfortunately, your recording places me at the scene. You owe me, and you'll hear from me soon."

He had to be lying about Mayfield. Although Jessica wasn't sure she cared. Let the sheriff solve that case.

He left as silently as he'd arrived. She'd come so close to the end of this case—Araceli gone and somewhere safe, Jace's arrest albeit for a different crime. Andres had pulled her back into the deep end, and she'd forgotten how to swim.

For someone who'd spent a good part of her life alone, Jessica had far too many choices about who to contact. She had to tell someone about the visit from Andres, but she couldn't unwittingly put another person in danger.

After two minutes, she grabbed her backpack and left the office. From the time she locked the door, to when she finally got in the rental car she'd picked up midday, she felt watched, as if Andres hovered somewhere close with a gun trained on her.

If she drove to someone's house to seek refuge, would he follow? That question made safety paramount. She thought about driving to police headquarters, but would he think that aggressive and take it out on her later? She wouldn't go to her lonely home with its burned-out truck carcass in the front yard.

Angus had taken Tela to her mom's after Araceli left, but she certainly wouldn't burden either of them with the evil that had walked into her office. She'd let Linda know what had happened once she found a safe place to land. They needed a better security system in the office.

Sal knew Andres, and he'd already offered her a place to stay. But the two men had a history that might escalate an already tense situation. She drove down Mesa Street, one of the main arteries on the west side of town. As she passed the university and the many eateries and bars surrounding it, she grew hungry. Maybe she'd think better with a burger in her gut.

As she pulled into the Charcoaler drive-thru, she relaxed a bit. The lane swept around a large lawn, and she could see every car already there and those that approached as well. Once she'd ordered a chiliburger and fries, she parked at one end of the large lot where she had a view of everyone coming and going.

Jessica pulled out the phone she'd picked up after she'd rented the car and called Jaime. He could serve as her way of getting to the police without driving to headquarters.

"Andres just came to see me at the office," she said as soon as he picked up.

"The guy at the Jeffries house?"

"Yes. And it's bad. He wants me to help him keep Jace in jail by testifying against him and forcing Araceli to do so also. He even wants me to find more women to make sure Jace stays in prison a while."

"Shit. Jace was released half an hour ago. I would have called you, but I just got word myself. Evidently, they brought in some judge who wasn't even supposed to work today, and now he's out on bail."

"Andres knew he'd get out. This is not going well." Would Jace come after her again? She needed a soft place to land and had to choose between cactus spines and agave spikes.

"What's his motivation?" Jaime asked.

"Honestly, I think he's pissed at the man, in this case meaning his boss, Jace's father. But it has to be more than that. This guy is a career criminal. Money must factor into it somehow." After all, if his only concern were race, he wouldn't want migrants shot or Hispanic women tortured in the desert.

"We definitely need to investigate. Besides, I'm sure the sheriff's department wants to question him about Mayfield's death. Did he threaten you? It's probably not enough to get a restraining order, but we can start building a case."

Jaime hadn't reached the heart of her personal dilemma, but he circled it. "He kind of threatened me, but it was more of a 'do what I say, and you won't get hurt' than a direct threat."

"Jessica, that is a direct threat. Can you meet me at the station? We need an official statement."

"I guess. I'm a little afraid he's following me and will see that as an act of aggression."

"Where are you?"

"At the Charcoaler."

Jaime laughed. "Did you at least order me a burger?"

"No. But I'd be happy to get back in line. It feels safe here. Also, I haven't seen him since I've been here, so I'm starting to think I'm not being followed."

She thought he'd hung up, almost pressed the red button on her phone, but then she noticed the call was still connected. She brought it back up to her ear.

"Hey, where are you sleeping tonight?" Jaime asked.

She went still, noticing only her thumping heart and the smell of grilled burger. "I'm not sure. I'm afraid to lead him anywhere."

"That's smart. Do you want to stay here?"

She did. But if Andres had found a way to follow her, it wouldn't help. "Again, I'm worried about him following me."

"I've got an idea," Jaime said. "Give me three minutes."

Jessica hung up the phone, while her shoulders unkinked one more knot. She grabbed a crinkly fry and dipped it in ketchup. She'd get through this. Cases ended. She glanced around. Nothing unusual or anyone out of place, yet she still felt eyes upon her.

Chapter 24

Twenty minutes later, Jessica parked in front of the Westside Regional Command Center, just like Jaime had told her to. He met her inside and took her to a room with a table and chairs. Officers Flores and Anderson waited for her there.

She recounted her visit from Andres, sorry she didn't have a video or audio recording to share with them this time. When she told them about the connection between the truck fire and Deputy Mayfield's death, they responded with crossed arms and angry faces.

"Why didn't you tell us last night?" Officer Flores asked. "We, of course, found out, but you could have made our jobs a lot easier. Also, for some reason the sheriffs didn't tell us about your involvement."

"I'm sorry," Jessica said. "I should have said something." But she wouldn't have. Not when she had Araceli to protect. She glanced at Jaime, desperate for him to understand. He'd met Araceli, knew how fragile she was.

"Where is Araceli?" Jaime asked.

"She's safe now. Gone."

"I think you need to tell the officers the rest of the story. If you don't, I will. It's the best way to keep you safe."

She kept it as brief as possible, a friend taken to the desert and beaten, following the trail that ended with Jace. And Andres.

They wanted to know Araceli's name and location. Jessica stalled. "She doesn't want to testify. And if her name got out, he'd be able to find her. I can't risk that right now."

"Someone burned your truck and someone else threatened you. You may be in grave danger, but we can't help you if you don't share all the facts." Flores's irritation rang through her voice and settled onto her face.

Normally, Jessica would have reacted in anger at the criticism, but she understood the woman's frustration. Just like she understood Araceli's fear. Everyone wanted this case behind them, but it kept growing new limbs.

Finally, the meeting ended. Jessica had walked the line between giving the officers enough to go on and not breaking her promise to Araceli.

Jamie asked her to give her keys to Detective Flores who would move her car around back to the fenced lot after they departed. Then Jessica waited by the back door until Jaime pulled up in a black-and-white cruiser and had her lie prone on the back seat.

"I'm pretty sure this is overkill, but there's no reason not to take every precaution," he said as he pulled out of the lot.

"I appreciate it. That guy scared the hell out of me when he showed up in the office."

"I know," Jaime said. "You've been in some tough situations, and that was one of the first times I've heard fear in your voice. I think you're growing up."

"I don't know about that. Most people would consider me a coward for hiding in the back seat of a vehicle. But this guy has the kind of scary that crawls under your skin."

"Good cops aren't good because they're not scared. They're good because they are scared and they use that as motivation to protect themselves and others."

"You know," she said, rolling over but staying below the window line. "I've dealt with some frightening people. But there's something different about these two. They attack without regard for their own safety. It shocked me when Jace pulled out his gun in a crowded bar. And did he think he wouldn't get caught when he set my truck on fire? That's either nervy or stupid. And Andres, he could keep his head down and let things unfold, but there's some kind of anger driving him to show up in my office, go up against his boss, and use the justice system to achieve his underhanded goal."

"I'm not surprised," Jaime said. "Everything that's happening in the country is polarizing. People think they can take justice into their own hands, but no one knows what justice is anymore. Instead, they go after what they think is right, whether it actually is or not. I see it in society, on the force, everywhere. No one works to find agreement anymore."

"That sucks." It was true. People took sides these days: pro or anti-immigration, for or against choice, Republican or Democrat. The same old issues had a new level of fervor. Don't like the way an election turns out? Storm the capitol. Unhappy about your friend dating a Mexican? Beat the shit out of her. Where would it end?

She couldn't solve the country's problems from her small slice of the desert. But she could help a friend. And she could do her best to outsmart a couple of criminals who made her community less safe.

***

The next morning, Jaime made Jessica coffee and eggs. When all this blew over, she'd be back to making breakfast on her own instead of having Araceli or Jaime wait on her. Unless Angus came home. Not that he made breakfast—she rose first and put on the coffee. But the real joy was having someone around.

When she'd called Angus last night and told him she'd spend the night at Jaime's, he'd immediately known something was wrong. But he seemed relieved that she'd gone to the police first, for once. Jessica wanted to speak of more important things, but it didn't help that the sound of his voice brought back how he'd lifted her against the wall and she'd completely come undone. She might never stop picturing him walking across the floor, shirt off, unzipping his jeans.

"Thanks for last night," she'd said, wondering if his mind was caught in the same sex trap.

But he'd said, "no problem," as if she'd asked for a sip of his beer or wanted him to sleep on the couch to protect her.

Her phone call to Linda had been completely different. When Jessica told her that Andres had come to the office, Linda put her on speakerphone. Sal was there, of course. Were those two ever apart?

Linda's concern turned immediately to action, and she suggested they put in the best security system possible immediately, including one that had cameras. The alarm system they set upon leaving the building was no longer adequate.

Sal reacted differently. He came across as tough, but under the gruff exterior, he cared about people. He'd helped Jessica overcome the trauma of being kidnapped and had molded her into a stronger, smarter version of herself. And the way he treated Linda—women dreamed about that kind of man.

But on the phone last night, she'd heard him turn into someone new. His voice changed from gravel to steel, and he ordered them to stay away from the office until he upgraded the security.

Linda said she'd work something out regarding the office. Jessica hoped it would happen soon. She didn't want to be a burden on Jaime and really needed to get some work done. She and Linda had been out of the office so often the last few days, she worried it would affect the business. People who paid a lot for an attorney expected you to answer the phone when they called.

They finished breakfast, and she told Jaime she'd clean up. He'd agreed to swing by her house so she could pack an overnight bag with some clothes and whatever else she needed for a few days away.

"I really can't keep imposing on you," she said. "You have a life."

He grabbed her in a side hug. "This is life. Doing things for the people you care about is the best part of life."

She never seemed to get the little things right. Angus would have said the same thing. Jessica's eyes filled. Such good people surrounded her, cared about her. Giving came so naturally to them.

"Thanks," she said, her voice shaky.

"Give me a few minutes, then we'll head down to your house."

Jessica's phone rang before she could respond. Sal.

"I've already told Linda," he said before she got a hello out. "I've installed a new camera security system at the office. When can you get down here? I need to train both of you on it."

———

Forty-five minutes later, Jaime dropped her off at the law firm, promising to return at noon to take her to get her car. He also extracted a promise from her. She had to call a tow service to take her truck to the junkyard before the neighbors complained.

Sal and Linda waited inside the front door. A few new lines seemed to have carved themselves into Sal's rugged face.

Linda rolled her eyes. "We'll never be unmonitored again."

"Given your clientele, you should have had a system like this years ago. Follow me."

He led them through the office, showing them where discreet cameras monitored the common areas such as the hallways, kitchen, reception area, and file room. Then he showed them the cameras he'd installed outside. The old house Linda had converted to her office had become an electronic fortress.

Back inside, Sal showed them how it worked and installed the surveillance app on their phones. When they activated the system after hours, it would ping them if anyone entered the building.

"He's also got it on his phone," Linda said. "The only spaces that aren't monitored are the boardroom, bathroom, and the two offices. Meet with clients in one of those areas."

Sal's face darkened. Clearly, he wasn't on board with that plan. Jessica raised a brow.

Linda turned to him. "It's not appropriate to record confidential meetings. Plus, you never know when we might need a little privacy." She gave him a wink.

"Gross," Jessica said. "I don't want to know what you two do here after hours."

"You definitely don't," Linda said before walking away with a smile on her face.

Sal just shook his head. "Women."

"Watch it," Jessica said. "You've got one standing right in front of you. By the way, did you work on this all night? It's only nine in the morning."

"Pretty much," he said. "I want you and Linda to feel safe in this office. It makes it worse that it's someone from my past showing up."

"You really don't like Andres, do you?"

"I respected him, once. But he ruined that, and he tried to ruin my service in the Army. Almost did."

"Do you think he's still pissed off about you getting him kicked out?"

"I do," Sal said. "You need to know that the past we share makes Andres even more dangerous."

"Got it." Just one more layer in this ever-evolving story.

Sal headed toward the door. "I'm going to go get some sleep. You two take care of each other while I'm gone. Also, I'll be checking the system periodically today."

"So be on my best behavior?" Jessica let the sarcasm drip from her voice. She appreciated the extra layer of security, but he'd pushed the guardian routine a little too far. Linda probably felt the same.

Jaime's comment about caring for others being the best part of life flitted through her mind and softened her heart. "Thanks."

Chapter 25

Jessica spent the morning focusing on the firm's active cases and letting the drama of recent events fade into the background. Going to the police, bringing in others like Sal, Jaime, and even her mom, who'd agreed to take care of Tela as long as necessary, had made things easier for Jessica. She owed them for their generosity, and hopefully after this case ended, she'd find a way to repay them. Especially Angus.

Linda walked by her desk on her way to a lunch meeting. "You'll be okay here?" she asked.

"Everything will be fine. It's broad daylight, and I swear, I've never had so many people taking care of me. Thanks for all you've done."

"You should lock the door when I leave," Linda said. "And I'm happy to help."

As if getting up in the middle of the night, showing up during questioning, and converting her office to a well-guarded palace had been easy. But at least with Linda, she could work hard to repay her boss's generosity.

The phone rang as the door clicked shut. Jessica answered and helped a new client register with the firm and schedule her first appointment.

Suddenly the door opened and Jace Jeffries strode in, slamming it behind him.

"Motherfucker!" Jessica yelled, jumping to her feet. "Do you need me to kick your ass here too? Get the fuck out of here."

She wished the desk weren't between them so she could lunge at him and tackle him to the ground before he pulled out his revolver. Anger, adrenaline, and fear pounded through her. *Get him out* played on repeat in her mind.

"Be quiet," he said. "We need to talk."

"The fuck we do. Get out of here before I call the police."

"No. Please, just give me two minutes."

"You burned my truck. You ruined it. You beat up my friend and left her in the desert to die. You pulled a gun on me. There is no way I'm letting you stay."

She picked up the handset on her desk to dial 911. Jace sprang at her and ripped the phone away.

"Please!" Jace yelled like a scared little boy. "Andres has gone crazy. I don't want to be here, but he said he'd kill me and my family if I didn't talk to you. I won't hurt you. I swear." Jace set the phone on the ground and raised his hands as if under arrest.

Jessica paused. How did this fit with the threat Andres made yesterday? She hated sharing space with this man, but maybe she could learn something from him. Something that would help her put him and Andres away.

"What do you want?" *You little twerp*, she finished the sentence in her mind to make her words come out doused in hate.

"Can I sit?" he asked and pointed at the chair facing her desk.

"Fuck no. Start talking or get the hell out."

Jace stared at her in shock as if no was an unfamiliar word. He opened his mouth, but nothing came out.

Jessica pulled her cell phone from her pocket. "I don't have time to stand around. Say what you came to say or leave. Either way, I'm calling the police. If you try to take this phone from me, I guarantee you I will kick your ass a second time."

"I just need to know the name of the girl we took to the desert." He had a hard time getting the sentence out.

Jessica had a harder time hearing it. Man, she hoped the security system had audio as well as cameras. If so, nailing Jace just got a lot easier.

"First," Jessica said. "She's a woman, not a girl. Second, saying you *took* her to the desert doesn't begin to describe what happened. You kidnapped her, right? Kidnapped, not took."

She stared at him for a long, uncomfortable minute. Finally, he gave a quick nod.

"Second, you need to acknowledge what you did to her out there."

He shook his head. Jessica sighed in disgust then turned to her phone and typed the number nine.

"Okay," he said. "We roughed her up a little."

"A little? You should have seen her bruises."

"She barfed on me." Outrage laced his words.

"Why did she barf on you, Jace? What were you going to do to her that made her so upset that she threw up?"

"Nothing, I swear."

"Liar." She looked back to her phone and pushed the number one.

"Please. He's going to kill me. I just need her name."

"Are you actually stupid enough to think I'd give you her name? I don't give a fuck if Andres kills you. Isn't that what you wanted to do to my friend? You left her in the desert to die."

"No. I . . . Why do you care about her so much? She's just a Mexican. Travis never should have defiled himself with her."

Ice settled into every cell in Jessica's body. She'd never wanted to kill anyone before. But some people didn't deserve to live.

"That was a huge mistake. Racism, actually, is a huge mistake. You do know that Andres is of Mexican descent?

"My dad will take care of him. Eventually."

"What about your friends? The ones in the bar who helped you brutalize my friend."

"They're my bodyguards."

That explained a lot. How much did daddy have to pay those guys to hang out with his son? She bet they felt about Jace the way Andres felt about his father.

"Have you ever thought about why Andres wants the name of the woman you brutalized? All of them, in fact."

"She's a loose end. We can't have loose ends."

"You poor, dumb motherfucker." This guy didn't have the brains needed to cross the street, much less run daddy's business. She understood why Andres would bristle at Jace being called his boss. "He wants you in jail."

Jace looked at her with the kind of shock Tela had on her face when you pretended to throw the ball but palmed it instead. She waited for the implication of her words to sink in.

"My dad would never let that happen."

"He thinks he can pin Mayfield's murder on you also."

"What? I didn't kill him. I swear. Andres told me I did, but I didn't even wake up until we'd left the house. I think he killed him."

Jessica shook her head. Andres had a plan and this guy couldn't see it. "You are definitely not the brightest bulb in this town. I'm sure he'll take care of your parents once you're locked away."

"What do you mean?"

She'd finished with Jace. He'd either figure it out or he wouldn't. She didn't want any part of it.

"Wait. He can't hurt my mom. I don't care what he does to my dad. That guy's an asshole, and he hates me. He thinks I'm nothing compared to him."

"Don't really care," Jessica said, and looked down to press the final one. The police should arrive quickly given that headquarters was only a couple of blocks away.

Before she could press send, the front door flew open. Sal rushed into the office and tackled Jace, slamming him to the floor. Jace struggled a moment, then went limp.

"I've got a message for Andres," Sal said. "Tell him if he ever comes around here again, he'll have to deal with Sal Guerra."

In one fluid move, Sal stood, jerking Jace up with him by the backs of his arms. Jace cried out in pain.

"You are going to jail for a good long while," Sal said. "This entire conversation was filmed and recorded. If you recall, you admitted assaulting a woman. Given all the deaths out in that part of the desert, the cops will be taking a good, hard look at you."

Sal spun Jace toward the door. "Go. Tell Andres. He needs to know his little game is over. Then turn yourself in. It's the best way to stay alive."

"He already knows," Jace said. "He's listening."

"How?" Jessica asked. Had Andres bugged the place when he'd come earlier? She hadn't noticed. Maybe he'd broken in some other time. Nice to know the good guys *and* the bad guys could keep tabs on her at work.

"Phone. Back pocket," Jace said.

Sal pulled Jace's phone from his jeans and stared at it like it had stung him.

"Hello, old friend." The raspy voice emanated from the device. "Send Jace outside."

"No. I don't work with criminals. Besides, you already heard the message I wanted him to deliver." Sal looked at Jessica, nodded at her phone.

She hit send and called the police. "We've got an emergency at 800 St. Vrain, related to an ongoing case." Jessica gave what details she could.

She listened to the response from the police dispatcher, at least until Andres's voice crawled under her skin.

"Jessica, I'm disappointed in you. I thought we had an agreement, and I told you what would happen if you didn't work with me."

Jessica didn't know what he'd do, not for sure. His broad threat hadn't specified who he'd hurt. He had his pick. He could harm her, or he could damage her worse by harming Araceli, or Angus, or her mom. He must have sent Jace when he realized she wouldn't agree to his deal. This was a test.

"Ma'am. Are you there? Did you hear me?" The voice came from Jessica's phone.

"I'm here." She wanted to tell the woman that someone had threatened her from a different phone. But it was too much to explain. And if Andres heard he'd get angrier, more destructive.

"Do not threaten people I care about," Sal said. "That won't work out well for you."

"Salvador Guerra. I've waited many years for retribution. Welcome to the war."

The line went dead. Jessica's heart beat in slow motion. Like they'd just pulled the pin from a grenade, things were about to get much worse.

"Ma'am. Are you there?" Jessica had dropped her phone to her thigh without realizing it.

"I'm here. We need help."

A siren blared, and within minutes a cop car with flashing lights stopped in the middle of the street. Two officers streamed in the door as Jessica hit send on a text to Jaime. One of the officers reached for his gun.

"No guns," Jessica said. "This man, the young one, Jace Jeffries, burned my truck two days ago, and Officers Flores and Anderson investigated. He paid me an unwanted visit here at my office today. It scared me. The other man, Sal Guerra, is an ex-sheriff's deputy and friend. He installed a security system here this morning because of escalating threats."

Another day, another interrogation room. Involving law enforcement had a huge downside, hours wasted telling the same story over and over. In the past, she'd played the Lone Ranger, investigating, question- ing suspects, and hunting down criminals all on her own. Streamlined cases with quick results.

By the time the questions ended, much of the day had passed. It wasn't worth returning to work, not that Sal would let anyone back in the office anyway. Not with Andres out there.

It came out in questioning that Sal had been a block away, catnapping in his Jeep when Jace entered the office. Because Sal couldn't spend his life hovering near the office waiting for something to go wrong, Linda had called a friend at one of El Paso's big law firms. Soon they'd occupy temporary space behind locked doors where they could work until this case cleared.

Jessica wanted so many things. She wanted to go on a run with her dog. She wanted to sit in front of Angus, stare into his eyes, and talk through their future. Frustratingly, she could do none of them, because she might unwittingly lead Andres to the people she loved.

Instead, she pulled up in front of Jaime's house, grateful yet unsettled. Jaime opened the door as she approached.

"Come on in, there's an update," he said.

Well, she'd wanted something to happen. It looked like she'd get her wish. She followed Jaime into the house and settled at the kitchen island.

"I'm throwing together a salad and have a chicken in the oven." Jaime was a genius cook and had the most tricked-out kitchen of anyone she knew. At least dinner would be excellent.

"Thanks, but you should let me buy dinner. I'm already imposing."

"It's no problem. It's nice to have you here." He opened the fridge, pulled out a beer, and set it in front of her.

"So, what's the news?" Small talk had never been Jessica's forte.

"I'll start with Jace. His dad tried to bail him out, but he refused to leave. Seems he's more scared of Andres than his father. I want you to press charges to hold him, since he's already made bail for burning your truck. I'm glad you recorded his confession, but this case needs to be watertight."

"Honestly, I don't really care what happens to him. Andres can have him. They deserve each other."

"He'll be in jail overnight. We'll see what happens tomorrow. Hopefully he won't make bail. The more interesting thing is we just got a call from the Tempe police department."

A chill went through Jessica, and it wasn't just the sip of ice-cold beer. Travis lived in Tempe. "What happened?"

"Travis Williams was admitted to the hospital. He was beaten up pretty good."

"Andres." Jessica recalled Jace mentioning him in their conversation earlier that day. You could pretty much walk into El Paso's airport and hop on a quick flight to Phoenix anytime. "He's probably on a flight back right now."

"He landed an hour and a half ago. He's back in El Paso. We don't know where."

"That sucks." Her mind whirred. He'd come see her again, track her down no matter where she fled. Even worse, he'd found Travis, and that guy folded fast. Andres had to have Araceli's name. It wouldn't take him long to find her.

Jessica texted her friend.

Bad news. There's someone out there worse than Jace. He works for Jace's dad and wants Jace in jail. He thinks you're the key. He went to Phoenix and beat up Travis. When he finds out where you live, he'll head your way.

Jessica looked up. "I just wrote the craziest text to Araceli. There has to be another way to go about this. Why don't we involve the dad? Andres is his employee. If he finds out his employee wants to take down his business and keep his son in jail, surely, he'll do something about it. From what I hear, he's got more money than God."

"That's not a bad idea," Jaime said. "Although the dad only knows about Jace burning your truck and going to your office. Things might not go well when he learns about his son's other activities."

"Yeah. It's not exactly Christian to beat up women and leave them in the desert to die." Jessica looked down at her phone as a text came in from Araceli.

Thanks. I'll tell my family. We'll take care of it.

Who knew what that meant? Araceli and her family lived on a very rural Mexican ranch several hours from El Paso. Andres might be frightening, but taking off into the wilds of Mexico to find a woman on a remote ranch protected by a large family might make him reconsider. Or get permanently lost down there. One could hope.

"Should I try and talk to his dad?" Jessica asked Jaime.

"Let's let tomorrow play out. Perhaps Mr. Jeffries will show up instead of having his attorney handle everything like last time." Jaime halved a handful of cherry tomatoes, then threw them into a bowl with baby lettuce.

Jessica considered the conundrum and all the different players. She'd like to see Jace and his crew in jail as well as Andres. At this point, she only assumed Andres killed Deputy Mayfield, but he sure seemed like the best suspect. As for Jace and friends, how many women had they hurt? Araceli couldn't be the only one. Finally, did these people connect to the murders of immigrants? Too many crimes and too many suspects with so very little of it clear.

Maybe she needed to go back to basic detective work. "I'm sure Jace and his crew hurt more women than Araceli. How can I find them?"

Jaime pulled out his phone and sent a text. "We can look into case files at the city and county. I just sent a text to Clint about this. I don't remember many beatings other than domestic violence and occasionally prostitutes around the base, but we'll look into it."

"Look into missing women as well. It took smarts and luck for Araceli to get away. Not everyone would have been so fortunate." How could they find those who didn't escape? Scour thousands of acres of desert? Maybe Jace would cave under questioning.

Jaime plated their dinner. "We have one other lead. The Tempe police didn't get to question Travis as much as they wanted. Evidently, the doctor gave him painkillers that made him a little loopy. If he's part of Jace's crew, then we might get information from him."

"We can only hope." She needed a clear path to follow on this case, but instead, she seemed stuck in shifting sands.

Chapter 26

The next morning, Jessica met Linda at one of the high-rise buildings in downtown El Paso. Guilt about the need to move the office, money spent on a security system, and all the time Linda had burned keeping Jessica out of trouble weighed on her.

"Well, this is exciting," Linda said as Jessica unlocked a door at the end of a long hallway.

Jessica turned on the light to a small reception area with a desk and a few chairs. Her new home. She laid the keys on the desk and hid her backpack behind it.

"Look at that." Linda strode down the hall with Jessica on her heels.

Two offices opened on one side, with a conference room opposite them. But Linda focused on a floor-to-ceiling window at the end of the hall. The view looked over the roof of Bassett Tower, one of El Paso's older downtown buildings. They stared at a steep copper roof whose patina had long ago turned green. The roof fell to a brick parapet topped by majestic concrete eagles that seemed to guard the skies.

"That has to be a sign of good luck," Linda said. "I feel like they're watching over us."

"The eagles are amazingly cool. And we could use some good luck. Sorry about that."

Linda turned to Jessica. "You have nothing to be sorry about. This is the work we do. I've built a career around helping women in trouble. You've brought a new aspect to that. You don't stop at wanting legal justice, you want actual justice. It's invigorating, but it's also dangerous. Finding the line between doing enough and going too far isn't easy, but I'm proud of your commitment."

It wasn't the reaction she expected. Probably not the grace she would have provided were their positions reversed. Once again, luck followed Jessica. "Thanks. How is Sal handling all of this? It seems like he feels responsible for Andres, although I'm not sure why."

"I agree. I think he feels like he should have pursued Andres harder when he was a deputy. But they were both kids from the barrio searching for a better life."

"Yeah, and one wore a white hat, the other black."

"Sal's a good guy, but he's got his odd streak." Linda returned her eyes to the window, as if not completely comfortable with her words.

"Yeah, like being able to kill a rattlesnake with a knife from yards away," Jessica said.

"And having a gun range in his home," Linda contributed.

"And an unhealthy obsession with drones."

The words stretched into silence. More could be said about the gruff, sometimes ornery man whose defense systems made him seem paranoid.

"The llamas are cool," Jessica said. She'd never approached the animals Sal kept on his property because he'd warned her they spit, but their comic-book looks made her smile each time she saw them.

"I really like him," Linda said.

"But . . ."

"I just never saw myself as part of a couple. Not at this late stage."

And Jessica had always seen herself as part of one since she married Angus. The two women stared out at the eagles guarding El Paso's pale blue sky, refusing to comment on mystery or trouble.

"Let's get the office set up," Jessica said.

"Good idea. Make sure the phone forwarded correctly."

They disappeared into their work. Jessica looked repeatedly at the desktop phone, which had forwarded without issue. She longed to call Angus, to continue the conversation their lovemaking had started. She also wanted to reach out to Araceli and learn when she would leave for Guadalajara and make sure Andres had left her alone. But she didn't want to bother them. And someplace deeper, she feared the answers to those questions.

The phone rang while she stared at it. Perhaps it was an auspicious call from one of them that would settle her concerns. More likely, a client wanted to schedule a meeting with Linda.

She picked up the receiver. "Linda Reed Law."

"It's me."

She'd know that voice anywhere. Why would Andres call her here? She almost hung up. But too much lay on the line. Araceli's future. Travis, Jace, his dad. Plus, she'd never forget how he'd threatened to find those she loved.

"What do you want?" Good. Her voice sounded angry, not frightened.

"Travis. I took care of him for you. He will admit to what he did and tell the police that Jace was the ringleader. Travis only went along with Jace because he was scared. If he testifies, the jury will believe him."

"I didn't ask you to do anything for me." She wouldn't let him pin any of this on her. Good to know he played dirty. Had this tactic worked on her dad?

"You needed to learn to trust me."

"Again. Don't need or want anything from you."

"That is not our deal." Anger now tinged his voice. "We need each other. You said you wanted Jace punished. Together, we can make that happen. I convinced Travis to testify. Tell your friend to do the same."

"She's a victim. She doesn't have to testify if she doesn't want to." Why was she even having this conversation? She should hang up, tell the police about the call.

"Where are you?" she asked. She could swear his eyes saw her every move.

"I'm at the Jeffries house. Don't think about sending law enforcement out here. You know what happened last time you did that."

The building seemed to spin. Mayfield. And he insinuated her call caused his death. "You killed the deputy. Not Jace."

Andres chuckled. The sound would have scared scorpions back into their holes. "I know better than to comment on that. You recorded me the first time we met. That was smart. Now the police know the terrible things Jace has been up to. You see, we can be good partners."

"You're a criminal. I'm hanging up now and calling the police."

"Your dad said the same thing, at first. Then he learned that if you go along, no one gets hurt."

Jessica's throat constricted and her lungs forgot how to work. What did this guy know about her dad? That was so long ago. Numbers turned themselves into answers. Andres probably had five years on her dad. He would have been out of the Army for a decade before her dad's conviction. He could have been a part of it.

"I can tell by your silence that you are starting to understand. Your father played the game to protect the people he worked with. To protect your mother, and you. All of that is still in play."

"No." The word sounded neither strong nor brave. Generational payback couldn't exist. It couldn't.

"There's really no choice. But you'll get what you want out of it. Jace is a monster. He deserves to be in prison. This is a two-way street, Jessica. We'll both get things we want."

Jessica couldn't get her bearings. The staid office had turned into a tumultuous sea. She'd always hated the water. She forced air in, then out. Again. History would not repeat itself.

"Two-way street." Her words held a hint of anger. "My dad was convicted, spent the rest of his life on house arrest, left his child. Me. That was no life."

"Be smarter than your dad. Don't make mistakes." Andres's voice rumbled into the phone, hurtling rocks.

Jessica hung up. This conversation would not happen. She'd fought other jackasses and won. Her father had lost his battle. It didn't mean she would.

So many puzzle pieces flew through Jessica's mind. Did her mom know who Andres was? Did she know anything about her dad's case that might be helpful? What about Sal? Did any connection between Andres and Sal exist after their time in the Army? And Linda. She'd arrested

Jessica's dad. It was like the network of the damned. And now Andres wanted her trapped in it as well.

The phone rang.

"Linda Reed Law." She couldn't get anything else out. For just a second, she let herself hope it was a client, even a wrong number.

"I don't think you understand. You don't have a choice. You've complicated my plans by involving yourself. I thought they'd get Jace for Mayfield's death. Then I find out you recorded your last conversation with him, the one from your office where he said he was unconscious when Mayfield died. You've already crossed me. Now you owe me. Just like with your dad, you'll do anything to save the people you love."

"I'm hanging up. Don't call me again." He couldn't force her to work with him. She'd just say no until he got it through his thick skull.

Another thing bothered her. How had he planned on pinning Mayfield's death on Jace? He couldn't have known the deputy would be the first to arrive. How did he even know she'd called the sheriffs? Unless Mayfield had already been on his way.

"I remember the first time I kept tabs on your mother. She was a beautiful lady." Andres's voice raked across her ears.

Jessica hung up again as her stomach turned. She sprang out of her chair and raced for the office door. She'd always chosen fight, but now flight seemed her only hope. The door led to the larger law firm. People at desks looked up as she barged through, but she didn't stop. She had to get away.

Finally, she passed the reception area, but then a bank of elevators stopped her. Of course, they had to be on the sixteenth floor. Nothing like trying to make a quick escape, then being forced to press a button and wait while Muzak played in the background.

Her body stilled, but her heart beat a wild rhythm completely out of sync with the soft hits coming through the speakers. Finally, a ding and then doors slid open. Sal stepped out and Jessica brushed past him on her way in.

"Jessica." He turned to her, worry crossing his brow.

She pressed the lobby button. The doors finally started to slide together. Sal stepped back in before they closed.

"Sorry, don't have time to talk. I need to take a quick walk outside." The words made no sense. Panic babbling. She did not want him to question her. Not yet. Not before her brain could process what had happened.

"What's going on?" he asked.

"Nothing." Christ. This had to be the slowest elevator in the universe.

Sal leaned against the wall, crossed his arms, kept staring with that concerned look on his face. Finally, the elevator dinged and the doors slid open to the tiled first floor. Jessica practically sprinted through the bank lobby, hoping she'd be able to breathe better in the outside air. She turned toward San Jacinto Plaza, the square in the heart of downtown.

People milled under trees and canopies, despite the hot, humid air. The pressure of a coming monsoon made breathing hard. Just minutes in the sunshine and humidity conjured sweat on Jessica's brow. Or maybe that was fear.

Sheer will kept her from running, not that she had anywhere to go. Just away. Away from the voice that had ensnared her in a trap she hadn't foreseen and wanted no part of. How had it happened? And how on earth could she extricate herself from this without someone she loved becoming a target?

Jessica crossed the street and turned west, finally stopping where she could see the trains pass beneath the city. One rumbled by. She watched it enter a tunnel under one of El Paso's tallest buildings. With all the land in this giant desert, why had someone chosen to build on top of an existing railroad? Just one more thing in this city that couldn't be explained, like extremely low crime rates, yet criminals who scared her senseless.

A shadow pulled up beside her. She could tell it was Sal without even looking. But she had nothing to say. No way to explain the phone call without pulling him into the morass. She'd find a way out of this. Maybe her mom could move. What, and Angus too? Linda?

She'd spent her entire adult life trying to be the opposite of her father, yet the very same people who'd entrapped him had set their sights on her. At least Andres had insinuated that. It could be a lie, although she doubted it. Lie or truth was a false battle, the threat remained either way.

"Were you involved in my dad's case?" Jessica finally asked.

"Yes. Peripherally."

She watched the sharp outline of his shadow next to hers as another train rumbled below them. "Was Andres?"

"His associates were. He was tied to the cartel, handled things for them on this side of the border. I was part of the sheriff's department team that worked on drug cases with the DEA. That's how I knew about your dad's case. They caught your dad but never implicated anyone from the cartel."

Jessica followed the crumbs. "So my dad, the local district attorney, who prosecutes drug traffickers, got turned by the cartel and destroyed evidence. Andres was their clean-up guy on this side of the border, so he was involved at some level. And Linda, who was with the police department, was the arresting officer."

"Yes."

"And now history has blown in from the past. The band is back together." Her panic left her body in such a rush she grabbed the iron railing to keep herself steady. She'd run from a trauma she thought she'd caused. Instead, this dilemma had birthed her, had entangled her from the beginning. No wonder those incels believed in red pills and blue pills. Her only remaining decision was which one to take.

"Tell me what happened." Sal's calm concern steadied her.

Jessica removed her jacket in the sweltering heat. She turned and jaywalked across the street to the small park in front of the library where an empty bench called to her. Sal followed. She wished she had a shot of tequila to take the edge off and a beer to cool her throat.

Instead, she had a hot summer day, and the company of a man who'd spent most of his life mired in crime on the border. At least he fought it. Andres, her father—they'd caused it. And now, if she didn't follow in daddy's footsteps, she'd risk the people she loved most.

She'd considered getting her mom to leave town to protect her, the same way she'd asked Araceli to go. What kind of life would that be, always afraid of getting too close because the people she cared about could be used against her? It helped her understand her dad a little bit better.

Instead of sending others away, she could exile herself. You couldn't use a tool that couldn't be found. Peace flowed through her like a river. She could save the ones she loved. Her mom could have a fresh start with the artist friend she seemed to like. Angus could stay with the family he loved, find someone new who would never chase criminals. Jessica and Tela could find a new home. Maybe a place where trees replaced cacti and where she could walk barefoot through grass.

Unlike many of her peers, Jessica had sworn she'd never leave El Paso. Other kids wanted to attend college out of town or out of state. But once her parents left, she wanted stability, not new adventures.

Perhaps the time had come to leave the only place she'd called home. If that's what it took to save those she loved, then she'd make that sacrifice a thousand times over. She wouldn't stay until something went wrong and one side locked her up or the other one killed her—or far worse, killed her loved ones.

Sal sighed beside her. Her silence had likely worn away his patience, but not so much that he'd ask her again.

"Andres thinks I should take my father's place in his operation."

"No."

It was the first time Jessica heard hate in Sal's voice.

"I think I should leave town. He can't use me if I disappear." He can't threaten me with the lives of those I love. She left that part unspoken, but as she glanced at Sal, she could tell she hadn't hidden the thought.

"Does he want you to meet him?" Sal asked.

"I don't think so. He said he was at the Jeffries house, not here, which is a small relief. I think he's fine interacting by phone."

"I will take care of this." Sal rose from the bench and walked away.

Now, Jessica followed him. "There's nothing you can do to take care of it," she said to his retreating back.

He didn't slow. He crossed the park, entered the bank, and took the elevator down to the parking garage. Jessica stayed on his heels.

"At least tell me your plan," she pleaded with him, but Sal remained stone-faced.

"You need to stay here," was the only thing he said.

In the garage, Sal strode to his Jeep and pulled himself into the driver's seat. Jessica rounded the vehicle to open the passenger door. She would not let him face Andres alone.

Sal locked the door before she could open it, then backed out of the space.

"Stop!" Jessica yelled, but he didn't.

Without thinking, she jumped into the aisle, throwing herself in front of the Jeep just as he put it into gear. He braked hard, stalling the engine.

Sal rolled down his window. "Jessica, you need to move."

"What are you going to do?" Panic came roaring back on a rollercoaster of concern.

"Something I should have done a long time ago. I'll be back soon." With that, he put the Jeep in gear, backed it away from her, steered around the corner, and then he was gone.

Jessica patted her pockets, looking for her keys, but she'd rushed out of the office without taking anything.

She ran to the elevator and punched the button. It seemed to take forever, as did the slow ride up to the sixteenth floor. Once that door opened, she trotted through the main office and back to Linda's little part of it. She spied the keys she'd left on the desktop.

"Hey Linda, I need to take off for lunch." Jessica swiped the keys and left before Linda could respond. As she hurried out of the office, it occurred to her that the people who worked here probably thought she was mad. Way to make an impression with future colleagues in the legal profession. But she couldn't worry about that today.

Back in the garage, she jumped into the rental car and peeled away. Sal had quite a head start on her, but she'd do her best to catch up in the compact rental car. She had no doubt about her destination, the Jeffries house.

Jessica had never driven so fast through town. If she obeyed the speed limit, she'd likely arrive too late. If a cop pulled her over for speeding, too late. But if she got lucky, speeding might just get her there in time. She had to convince Sal to stop. She could only end this by leaving. It was safer for everyone.

Ten minutes into the drive, a miniscule amount of the panic subsided. She should call Jaime. Unfortunately, she'd only grabbed her keys. Her backpack and phone remained tucked behind the new desk. She pressed the accelerator. She'd just have to catch Sal in time to talk him out of confronting Andres.

The trip went quickly as she wove through traffic on the busy freeway. Once she reached the smaller state highway, time slowed. The desert stretched before her. Made of nothing but sand and distant hills, the landscape played tricks on her, making her think everything remained the same distance away. It reminded her of being on a treadmill, moving yet going nowhere.

Finally, the hills drew closer. Then they rose above her and the small car climbed the road, engine protesting. At long last, she arrived at the turnoff, then passed the place where she'd talked to Keith. She hadn't caught up with the Jeep. At the very least, she hoped she'd arrived on his tail. If she had, dust would have hung in the air, spewed up by tires on dirt. But the air was crystal clear.

Did she have it wrong? Had he not come here? Maybe he'd gone to the police like a normal person. Maybe he'd called Keith. If she made it to the house and the Jeep wasn't there, she'd turn around and leave before anyone could stop her. If it was there, then perhaps she still had time to talk him out of whatever he'd planned. Or she'd face it with him. He'd given her so much. She wouldn't leave him alone.

This issue might have spawned from earlier times, but Jessica had involved herself in it. She had made herself a target by coming out here the first time, by tracking down Jace in a bar, and before that, following Travis to Arizona. Those had been choices, this was the consequence.

Jessica pulled up to the house. Sal's Jeep stood empty in front.

Chapter 27

Jessica rolled the car to a stop. The door of the house stood open and ominous. The heavy air hinted at fear, and storm clouds darkened the horizon. But her panic from earlier had fled. Resolve replaced it, resolve fed by love.

On the drive, she'd recognized how much she loved Sal, who'd volunteered to mentor her at a true low point in her life. Back then, she'd thought he was the toughest person she'd ever met. But, like her, emotions ruled him. He'd do anything to protect her or Linda. Just like Jessica would do anything to protect the people she loved.

It pissed her off that Sal had stormed off to the desert alone to fight the bad guy. And then she realized some cosmic dial had turned. She'd switched to Angus's role, the worried one, while Sal had become her.

She understood Sal's guilt. He hadn't stopped Andres earlier, a whole lifetime ago. Guilt had fueled Jessica into many stupid reckonings. The kind Angus hated.

She unbuckled the seatbelt and got out of the car. She had no weapon, no adequate skill. But she would match her friend's courage. Hopefully, they'd save each other.

Jessica approached the eerily silent house. Suddenly, a crash, and then a shuffle came from inside. Then nothing.

She peered around the door and let her eyes adjust to the dark interior. Andres and Sal faced each other across the coffee table. Both men had their knees slightly bent and their hands rested in front of their chests in guard position. They seemed completely relaxed, but the tension in their intense focus sent a current through the room. This was a fight.

"Leave, Jessica." Sal didn't look her way.

She thought she'd approached quietly. She should have remembered Sal's sixth sense for danger. She glanced at Andres. Did he have the same ability?

"I'm so glad you've returned," Andres said. "I knew we'd be able to reach an agreement." He turned his head toward her, teeth bared in either a smile or hungry anticipation.

She wanted to punch back with words, assure him she would never do his bidding, but Sal leapt onto the table between them, then seemed to hang in the air a moment before slamming onto Andres.

They hit the floor, then rolled away from each other before staggering to their feet. Jessica thought Sal had landed a direct hit, but Andres must have avoided the worst of it.

Sal tiptoed back, leaving plenty of space between himself and Andres. He turned to Jessica. "Leave." He spit the word at her.

He didn't have time for anything else. Andres attacked, throwing his left leg directly toward Sal's gut. In a move that curved his spine, Sal just avoided the foot that should have sent him sprawling to the floor. He continued the motion, spinning until he met Andres's side with a punch that must have shattered a rib.

Jessica watched her mentor's next move as he followed the forward momentum from the punch to hook a leg around Andres's ankle and drive the man to one knee. Hope welled up in her. The fight could end quickly. Andres would go to jail, and they could go home.

Sal began a swing headed straight for the back of Andres's head. But Andres moved too quickly, diving to the floor and wrenching Sal's leg along with him. Jessica heard a sickening pop as Sal sank to the tile, his ankle twisted at an unnatural angle under Andres.

Andres roared, rolling his body across Sal. Sal delivered a punch to Andres's ear as it passed. It pushed Andres's head to the side, but his body continued its momentum until he'd risen to his knees alongside Sal. Jessica didn't see Andres's fist, which seemed to move faster than light, but the sound of it slamming into Sal's head would never leave her. Sal's body went limp, while his foot unnaturally splayed to the side.

Andres didn't stop, delivering another blow to Sal's cheekbone, then one more to his chin. He wanted to kill him.

"Stop," Jessica yelled as she stepped into the room.

Andres stared through her. "I should have done this forty years ago," he said, fist raised and eyes full of fury.

She couldn't let him kill Sal. Jessica ran toward them, the opposite of what Sal had taught her in their classes. Her mind went blank, all moves forgotten.

She kicked, trying to aim her boot where she imagined his kidney. It connected, but he had already begun to spin away from her attack. He grabbed her ankle, would take her down just like he had Sal.

She stared into his evil eyes and kicked her other leg straight toward them with all the power she had. She felt a connection, then her back slammed into the tile. She remembered too late how Sal had taught her to protect her head from a fall. All went black.

***

Jessica jerked awake to a horrible smell. Her head hurt, and she couldn't make her eyes focus. The smell returned, searing her nostrils.

"Wake up."

She tried to place the raspy voice. She closed her eyes tight, then opened them again. The light hurt.

"Better." Andres came into focus. He closed the vial that contained the horrid smell that woke her.

"I will never work for you." Her voice had to fight its way through the ringing in her ears. "Not ever." Just in case he hadn't understood.

"That is a mistake. So was coming here. I don't work with people who make mistakes. Now get up and get the fuck out of here."

Jessica lay flat on her back. She tried to rise, but her head exploded in pain as if a cleaver had run through it. The room spun like a tilt-a-whirl. She slumped to the side and threw up.

With a shaking hand, she pulled her shirttail up and wiped her mouth. Then, she rolled away from the vomit and got to her knees. It seemed impossible to push herself up. All her energy pulsed through the ache in her head. She forced herself upright anyway.

Fighting the nausea, she managed to not barf again. She looked around the room. Sal was gone.

"Leave," Andres barked. "Walk to your car. Get in. And never come back here."

"Where is he?" Sorrow filled her voice and tears burst from her eyes. This couldn't happen.

"Don't go all girly on me now. I thought you were tough." Andress grabbed her arm and pulled her across the room and out the door.

The brightness outside exploded in her head. She covered her eyes with a hand and let him lead her to the car. Finally, he shoved her against it.

"Leave."

She hovered over the windshield. Inside, Sal's body lay in the passenger seat. He looked dead: no movement, eyes closed, face and torso bloodied. She scrambled for the door handle, poured herself inside. She pulled the keys from her pocket, then remembered the car had a start button. She pressed it.

Andres knocked on her window. Fuck. It had been too good to believe. She lowered the window, and any modicum of safety the glass provided slid out of sight.

"Why are you letting us go?" Her broken brain wouldn't let her stay quiet.

"Everything is already in motion. Your deaths would bring too many questions. But you must never come back. And you must testify against Jace. Just tell the truth."

"What is in motion?"

"Questions will only get you into trouble. Take this gift, and your life is a gift, and drive away." With that, Andres left. He pulled himself into Sal's Jeep and steered around the back of the house.

Jessica put the car in gear. The second she could no longer see the house, she reached for Sal. His body remained warm. She held his wrist but couldn't feel a pulse. She wanted to pull to the side of the road and bawl. The emptiness inside her at the thought of this man's death clawed a chasm in her soul.

Yet all she could think of was Angus. She finally understood. She'd done this to him time and time again. It didn't hurt to chase criminals into danger. It hurt to be left behind, wondering if the person you loved would survive. Even if they were just a friend.

She longed to howl at the world. All the pain and misery she'd caused, that she dealt with still, that lay beside her, unmoving, she couldn't survive it. But instead, she drove. Just in case he lived.

This time, she pushed the car beyond the limits of safety. They swerved down the hills, and once the road straightened, she pushed the pedal to the floorboard. The vehicle's safety system chastised her, beeping until she had to slow because each sound hammered her aching head.

She didn't know where the nearest hospital was. The base had a VA hospital, but she'd never get through the gate with a possibly deceased man beside her. Driving all the way to the county hospital would take forever. There had to be a place to go on this side of the city, but where?

Finally, she reached the outskirts of El Paso. Junk yards and tire shops gave way to convenience stores and strip shopping centers. The sky darkened and the air seemed to sparkle with the electricity of the coming storm.

She passed a firehouse. Firehouses in El Paso had ambulances and EMTs. She pulled into the center lane that divided both directions of traffic and slammed on the brakes. Sal slid down the seat.

The second oncoming traffic cleared, she did a U-turn, squealing the tires so hard they smoked. She pulled into the fire station and parked at the human-sized front door. She jumped out of the car, not bothering to close the door, and ran into the building screaming that she needed help. Two firefighters appeared almost immediately.

"In the car, there's a man, a friend. I don't know if he's alive."

One of the men trotted away and the other followed her to the car. Soon she heard a siren, and one of the huge garage doors began to rise.

Meanwhile, the other man moved to Sal's side, checking his pulse and surveying his wounds. "He's alive. What happened?"

Relief hit like a train, making her sway. Maybe he'd make it.

"Ma'am. Are you alright?" the firefighter asked.

"He was in a fight with another man. This is Sal Guerra. He's a retired sheriff's deputy." The tears started to come. She let them. "He's a really good fighter. He's been teaching me self-defense. But the other guy . . ."

She couldn't finish her sentence. It seemed rude to say Andres fought better. Even if Sal couldn't hear her, he'd put himself at risk trying to take care of her. It hadn't been worth it.

"Were you hurt also? Are you okay?"

How the hell should she know? She didn't feel okay.

"Were you in the fight too?"

"I'm fine. Just upset."

"We're going to transport him to the University Medical Center. Do you want to ride with us, or can you drive yourself?"

Two men approached with a stretcher. Jessica watched as they carefully moved Sal from the car to an orange board and then placed the board on the stretcher.

"We need to stabilize his leg," one of the men said. More people moved toward Sal.

One man, older than the others, approached Jessica. "I'm Captain Olivo. Can you answer a few questions for me?"

"I'm going to the hospital. I need to be with him." Jessica stepped toward the stretcher.

"Are you related to him?"

"No, sir. He's my self-defense instructor. And friend."

They rolled Sal to the back of the ambulance, then slid the stretcher inside. Lights swirled and the siren blared, attacking Jessica like a punch to the head. She clamped her hands over her ears and squeezed her eyes shut.

"Ma'am. Do you need medical attention? Are you on drugs or any medication?" asked Olivo.

Jessica stared at the man, dumbfounded. Rage would have followed, but it couldn't make it past her aching brain.

"No. I need to leave." Thunder clapped as if God agreed.

"Your friend is in good hands. Let them do their jobs. Come into my office. I need some information."

Jessica strode toward the driver's-side door. "My name is Jessica Watts. The man in the ambulance is Sal Guerra. The hospital will also need information about him, and that's where I'm going."

She slid into the front seat and locked the door before starting the engine. Captain Olivo watched her retreat. Then the skies opened, drenching him as Jessica sped away.

She had to keep it together for twenty more minutes. She wished she could call Linda and let her know what had happened. Linda would want to be at the hospital. For the hundredth time, she chastised herself for leaving her phone at the office. Andres's phone call, running through the park, that all seemed like days ago, not mere hours.

It took all her remaining energy to focus on the road. Her head pounded and her back hurt so badly, she wanted to pull over and stretch. But there'd be time for that at the hospital, probably lots of time.

Just let him be okay. She repeated the prayer like a mantra. It calmed her as she drove street after street, slowly closing in on the hospital.

Located in an old part of town and morbidly set next to a large cemetery, the University Medical Center loomed alongside El Paso's new medical school. Once the county medical hospital, the emergency room had seen every type of trauma and had the medical team to deal with it.

She spied the school and hospital rising above the low buildings surrounding them long before she arrived. When she finally turned into the driveway, still repeating her mantra, she thought about leaving the car at the emergency room door and crawling inside to ask for help and an update.

Instead, she drove the vehicle into the parking structure, took the ticket the dispenser shot out, and then circled the multistory garage, searching for a space. She found one on the fourth floor. She had to get to Sal, but pulling herself from the car was like swimming against the tide. She closed the door, then slumped against it for a moment to regain her strength.

Buck up. She wasn't the one whom Andres had almost killed. Jessica staggered down the aisle toward the elevator door. So many elevators had impeded her progress today. Once inside, she smashed the button and leaned against a wall, happy for a steel interior instead of a mirrored one.

On the ground floor, she quickly walked to the emergency room entrance. The rain had stopped, leaving behind the spicy aroma of desert petrichor.

Jessica made it to the emergency room, where she told the gray-haired woman she was a friend of Sal Guerra's who'd been brought in by ambulance. Jessica leaned on the woman's desk to steady herself.

"You need to fill out this information," the woman said, handing her a clipboard holding a sheaf of papers and a pen.

"I need to use a phone," Jessica said. "I have to contact his family and friends."

"I'm sorry, we don't have phones for public use."

"Please, ma'am." A dizzy spell came on, and Jessica grasped the desk tighter.

"I'm afraid I can't help you. Please take these papers and step aside. I have other people to assist."

Jessica took a deep breath and pushed herself off the desk. She would not give up. She turned around to a room filled with beige chairs on a cold tile floor. A couple of dozen people, many looking like they desperately needed medical attention, clustered around the room.

"Does anyone have a cell phone I can borrow for a couple of calls?" Jessica's voice boomed through the open space. "My friend was badly hurt, and I need to let his family know."

A family in the front row watched her with big eyes. The mother grabbed a teenage boy's arm and nodded at Jessica. He brought her his phone.

"Thank you." She sank into a chair near the family and dialed Linda.

"Hello?"

"It's me."

"Jessica. Where the hell are you?" Anger threaded through Linda's voice, but it sounded wonderful to Jessica.

"You have to come to the emergency room at University Medical Center. Sal's in bad shape. He went after Andres."

"Shit. On my way. Stay on the line and tell me what happened."

"Sorry. Can't. More calls to make."

She dialed Angus's number, her heart bursting with all she had learned. When he answered, his voice almost made her swoon.

"You were right about everything," she said.

"Jessica."

"I'm at the University Medical Center emergency room. Sal was in a fight. It's bad."

"Are you okay?"

"Not really." Jessica started to cry.

"I'm on my way. Hang in there, I'll be there soon."

Oh, the relief of hearing his voice. She clasped the phone to her chest for just a moment, held it where her heart was. He'd be here soon.

She rose to give the kid his phone back, but it slipped to the floor as she crumpled into blackness.

Chapter 28

"She should wake up soon." An unfamiliar voice wafted through Jessica's consciousness. She tried to sink back into the quiet, dreamy world of rest. Gradually, beeping and whooshing reached her. People shuffled about and spoke in the distance. Light made it through her closed eyelids. She just wanted to go back to sleep.

Until the memories hit. Her eyes slammed open. Where was Sal?

The brightness assaulted her, and she tried to raise her hand to cover her eyes but couldn't. Something warm covered her hand. She turned her head and saw Angus.

"You're here." The words struggled to come out of her dry throat, but they echoed through her body. Everything would be okay now.

"Hey, babe. How are you feeling?"

Jessica struggled to sit up. "What happened? Why am I here? Where is Sal?" One memory after another battered her. The fight. The drive. The waiting room. Nothing beyond that.

"It's okay," Angus said. "You passed out in the waiting area, so they brought you back here. A doctor will examine you soon."

"Sal?" she croaked.

"He's alive. Linda is with him. They're working on him."

What did that mean? "I need to see him."

"No way. He's going to be okay. He's conscious, but he needs rest. You both do."

She sank back, letting the pillow support her. Thank god Sal had woken up. The fear that he'd died had been a tangible, visceral thing. It had made her desperate. She'd attacked Andres without a thought or a plan, exactly opposite of the way Sal had taught her. The harrowing drive, going too fast when she probably shouldn't have driven at all, had endangered them both. She'd almost lost him.

Jessica looked at Angus. His warm brown eyes shone with love and worry. She'd put him through hell, yet he'd come to save her once again.

"I know now," she said. "I understand everything I put you through. It takes so much more courage to let someone you love face danger than to face it yourself. I'm so sorry. I don't know how you were brave enough to let me leave when you knew where I was going."

The pain in his eyes threatened to undo her. How could she have hurt him like this when she loved him so much?

"I didn't want to be the kind of guy who held you back. You deserve better than that."

"But it can be too much," she said. "The way it squeezes your heart until you can't breathe. I thought he was dead."

"Yeah. That's exactly how it feels. The last time, when you were gone for days, I almost lost my mind." He pressed his lips together as if trying to staunch the pain. A tear rolled down his cheek anyway. "And when you came home, you were so broken that I set my worry aside to help you heal. I don't think I ever did."

"And then I left again."

"I didn't want to leave you. I just didn't know how to stay whole and stay with you."

Jessica might have arrived with head trauma, but that didn't compare to her wounded heart. A completely self-inflicted injury.

A part of her wanted to wallow in the grief she'd caused him, use it to flagellate herself and convince herself she didn't deserve him, had never deserved him. But surely all they'd been through together had molded her into a better person than that.

From the very beginning, he'd volunteered to be her best friend, then her lover, her husband. She needed to stand up for him, acknowledge the things important to him the way he'd let her chase the heady mix of justice and peril.

But could she be that person? The one who thought of him first? Even when she knew he thought only of her? Crap. That circular logic always led back to her. To her not caring whether she lived or died as long as she could be part of the chase, avenging the mistreated.

The thoughts were almost more than her aching brain could handle. What inside her made her care so little for her own safety? Is that how Sal felt when he went after Andres? No. Sal had done it for love. He loved her and Linda and his community. He wanted to make it safer, as did she.

But there had to be a balance. She cared about the man in front of her. She'd put him before anything. And he'd always put her first.

Fuck. It was time to grow up and become a fully functional adult. She could see the path so clearly now—one she hadn't known existed mere minutes earlier. It was okay to pursue justice without constantly putting yourself in the firing line. Look at what Linda did. She'd helped hundreds of women over her long career. And she'd probably been in a few dangerous situations. But she didn't make a habit of it. She didn't have to prove her worth by single-handedly stopping bullets and bringing down criminals.

Jessica had behaved like an addict in need of a fix, not caring who she hurt in her quest for danger. Fuck that. Her life could be so much bigger than she'd made it.

Tears streamed down her face. She wanted the big life. One filled with family, friends, and community. She wanted work she loved that wouldn't get her killed, so she could enjoy a long and fruitful career. She wanted to live in El Paso, which had always stunned her in the way it combined harshness and beauty. She wanted Angus, wanted the way his love wrapped around her and honored her, and she wanted to give him that in return. And she wanted herself, healthy and happy, in the mix.

"I'm sorry for what I've put you through. I want so much more than that. For you and for me." She sniffled, wiped her cheek. How could she share the revelation that had happened in her psyche?

Hurt filled his eyes. "Does that mean you're moving on without me?"

She searched his face. How could he not know? "Of all the things in this world, you're the one I want the most."

The sage-and-sand patterned curtain around Jessica's hospital bed whooshed open accompanied by a metallic clatter. A tiny Asian woman who couldn't be older than thirty-five stood before Jessica in a white lab coat.

"I'm Dr. Namba. Let's take a look at you. I hear you passed out in the waiting room."

"That's what they tell me," Jessica said.

The doctor approached, checking Jessica's heartbeat, eyes, and ears, all while firing questions at her like an automatic weapon: name; birth date; injuries.

When Jessica said she'd fallen onto her back and hit her head on a tile floor, the doctor asked her to lean forward. She did, with Angus's help. Moving felt like taking a bludgeon to the skull. She cried out when the doctor touched the center-back of her head.

"Wow. That's quite a contusion. How did you fall?"

Great. How did one explain the injury to rational human beings? "I was with a friend, Sal Guerra. I think he's here. We were in a fight with someone, and I fell. Do you know how he's doing?"

Dr. Namba glanced at Angus and then at Jessica. "I can't disclose the condition of other patients in the hospital."

"But I'm the one who brought him in." If she had to get up and search bed by bed, she would.

"I'm pretty sure he came here by ambulance."

Jessica couldn't tell if the doctor's face contained confusion or suspicion. "I drove him to the fire station, and they brought him here in the ambulance. I followed."

"You operated a car with a concussion? That is extremely hazardous. No driving for at least forty-eight hours. Longer if you still have symptoms like headache or dizziness."

"At least I'll get to turn in the rental car," she quipped to Angus. "Although I'll be stranded."

"Stranded is good if it means you'll rest," said Dr. Namba. "Dark room, no TV or computer for a few days. No sports or similar activities until you feel better. Drink lots of water."

"Can I take painkillers? I have a raging headache."

"Tylenol only. You may have trouble sleeping and might become nauseous. If your vision gets blurry or you pass out again, get to a doctor. Other than the concussion, you seem healthy."

"Thanks."

"Are you here to take her home?" The doctor nodded at Angus.

"Yes. I'm her husband."

A woman in pink scrubs came into the curtained cubicle. "There's a woman in the waiting area causing a disturbance. She says she's Ms. Watts's mother."

Jessica glanced at Angus. "You told my mom I was in the hospital?"

"Yes. But I made sure I got here first." He gave her a wink.

"She can be discharged. I'll go tell the mom she's okay." Dr. Namba started to leave, then turned back. "No alcohol for at least four days. Let your brain heal."

Damn. That woman could read minds. A bed rolled by, and Jessica saw Linda trailing it.

"Linda," Jessica called.

"Oh my god. Are you okay?"

"Fine. Just a little concussion. How is Sal? I haven't heard anything since I took him to the fire station." She wanted to see him, but the orderlies had kept the bed rolling.

"He's doing better. At least he's conscious again, although he hasn't said much." Linda glanced down the hallway after Sal. "I've got to stay with him. They've admitted him and are taking him to a room. Call me. I want to know what happened," she said, already moving down the hallway.

Clearly, explanations could come later. Jessica gently relaxed back into the bed. Sal would be okay. Frankly, she ought to be worried about Linda. For someone usually extremely put together, her clothes and skin looked like they'd been tossed around and rumpled. But it also looked like love.

She turned to Angus. "You are my hero. You may be a reluctant hero when it comes to me, but I sure appreciate you." She squeezed his hand and smiled into his handsome face. "And thanks for calling my mom."

"You bet. We need to talk about where you're going to stay tonight. Do you want to go back to Jaime's? I can't imagine it's safe for you to stay at your house, but you also need someone to look after you."

Jessica hadn't thought about where she'd go next, and it hurt her brain to consider the options. "I don't think I'm in danger anymore." Thinking hurt so much. "I just don't know."

"I bet your mom would love to take care of you." Angus's lips curled up in a smile.

"I would really love to see my dog, but that's probably a little too much care. I'm not sure even the doctor would agree to that one, especially if she's causing a disturbance outside."

"I've got an idea," he said. "Robbie's place sucks. It's a studio with almost no room. It kind of reminds me of the dump you used to live in."

"Hey—we had some fun in that dump."

"We did. But I wouldn't want to go back there. What would you think about staying at my parents', at least for a few days? Mom would be there to take care of you, and we'd get her fantastic cooking."

"We?" Her voice broke.

"Yes, Jessica. We. As hard as it can be to live with you sometimes, I don't want to live without you anymore."

She couldn't stop the tears. He was everything. And he'd been right about her. She'd promised him she'd change in the past. But this time, she was the one who wanted to change. She wanted to pursue that bigger life, especially if he was a part of it.

"I'll go anywhere with you, Angus Delgado," she said, squeezing his hand like she'd never let go. Which, she wouldn't.

The woman in the pink scrubs came back in. She took one look at Jessica and dashed to her side. "Oh, honey. Are you okay? Where does it hurt?"

Jessica must have looked ridiculous with tears streaming down her face. "I'm completely fine. Just happy."

The nurse gave her an odd look but let it go. Jessica signed some papers, and Angus provided their insurance information. Even with a concussion, with one criminal in jail whom she needed to testify against and a more dangerous one on the loose, Jessica felt better than she had in months.

Chapter 29

The second Jessica and Angus exited the emergency room doors into the lobby, a shriek made Jessica wince and then her mother full on ran toward her to envelop her in a hug.

Jessica threw her arms in front of her. "Head injury," she said, loud enough to stop her mom in her tracks.

"Can I hug you?" Clarice asked.

"Gently." Angus spoke up this time. "And no loud noises."

Jessica glowed at his response, at least inwardly. She didn't want to hurt her mom's feelings, and Angus had relieved her of that.

Clarice wrapped Jessica in the softest hug of her life. "I was so worried when they said you were in the hospital again."

Jessica almost reminded her mother that she'd always been fine. She could even imagine the chastising voice she would have used. And then she remembered her anguish at seeing Sal knocked out. It had ripped her in two, causing momentary insanity. Jessica had scared her mom, and she needed to be gracious and thankful the woman cared enough to show up.

"I'm going to be okay, Mom. I just need to rest for a couple of days, and Angus is going to take care of me."

"Bless you," her mom said, wrapping Angus in a vicious hug that allowed her to use all the mom energy she'd wanted to spend on Jessica.

A man came up behind her mother. Keith's tall form shadowed Clarice.

"Have you heard anything about Sal?" Worry creased his brow and flooded from his eyes. "Linda called me, but she hasn't responded to my texts since I arrived."

"We just saw her. They're moving him into a room. I'm sure she'll let you know where they are shortly. He's okay. He regained consciousness in the ambulance."

"What the hell happened?"

Jessica heard the accusation in his voice. She'd only earned part of it. Like her, Sal had chosen his path.

Jessica pulled them into a quiet corner. "He went after Andres. There's a lot of history there, and he didn't like that he'd threatened us. Me. It goes all the way back to my dad."

"What?" Her mom raised a hand to her chest.

Jessica looked at the circle they'd formed. The past and present met in an awkward ring.

"I guess introductions are in order. Keith, this is my mom, Clarice Watts. And this is my husband, Angus Delgado. This is Keith Guerra, Sal's nephew."

Both men visibly stiffened.

Keith broke first, reaching his hand toward Angus. "It's nice to meet you. I've heard a lot about you."

"Likewise," Angus said, shaking Keith's hand.

Keith glanced at her and then back at the door she'd just exited. "Were you hurt?"

"Just a little concussion."

"What happened?" he asked.

"Yes, Jessica. What exactly happened? And what does it have to do with your dad?" her mom chimed in.

Suddenly, the exhaustion of the day cratered into Jessica. "Let me give you the short version. Andres called me and wanted to use me—I guess the way he used Dad." Jessica's words would likely hurt her mother, but the truth needed airing.

She continued. "Sal found out and went after him, and I went after Sal. We went to Jace Jeffries's house in the desert. They were already fighting when I arrived."

She stopped. Recounting the story put her back in that room, and that took a big toll on her. She took a deep breath and braced herself.

"Andres knocked him out."

"Impossible." Keith's voice came across like a whip cracking.

Mucky sadness flowed through Jessica. "If only. I, well, I wasn't thinking. I tried to attack Andres and pretty much knocked myself out by hitting my head on the tile floor."

"Oh, Jessica." Her mom's anguished cry was quickly followed by Keith's "No."

"Anyway," Jessica said. "Long story short, I drove Sal to the fire station and then followed him here, passed out, and they fixed me up. I know that leaves a lot out, but I need to rest now." She gave her mom and Keith a smile, then leaned on Angus.

"Let's get you out of here," he said and led her to the door.

And just like that, the world looked brighter.

———

It wasn't until Angus had parked in front of his parents' house that Jessica remembered the potential danger of her situation. The relief at Angus rescuing and caring for her, and perhaps her tortured brain, had erased the danger of Andres, and even Jace if he got out of jail. She couldn't let Angus's family become potential targets.

"Wait. Maybe this isn't such a good idea. I don't want your parents targeted because they tried to help me."

Angus sighed. "I've thought about that. But I also can't think of a safer place for you to be. I plan on calling Jaime to let him know what happened." He shifted in the seat to face her. "How likely is it that this guy is still after you?"

Jessica shook her head, then stopped when that caused waves of pain. "I'm not sure. I'm not even sure why he let us go. He could have killed us both. I passed out, and he actually used smelling salts or something to wake me up. He told me to leave, basically pulled me to my car. When I got there, I saw Sal in the front seat. He must have put Sal there."

It didn't make sense. But somewhere, lost in her memory, she found a thread. "He said something about not wanting to bring more attention to what he's doing. I think he's got some grand plan."

Dread reared up like nausea. "He wanted me to be a part of it, to work for him or something. He insinuated that the same thing had happened with my father. I couldn't be like him." She reached for Angus, pressed her hand against his warm thigh.

"You'll never be like your dad." He covered her hand with his own.

"That's when I ran out of the office. I just panicked. I didn't even take my phone. I think I was afraid he'd call again, although that doesn't make any sense." A tremor started in Jessica's chest, like that little bit of trauma had its own beating heart.

"Sal came after me. When I told him what happened, he must have been furious. He took off, and I followed him, all the way to Jace's house."

"After Andres hit me and then woke me up, I told him I wouldn't work with him. He still let me leave. He does want me to testify against Jace."

"How do you feel about that?' Angus asked.

"That jackass hurt Araceli and burned my truck. I want to testify against him." Jessica sighed. It was all so much. "Maybe it will be over after that."

"Let's go inside," Angus said. "You need rest. I'll talk to my parents and Jaime about what's best. But I think this is a safe space for everyone, at least for now."

"Thank you for being there for me, again. I love you."

"I love you too. It feels like my life is sliding back into place," Angus said.

They walked through the front door together. Jessica took in the comfortable, modern Norman Rockwell scene. Angus's dad relaxed in his La-Z-Boy, a cop show on the TV in front of him. Angus's sister wandered in from the hallway, a baby in her arms and a toddler zigzagging behind her. Plush wall-to-wall carpeting, exposed brick, and comfy furniture decorated the room. And the whole place smelled like enchiladas.

Angus led her to his bedroom, just like when they used to sneak back there in high school for epic make-out sessions. He had the same full-sized bed, although his mom must have upgraded the bedding since he left. She'd definitely taken down the AC/DC posters.

"Do you want to shower?" he asked.

"Sleep first. I'm so tired."

She stripped down to her underwear. Angus opened a drawer and pulled out an old KLAQ T-shirt she hadn't seen in fifteen years. Soft and thin, it provided cashmere level comfort.

He pulled back the covers and once she'd slid in, tucked her in.

"Stay with me?" Sleep already drew her downward, but she didn't want to be alone.

Angus stripped down to his boxer briefs and climbed in. He stretched long and lean beside her, his soft, warm skin its own kind of lullaby.

"I'm so lucky." She placed a hand on his hip, felt him do the same, and drifted off.

Chapter 30

After days of care, great food, and almost too much rest, Jessica wanted to split herself in two and leave her kindness and gratitude with these wonderful people. She'd take the less savory part of herself back out into the desert where she could hear herself think and figure out what came next.

Last night, tucked closely into the full-sized bed of Angus's youth, he'd said, "I want to move back into our house."

Her heart had soared with joy, then she'd taken those feelings and wrapped them around him, along with her body, in an attempt at silent lovemaking. Everything seemed right with the world.

Now, they drove home, where her mom waited with Tela. A wild happiness filled Jessica. After days of evening rain, her brown desert had turned green. Grasses appeared out of nowhere, sage bloomed purple and magenta, and yellow flowers exploded from trees and shrubs. The crisp air had shed its humidity, and she bet she could see a hundred miles or more from the mountaintop.

As they pulled into the driveway, home settled into her bones. The sienna color of the adobe cottage glowed in the sun, the large plate-glass window reflecting the morning rays. Her mom opened the front door the second Jessica exited the car, and a blur of brown and white streaked across the yard toward her.

Tela barreled into her arms, but only for a moment. The dog ran to Angus next, practically knocking him over in her excitement, then she returned to Jessica, running a few circles around her before charging back to Angus. Finally, she zoomed around the front yard as if trying to burn off the excitement her body couldn't contain.

Angus came over and put an arm around Jessica. "I think I'm just as happy to be home," he said, nodding at the dog.

"Me too."

Clarice stood on the stoop, her face lit by a huge smile. Jessica stepped toward her mom and wrapped her in a tight hug. "Thank you for taking such great care of her."

"Oh, honey, I love that dog." Emotion trembled through her voice. "I have something to show you."

Jessica followed her mom into the house. As soon as she stepped into the living room, she stopped so quickly that Angus ran into her back. An oversized painting now covered the living room wall.

A field of tangerine poppies studded with cactus and sage led to shards of purple mountains reaching toward an azure sky. It was El Paso. It was hope. It was every emotion inside Jessica's heart. She swelled with gratitude for her mother who had somehow seen inside her soul and painted her every aspiration onto canvas.

Angus's arms wrapped around her, and she wanted to stay in this perfect moment forever. She grasped her mother's hand and tried to transmit feelings too big for words.

Finally, Tela, who'd followed everyone in and couldn't understand why they just stood there, barked. It broke the moment, and her mother laughed.

"Thank you," Jessica said. "It's your most beautiful work, and it means so much to me."

"Clarice," Angus said, then he hugged her mom so thoroughly her feet lifted off the floor.

"I'm glad you like it," Clarice said after Angus let her go. "I'm grateful to be a part of your lives. That's the feeling I had when I painted it."

Jessica filled with so much love it spilled out of her eyes and down her cheeks. Family, home, love. Protecting it didn't just mean chasing bad guys. It meant showing up for these people in the ways they needed her and caring about herself as much as they did. It was a new world, that big world of her dreams. And she was ready for it.

"We better get the car unpacked," Angus said, his voice rough with emotion. "People will start showing up soon."

Jessica probably should have waited to call a meeting about everything that had happened over the past two weeks. But part of stepping into the future meant dealing with the past.

They'd invited Jaime and his partner Clint over for an update. Linda and Sal would arrive soon also. Jessica hadn't seen him since the hospital, but heard his recovery was going well. She'd also invited Keith. Jessica had dragged him into this mess, and he deserved to know everything she did about how it had progressed.

"I picked up a couple of boxes of coffee from the local shop," Clarice said. "I know Jaime is bringing breakfast, but the pastries looked delicious, so I bought some."

"Fantastic," Angus said. He strode into the kitchen and opened the pink box on the counter. "These look amazing."

When he turned around, he had something resembling a bear claw in his hand and a giant smile on his face. Tela had followed him and stared up with hungry eyes. It made Jessica laugh. This was exactly the life she wanted.

Soon, the doorbell rang, and Jessica opened it to Jaime carrying an aluminum catering tray. The scent of roasted chiles accompanied him. Clint followed, a grocery bag in each hand filled with who knows what.

Jessica cleared space on the counter, and Jaime let her peek under the foil top of the tray. He'd made her absolute favorite, chilaquiles with red sauce. She could barely wait to dip into the heady mix of tortilla chips, cheese, and scrambled eggs.

Keith arrived and Angus met him at the door. Jessica watched from the kitchen, not worried so much as curious.

"Welcome," Angus said, a warm smile on his face. "I'm glad you could make it."

"Great to see you. Thanks for having me over." Keith returned the smile, not in the awkward way Jessica had feared, but like he'd just met up with an old friend from high school. Jessica loved how some guys could put rivalries behind them like nothing had ever happened.

Clarice took over introductions, leaving Jessica to observe from the kitchen. Angus glanced at her, then came over.

"How are you feeling?" he asked.

"Great. I'm so happy to be back here." She gazed at him, then raised a hand to his cheek. "With you."

He leaned in for a kiss, but the doorbell rang again. This time, Sal and Linda entered the house.

Sal looked like he'd aged ten years. He'd always had that craggy, desert cowboy look, the kind of guy who inhabited harsh landscapes and Western movies. Today, he appeared smaller, the lines in his face more deeply drawn. Not to mention the cast and cane. He didn't lean on Linda, but he didn't appear steady either.

Jessica's heart ached at seeing him diminished, even while her mind raced back to him limp on the floor, then unconscious in the seat beside her. Gratitude at seeing him at all smothered the sad ache. They could move forward from here.

Jessica waited until he'd said hello to everyone else before she approached. "I'm so fucking happy to see you." She hadn't meant for her voice to break or for her eyes to fill.

"Jessica." The low rumble of her name was followed by a grin. "You do not know how to stay out of trouble, but I owe you one. Linda told me what happened. I don't remember much after arriving at that house. She said you got me out of there and drove me to the paramedics even though you had a concussion."

"Kind of. Andres put you in the car while I was passed out. I'm so glad we both made it. Let's make a pact never to visit scary houses in the desert again. It's gotten us into trouble twice in a row."

He chuckled. "That sounds like a good plan."

"We should eat," Angus said.

They herded into the kitchen and served themselves from the feast on the counter. Angus and Keith pulled chairs from the kitchen table into the living room so they could all dine together, plates balanced in their laps or atop the coffee table.

The small talk and sounds of eating didn't last long. Despite the great food and companionship, the cloud of what needed to be said hovered above them. As much as Jessica loved the black coffee and Mexican breakfast, she couldn't wait to break down where everything stood and what dangers remained.

"So, where are we with the case against Jace Jeffries?" she asked Jaime.

"We picked up three of his four buddies. The last one is still missing, but we hope to get him soon. Jace won't be out of jail for a while. He made bail on the felony arson, but now he faces charges of kidnapping, aggravated assault, and attempted murder. He'll stay in jail until the trial."

"I think I read about that," Clarice said. "Isn't he associated with one of the big churches?"

Clint jumped into the conversation. "Yes, his uncle founded The Way and has publicly condemned Jace and removed him from the church. He says the devil took the boy and invaded his soul. Weird stuff. Evidently, it caused a rift between the brothers, although we don't know much about it since his father won't talk to the press or the police at this point."

"How can that be?" asked Jessica. "Crimes occurred on his property, including the murder of a deputy for which his son, or more likely one of his employees, is responsible."

Jessica looked around the room hoping for answers. Her gaze landed on Keith.

"What's the latest on the Mayfield investigation?" she asked.

Keith's face darkened. "I'm not sure. The case seems to be stalled, although it shouldn't be. They've frozen me out, allegedly because I was first on the scene." His eyes slid toward his uncle. "And because of Sal's past relationship with Andres."

"No." Sal shook his head, suddenly looking a hundred years old. "They can't do this again."

"What do you mean?" Jessica asked. He sat beside her and she reached for him.

"Nothing." He kept his eyes on the floor, very un-Sal-like behavior. "It's nothing. It just reminded me of a case I wanted to work once that never really got resolved."

Silence stretched in the room, and Linda's face revealed her extreme concern for Sal. Protective of him, Jessica wanted to turn everyone's focus elsewhere.

"Speaking of past cases, I'm still not sure how my dad is connected to all of this."

Linda gave her a grateful smile. "From what I remember when I was with the police force, we knew the cartel had pressured your dad. That's another case that fizzled out. I think we could have brought down some of the cartel bosses back then, but the governor got the Texas Rangers involved and basically took us off the case. It never went anywhere."

"That's exactly what happened," Sal said. "The old sheriff back then wouldn't let me work it, which didn't make any sense since I was working as the DEA liaison. After your dad's conviction, the case just sort of disappeared. I never did understand it."

"It was one of the things that made me leave the force," Linda said. "I need to be able to see cases through to the end. It also made me mad that your dad was the only one convicted. His case made it clear that he was just trying to protect the people around him."

"He did break the law," Clarice said.

The comment shocked Jessica. Her mom had never openly admitted her father's wrongdoing.

"Absolutely," Linda said. "And I thought his punishment was fair. He just shouldn't have been the only one to fall."

"I wonder if history is going to repeat itself." Jaime might as well have detonated a bomb in the room. "This is pure speculation, but if Andres was involved with the cartel back then, he probably still is."

"He'd be dead otherwise," Keith said. "It's not exactly a job you retire from."

"If he works for the cartel and for Jeffries, which boss does he truly answer to?" Jessica asked. "It has to be the cartel, doesn't it?"

"I'm not sure," Jaime said. "The Jeffries family is extremely well-connected in the state capital, and The Way gives them a huge platform. Some of the richest men in Texas subscribe to that religion, or at least to the politicians it buys them."

Dread threaded through Jessica. "It sounds like we're headed for a war."

The silence stretched. Jessica looked at the beautiful painting on the wall, then at the woman who'd created it. Her eyes moved around the room, resting on each person she cared for. Finally, they landed on Angus.

"I want to stay out of this one," she said.

"Then let's focus on the things we can control." Jaime took charge. "Convicting Jace has to be our top priority."

"I'm definitely testifying against that guy," Jessica said.

"So is Araceli." The comment from Clint shocked Jessica.

"We've stayed in touch," he said. "She's a fantastic young woman. I talked to her yesterday, and she's settling into Guadalajara. Her aunt is going to stay with her for a couple of months, and she starts at the university next week. I think the distance has given her perspective. She wants to come back to testify. With her testimony and Travis's, we're hoping for a conviction."

"Isn't his dad trying to have the cases against him disappear?" Jessica asked.

"Yes, but it's going to be harder now. That Travis Williams kid sang like a sparrow," Clint said. "My guess is that Jace's attorney will try to place the blame on the other guys and say Jace went along with it because he feared for his life."

Jessica pictured the other men from the bar. "According to Andres, they're all employees on the payroll. Jace called them bodyguards, but they looked more like paid friends."

"That doesn't make them innocent." Jaime said. "But it definitely makes Jace look guilty."

"They'll still be prosecuted, won't they?" Jessica asked.

"You bet," Clint said. "All those young men should do some serious time."

Jessica took a deep breath. With Jace and his crew behind bars, she had accomplished her goal. They could no longer hurt others.

"The problem we haven't solved," Keith said, "is Andres. Until we find him, I don't think either of you are safe." He looked at Sal and Jessica.

"I'm not sure," Jessica said. "I mean I don't like that he's out there, running free. But doesn't he have bigger things to focus on? The sheriffs are looking for him, I'm sure Jace's father has goons out looking for him, and the cartel has got to be either hiding him or hunting him."

"But we don't know for sure, and he's still a danger," Jaime said.

That old, comforting spark of anger returned to Jessica. "I'm not going to let some asshole keep me from living my life. I want to testify against Jace. I want to return to work and school. I can't be looking over my shoulder for some bogeyman every day."

"We don't really have a choice. He'll either show or he won't." Angus spoke with both resignation and confidence. It made Jessica proud to be with him.

"We'll take the precautions we can. For now, we'll work in the bank tower office," Linda said. "And I'm moving in with Sal."

Keith's eyebrows rose, and Jessica felt hers do the same. She side-eyed her boss, but Linda ignored her. Sal visibly struggled to keep the smile off his face.

"How much of a danger do you think Andres is?" Jaime asked Jessica.

"I'm not sure. I think Andres got excited about my doing his bidding the way my father did. Hopefully, he has reevaluated that thought." She looked around. "It's weird the way the past has returned. But it's El Paso. It happens here. Even the people who leave eventually come back."

"Yeah," Jaime said. "Everyone wants to escape. But when your family is here, you usually make your way home."

Clint chimed in. "And for folks like Andres, when the cartels entrap you, it's hard to escape their talons."

Jessica thought about the last phone call from Andres, remembered the caged feeling that made her flee. "I understand that. I thought I could only protect the people I loved by leaving town. Even that wouldn't have guaranteed anything, but working for him would have ensured constant exposure to danger. But I want to stay. And I don't ever want to work for him."

"Do you think the only thing he wants now is for you to testify in Jace's trial?" Jaime asked.

"As far as I know"

The layers went deep and stretched back years. Jace and his friends. Andres, Jace's dad, and possibly the cartel. Jessica's dad. The Way and local and state politicians. How would Jessica carve out a safe space in the midst of so much evil?

Then she looked around the room. This was how. By locking hands with the wonderful people around her. No one could tell what the future held. Or maybe everyone could. It held the ugly and the beautiful. Her eyes found the painting on the wall. The world brought hate and violence but also love and hope.

Jessica reached for Angus and clasped his hand while still holding on to Sal, forming an unbroken chain. A swell of emotion passed through her, acknowledging how they each matched their vulnerability with passion. The people in this room and the sacred world they'd created were worth fighting for, when necessary. Perhaps the battles would find them again, but for once, she wouldn't go searching for them. She had way too much to live for.

THE END

Thank you for reading *El Macho!* This is the fifth book in the Jessica Watts Southwest Suspense Series. You can find these and other novels by Kathryn Dodson wherever books are sold online. For updates and information visit www.KathrynDodson.com.

Acknowledgements

Thank you to all the fans who have stuck with Jessica Watts (and me) through five books. This one dealt with some tough subject matter, but it felt important to tell this story – and to show that love and community can triumph over the evils in the world – at least some of the time.

There are four people who really helped me shape this story into something I'm proud to put out in the world. They are my incredible critique partners, Sydney Clark and Claudia Armann. I'm lucky to have partners who know my writing (and my many grammar vices) so well. Kate Underwood copyedited the book, and her valuable comments made the book better. Lori Diedrich proofread the novel. She's proofread all of my novels, and not only does she make the book far more readable, the comments she leaves often make my day. By the way, she let me know she was firmly #teamAngus in this one (me too).

I literally could not write without the support of my family. I owe many thanks to my parents, Diane and Jody Lawrence, and my in-laws, Laurie and Rhett Dodson for helping make this dream come true. My husband Tom has always encouraged me, through all of my endeavors, and I'm grateful to him for many wonderful years together. Finally, my son Jack is my inspiration.

Thanks for reading to the end. For updates, book information, and more, join me at www.KathrynDodson.com.

About the author

Kathryn Dodson grew up writing and riding horses in far West Texas. She graduated from SMU in creative writing and went on to get an MBA from Thunderbird and a PhD from Clemson.

She has worked on both sides of the US/Mexico border and has held jobs with governments, chambers of commerce, and other businesses. Now she spends her days writing about interesting women in fascinating places.

Join Kathryn for updates and extras and receive the *Tequila Midnight* prequel, *La Paloma*, at www.kathryndodson.com/

www.ingramcontent.com/pod-product-compliance
Lightning Source LLC
Chambersburg PA
CBHW061435150726
47987CB00001B/223